D1042371

DARLING

DARLING

K. ANCRUM

〔Imprint〕
MAKE YOUR MARK
New York

[Imprint]
MAKE YOUR MARK

A part of Macmillan Publishing Group, LLC
120 Broadway, New York, NY 10271

Library of Congress Cataloging-in-Publication Data is available.

ISBN 978-1-250-26526-5 (hardcover) / ISBN 978-1-250-26529-6 (ebook)

Our books may be purchased in bulk for promotional, educational, or
business use. Please contact your local bookseller or the Macmillan
Corporate and Premium Sales Department at (800) 221-7945 ext. 5442
or by email at MacmillanSpecialMarkets@macmillan.com.

Book design by Elynn Cohen

Imprint logo designed by Amanda Spielman

First edition, 2021

10 9 8 7 6 5 4 3 2 1

fiercereads.com

To stay in one place, static and unchanging,
surrounded by growing, evolving things,
is the greatest curse of all.

I would like to dedicate this book to the kids who get a thrill from running in the dark of night, and to kids who get a thrill from reading about them.

"The boys on the island vary, of course, in numbers, according as they get killed and so on; and when they seem to be growing up, which is against the rules, Peter thins them out."

"He often went out alone, and when he came back you were never absolutely certain whether he had had an adventure or not. He might have forgotten it so completely that he said nothing about it; and then when you went out you found the body; and, on the other hand, he might say a great deal about it, and yet you could not find the body."

Peter Pan, by J.M. Barrie

CHAPTER 1

Wendy scowled, scrunching herself down in the car seat angrily.

"I said no," Mr. Darling declared.

"I know you did, but seriously? I've done a background check on her. Like, a literal criminal background check, Dad."

"You never know who you could be meeting online," Mrs. Darling said gently. "I know you've been friends with her for more than a year, but that doesn't mean anything. She could be a serial killer for all you know. Besides, we didn't bring you here to go running around with strangers in the night. We came here to—"

"—adopt other kids that you also won't let go outside," Wendy snapped.

"Wendy . . . darling," Mr. Darling said, eyes crinkling at his own tired, ancient joke. "Can we please discuss this at another time? You can meet this 'Eleanor' person after you've had more time to get used to things and made a few new friends at school."

"Boring prep school friends," Wendy muttered.

"Lucky you!" Mrs. Darling said brightly. "We've just arrived at your boring new prep school! Aren't you excited and thankful that you have parents who can provide you with a quality education in a safe neighborhood where you don't have to take a bus to school and can walk instead?"

1

Wendy scowled deeper. She couldn't say anything to that. She was well aware that her mom had grown up in much rougher circumstances, and it would feel like a punch in the chest for her to hear Wendy say that she wasn't thankful. No matter how much she wanted to go out on her first night in Chicago.

Wendy kept up her silence all the way from the car through the building and into the principal's office, taking the opportunity to look around. A lot of things were the same as the prep school she'd gone to before the move. But there was a lot more diversity. She wouldn't be one of the only Black students, which seemed like it would be kind of nice. The uniforms everyone wore were a bit less stylish than the ones back in Hinsdale, but the girls rolled their skirts up and wore rule-breaking flourishes here, too. There were cuter guys, but that might just have been due to the quantity of them to choose from. There had to be three times as many kids in this building as there were in her entire town.

It looked like schools in Chicago had an alarming amount of security. She was familiar with the whole metal detector song and dance. But here they had a whole conveyor belt you put your backpack on, just like in the airport. There were also a ton of actual cops just standing around indoors. Her old school only had a regular security guard on staff, and he mostly just stood around looking bored outside the front door.

Mr. Darling clamped a hand on Wendy's shoulder and

steered her toward the administration office. "We have an appointment," he reminded her crisply.

The Darling family settled down outside of the dean of admissions's office to wait. Mrs. Darling filled out a registration form and handed it back to the secretary. Wendy watched as her mom tugged nervously at her skirt and combed her fingers through her flat-ironed hair to settle it more perfectly on her shoulders. Mr. Darling squeezed Mrs. Darling's hand gently and raised his eyebrows at Wendy. *Don't fuck this up,* his eyebrows said.

After a few minutes, the dean cracked the door open and called her name.

Wendy stood, but Mr. and Mrs. Darling stayed seated.

"Just me?" she asked her dad.

"Just you," the dean's secretary said sternly.

Wendy left her jacket on the chair and made her way into the dean's office. It was a large room, bigger than some of the classrooms at her old school, and it was completely crammed with plants and bookshelves.

The dean sat in front of a wide window. His hair was gray, his suit was expensive, his desk was massive, and his chair was tall. The chair that Wendy was supposed to sit in was small and pushed far enough back from the desk to feel awkward.

Wendy sat in it anyway.

The dean shuffled through the papers Mrs. Darling had filled out, seemingly just to create suspense, before finally looking up at her.

"Welcome, Wendy. So—" he paused, looking down at his papers to check, "—you're . . . seventeen, and you'll be entering senior year in the middle of the school term. Do you feel as though your previous institution has prepared you adequately for shifting into a new environment?"

"I think so?" Was this an interview? This was alarmingly beginning to feel like an interview. Wendy glanced down at the tight church shoes her mom had forced her into this morning and a wave of dread crashed over her body. "I . . . um . . . I did okay on the ACT prep, and I have a three-point-oh—"

"Which is a little low in comparison to the rest of our higher-performing students, but I've been led to believe that you're accomplished in your extracurriculars?"

"Oh yeah. My parents didn't usually get home until late, so I did a lot of clubs. I'm good with home ec, I won fourth place in the regional track-and-field four-hundred-meter dash, and . . ."

"And?" The dean peered at her over his glasses.

"And I write stories sometimes."

He grimaced, then folded his arms and leaned back in his giant chair. "Well. They any good?"

"I think they are," Wendy snapped before she could stop herself.

To her surprise, the dean smiled. "That's a lot of confidence. If you're as forthright about your work as you are about handling new experiences, you'll adjust just fine." He shuffled the papers in front of him and then shoved them to the side. "Now, do you have anything you'd like to say that you think will influence whether or not we accept your scandalously late application?"

Wendy looked down at her shoes. "I—" she started, then stopped. "My mom wants me to go here. I wanted to go to public school because I wanted to have a new experience, but I think that it would be really painful for my family if I didn't at least try my best to get in here. My mom used to live here, and I think she always wanted to go to a school like this. Giving me the chance to go is the closest she'll get to that."

The dean watched her curiously but didn't say anything, so Wendy continued.

"I know a lot of kids do things for their parents that they don't want, and it's always some big sacrifice. But I know the difference between wants and needs, and my want to go to public school is smaller than my mom's need to see me go here. And that's important. If my grades aren't good enough, then maybe my extracurriculars will help."

The dean nodded. "That was a good answer." He folded his hands on his desk. "You're an interesting applicant, Wendy Darling."

He wrote something on the papers and then stamped them.

"You can go out to the lobby. If I need anything else I'll give your mom a call. Have a great rest of your day."

When Wendy stepped back into the lobby, Mr. Darling immediately stood. "How did it go?"

"Okay, I guess?" Wendy said. "He stamped the forms and said we can go home."

The dean's secretary looked up. "You're probably good to go then. Believe me, he doesn't stamp much. You'll get a confirmation call next Monday that has her start date, and an email with information about what supplies she needs and where to purchase your uniform."

Mrs. Darling sighed in relief and leaned against her husband. "Thank you!"

The secretary snorted. "Usually I wouldn't call it this early, but you looked like you were about to pass out. Figured you could use the good news. Have a nice rest of your day, Mr. and Mrs. Darling. And good luck, Wendy."

Wendy's quiet mood followed her all the way back to the brownstone they'd just moved into. They had unpacked the car and promptly hopped back into it to register her for school, so all her things were still sitting on the floor in the living room.

While her parents focused on unpacking boxes in the kitchen, Wendy began lugging her suitcases and boxes up the stairs to her room. Her parents' bedroom was on the first floor, but her room and the room where her new sibling would be living were both on the second floor, with their own bathroom. After Wendy was done shoving boxes into her room, she took a break to go into the second room. It was white like hers, but had a bigger closet and one more window. Normally, she would have taken this room, but whoever they were adopting probably deserved to enjoy having a nice big space after what they went through a bit more than she did. Wendy scrunched her toes in her socks and looked at the ground. They hadn't had wood floors at their old house, only carpet and linoleum.

"Are you unpacked yet?" Mr. Darling yelled from the first floor. "I don't hear unpacking noises."

"I'm getting to it!" Wendy yelled back. She ducked out of the empty room and into her significantly more crowded one.

She set up her phone on the windowsill and started a video call, then she sat on the ground and started assembling her bed.

"Wendy?" Eleanor's twangy voice blared loudly into the room. "Is that manual labor I see you doing? Very butch. I'm loving it."

Wendy huffed. "I'm not doing it for your entertainment, Eleanor, I'm doing it so I can have a place to sleep."

"Yeah, yeah, yeah. So are you able to meet up tonight? I want to take you to Ann Sather so you can understand what real cinnamon rolls are supposed to be like. Then I was thinking we could go to Boystown and see if we can get into a club or something."

Wendy sighed loudly and wrenched at her headboard. "No. My dad says we can't meet up today. My mom thinks you're a serial killer."

"Why does she think I'm a serial killer? I'm vegan."

"You're vegan because you like animals. Not because you don't want to kill people. Those two things are not mutually exclusive. You think there aren't any vegan serial killers?"

"Anyway, didn't you tell them that I couldn't possibly be a catfish because we video chat? Catfishes always work really hard to make sure people never get a chance to video chat with them. Plus, if I was a catfish, I would work harder to look better than . . . this."

Wendy looked up. Eleanor had her curly blond hair bundled up into a pineapple on the top of her head and was wearing a gel mask.

"What? You look hot." Wendy snorted. "Why are you dressed for bed? It's like four thirty."

Eleanor rolled her eyes. "Well, I WAS going to take a nap so I would be awake enough to take you on a tour of the city, but I guess that's no longer a thing." She whipped the scrunchie off her head and shook out her curls. "Why are your parents so strict? Aren't they tired?"

"Dude, I don't know. I'm so well-behaved. I genuinely don't get it. I've literally never done anything that they wouldn't approve of, but they treat me like a criminal."

Eleanor shrugged one shoulder. "Well, at least you'll be eighteen soon. Maybe they'll let you go outside then."

Wendy dropped the slats over her bed frame, then tugged her mattress across the room. "Mmm. I don't know. Whenever anything happens that reminds my mom that I'm growing up, she gets all weepy and excuses herself to go feel feelings in another room. Just . . . like . . . what do you even say to that?"

Eleanor laughed. "Aww, that's cute."

"It's not cute, it's annoying," Wendy griped as she tucked in her sheets.

"It's cute," Eleanor insisted. "She'll probably calm down when the adoption goes through. Then she can focus all her mom-energy on momming someone else to death, and maybe we can finally see each other face-to-face."

"You wanna see my face, sweetheart?" Wendy pushed her face up close to the camera so it was nothing but a big brown blur.

Eleanor cackled. "Go finish setting up your room. I'm just a distraction at this point." She grinned at Wendy fondly.

"No, no! Give me five more minutes," Wendy said. She opened the box that held all her books and dumped them out onto the floor.

"So needy," Eleanor scoffed. "Okay, five more. What was the school like?"

"Bland. The guys there were actually hot, though."

"I'm going to stop you right there and let you know that prep school boys aren't 'hot.' You're just confused because there were, like, eight boys at your old school and all of them had faces like a loaf of bread."

Wendy scrunched up her nose. "You don't even like boys."

"Not again. Don't say it—"

"How do you even know which ones are cute?" Wendy continued, louder.

"Ugh. I'm just gay; I still have eyes. Please, Wendy, love yourself. Do you want to end up with some boy with a bowl cut named Chet who takes you to dinner with his parents while wearing khakis and sweating a lot, or do you want to get fingered in the back of a club you're technically too young to be in by a gorgeous fucker named Montana who has a dirt bike, plays bass, and had to retake algebra? These! Are not! Hard choices!"

Wendy covered her face with both hands.

"You want dumb hot Montana, don't you?" Eleanor asked.

"I want dumb hot Montana," Wendy groaned through her fingers.

"Exactly. So hold off on whatever options are in your native area, and when your parents finally let you out of prison, I'll introduce you to Montana."

"You'll WHAT?"

"Introduce you to Montana. He's single. And pretty okay."

"I THOUGHT THAT WAS A HYPOTHETICAL."

"It was both. Two birds, one six-foot-two stone named Montana."

"I can't. Why are you so good at making me feel embarrassed? I'm gonna finish unpacking." Wendy crossed her room to get to her phone.

"He failed algebra *and* US history," Eleanor said quickly, trying to cram in more about Montana. "But his arms are great, he can blow smoke rings, and he has a buzz cu—"

Wendy turned the video chat off.

She flung herself backward on her bed and laughed semi-hysterically while she waited for her heart to stop racing.

Eleanor was the only online friend she'd managed to keep for long. Wendy was pretty good at making friends in real life, so relying on an online community for close friendships never really appealed to her. Eleanor just happened to like all the same weirdo stuff that she did back in sophomore year, and even though they lived in completely different cities, they were online around the same time every day.

When her parents announced they were moving to Chicago, it was purely coincidental that Eleanor lived there. Wendy and Eleanor were both super excited to randomly be placed in each other's paths like that, and it seemed perfect right up until Mr. Darling firmly put his foot in the way of their in-person introduction.

Wendy pulled up her maps app and figured out how far her new school was from Eleanor's. It wasn't that bad. She could probably figure out some way to meet Eleanor halfway between their schools after class was over and manage to get back home before anyone knew she'd been missing.

Wendy did things like this back in their hometown, so it wasn't nearly as stressful to imagine doing it here. Of course, the city was bigger, but that just meant there's better public transportation and more emergency services in case anything went wrong. Back home if something happened, you had to wait half an hour or more for an ambulance. Here, she could probably just look up an urgent care center and take a cab.

Some of the books she'd dumped on the floor fluttered their pages angrily as a huge gust of wind blew into her room through the window.

Wendy grimaced and stacked them neatly against the wall. She wasn't normally this careless, but the bookcase they belonged in needed to be rebuilt from scratch, and after doing the bed, she simply did not have the energy.

Then Wendy slammed the window shut. It rebounded off the bottom of the windowsill and reopened itself, leaving a crack more than an inch high. Wendy scowled and pushed it back down again much slower, and this time closed the lock on the top. Then she paused and tugged the window just to check it, and to her great irritation, it swung right up again, even though it was supposed to be locked.

Wendy shifted the lock to the other side and pulled on the window.

Up it went.

Great. She looked out at her new neighborhood. Things seemed quiet, and it was well-maintained enough to not immediately suggest they were about to be burgled, but this was still a problem.

"Mom!" she yelled down the stairs. "The window is broken!"

"Which room?" Mrs. Darling yelled up from the kitchen.

"Mine," Wendy yelled back.

She went into the empty room next to hers and tested all the windows. They all worked perfectly fine. Even the bathroom window locked tight when she tried it.

"We gotta fix this, Mom!" she yelled down the stairway.

"Just put something heavy in front of it. Your dad will fix it on Saturday."

Wow. Wendy felt super loved and cherished now. She went into her room and picked up her hardcover copies of *Les Misérables*, *Crime and Punishment*, and *Infinite Jest*, the bulkiest books she had, and dropped them in front of the window. For now, that would have to do.

CHAPTER 2

Wendy came downstairs the next morning to find her parents making breakfast, and exactly none of the rest of the boxes unpacked.

"So . . . are we just going to live this way?" she asked, sliding into a kitchen chair.

Mrs. Darling glanced at her reproachfully, then went back to scrambling eggs. "We bought unpacking as part of the moving service, but the unpackers aren't coming until Sunday. Your father got twenty percent off on the deal because of the inconvenience—and it *is* an inconvenience."

Mr. Darling shot Wendy a look over his newspaper and wiggled his eyebrows. Wendy smirked back at him and dug a bagel out of the bag on the kitchen table.

Mrs. Darling continued to complain. "And aside from all that, we still have to pick up the dog from the airport, and your father is taking the car, so we'll have to pick Nana up on the train."

The train? "Like . . . Amtrak?"

"No. The city train, and you have to come with because we can't have Nana on a leash on the train. She has to be in a gosh darn carrier, which means I need you to help me carry the other side of the kennel."

"If you used the CrossFit membership I got you for Christmas last year, you wouldn't need Wendy's help with your 'sick lifts' because your 'gains' would more than cover the weight," Mr. Darling said, hiding his grin in the curve of his paper coffee cup.

"You can't distract me with jokes while I'm frying eggs on a baking sheet that I had to buy this morning at a corner store, George," Mrs. Darling snapped.

"We could just unpack the stuff ourselves," Wendy said nonchalantly. "Then maybe, instead of supervising movers on Sunday, I can go to brunch with my fri—"

"No. We already paid for it. And you're not going anywhere with anybody until I get to speak with their parents live and in person." Mrs. Darling sat down and started spooning eggs onto her bagel. "I'm not going to have you get kidnapped within the first seventy-two hours we've been in this city."

"But if you *do* get to speak with Eleanor's parents . . . then I can hang out with her?" Wendy asked.

Mrs. Darling chewed and looked Wendy over. "I suppose."

"Okay, great. I'll work on arranging that. Also, if we're making efforts to not have me be kidnapped, could we also work on getting my window fixed? Because it would be super ironic if I got kidnapped out of our own home—"

"Yes, fine," Mr. Darling interrupted. "Just go upstairs and get ready to pick up Nana."

Wendy shoved the last bite of her bagel into her mouth and went to her room. She dialed Eleanor and laid back on her bed.

"It's ten a.m. and it's Friday," Eleanor said quietly, her

face super close to the screen, with one of the edges of her hand blocking most of the light. "I'm literally in homeroom and we aren't allowed to have our phones out, so make it quick."

"Oh crap, I forgot it's not the weekend. I probably won't have class until next Tuesday," Wendy said. "Sorry."

"Yeah, enjoy it while it lasts. What's up?"

"My mom said we can meet up unsupervised if she has some sort of weird conference with your parents. Do you know if they're free any time in the next couple of days?"

"Not until Sunday," Eleanor replied. "My parents are at work right now, then after work we're going to some Friday night church thing. Then on Saturday we're going apple picking before it gets too cold. Maybe Saturday night might work? I'll ask."

"Apple picking with your parents? Your life is so wholesome. I still can't believe my mom's making us go through this."

"Yeah, yeah, it's great," Eleanor said quickly. "I've gotta go. My homeroom teacher is looking directly at me and can clearly tell that I'm on the phone. Call you later."

Eleanor hung up.

"DOES SATURDAY NIGHT WORK FOR YOU?" Wendy shouted out her open bedroom door.

"Saturday night is your father's work party," Mrs. Darling called up the stairs. "How is Sunday?"

"SHE SAID SHE'LL LET US KNOW," Wendy shouted

back. She chewed her lip for a bit and then continued. "THEY GO APPLE PICKING TOGETHER, YOU KNOW. THIS IS WHO YOU'RE BARRING ME FROM SEEING. A GIRL WHO GETS EXCITED TO PICK APPLES WITH HER PARENTS."

"Are you getting ready to pick up Nana?" Mr. Darling asked. "You've got ten seconds to get dressed or we're coming up. One . . . two . . ."

Wendy pushed her door closed and shoved on jeans and a sweater. She got her feet into her shoes just in time for Mr. Darling to knock on the door.

"Come in."

Mr. Darling headed straight to her window and started jimmying the latch. "This is really broken."

"I wouldn't lie about my window being broken, Dad," Wendy said dryly.

"No, I meant this is really, *really* broken. I don't know if I can fix this by myself. The latch on the back of the window was pried off from the outside. We might have to replace the whole frame. Do you want to sleep in the other room for a while?"

Wendy shook her head. "It's fine. I'll just . . . put books in front of it like I did yesterday. We can figure out the window situation when things aren't so stressful."

Mr. Darling huffed and leaned back against the window-sill. He watched her as she pulled on her jacket and hat. "Thanks for being a good sport. I'll make it a priority."

He was lingering, so Wendy turned around to face him.

"You know," Mr. Darling continued, "your mom and I just want to make sure you're safe. Anything can happen out here. It's not like back home where most people know each other . . ."

"I'm seventeen, Dad. I get it," Wendy said.

"And there are a lot of things out there that you haven't experienced," Mr. Darling finished.

Wendy scowled. This wasn't her fault. Maybe if they let her out to experience things more, they wouldn't have to be worried about her "experiencing things." But it didn't seem like the best time to say that so she just stayed quiet.

Eventually, Mr. Darling nodded at her open bedroom door. "Go on. Mom's waiting. She'd never admit it, but she's nervous about riding the trains again. Can you be a *darling* and help her out?"

Wendy walked to the top of the stairs, then looked back at him over her shoulder. "Sure. I'm going to college next year; I can handle a train."

Nana's kennel fit neatly in the area near the back of the train car, and she was behaving very well. The woman at the train kiosk had eyed the crate warily as Mrs. Darling and Wendy hoisted it over the turnstile. Nana had remained silent the entire time, paws folded primly, so the woman had held her tongue and allowed them to continue.

Mrs. Darling sat next to Nana, her hand tightly clenching the bar next to her seat. Her eyes were glued to the map above the door with the words PURPLE LINE TRAIN above a list of train stops; she was running over the map with near-religious persistence. Wendy stood by the doors so she could watch the city. Mrs. Darling had been so nervous on the ride over to the airport that Wendy felt responsible to make sure they got off at the right stop and couldn't really relax and take everything in, so she was using the opportunity to do so now. She couldn't really understand why her mom was so antsy; the system was simple enough.

Each train had approximately eight to ten cars. Each car had a door on each side for traveling between the cars if necessary. The trains ran both ways at about the same pace. That way, if you got off at the wrong stop, you could easily transfer to the other side of the train platform and head right back in the direction you came from. All the stations had people to assist you on the platform itself and where you purchased tickets. You only needed one ticket to get past the turnstile, but once you were through, you could ride the trains all day in any direction, transferring from line to line on the $2.50 it took to get in.

It was a much better system than the one they'd had to endure on their trip to Europe last year, where you had to pay based on distance. Chicago made it easier to get lost without any real financial consequences.

Wendy glanced back at her mother, who was clutching

the bar behind the seat so hard her brown knuckles were beginning to go yellow from stress.

Really.

"Can you tell me about what it was like when you were living here?" Wendy asked. Hopefully a distraction would help.

"Well," Mrs. Darling started. "We didn't live in as nice of a neighborhood as we do now. We were in this part of the city called Logan Square, over here on the blue line by the California stop. There were a lot of families there, which was good. But the city didn't take much care of the infrastructure, so there were a lot of crumbling buildings and crumbling roads . . . I'm a lot more familiar with that area than the neighborhood we're in now."

"What did you do for fun?"

Mrs. Darling's mouth twitched into a small grin. "We mainly got into trouble. It was the early 2000s; it was much more common for everyone to be out running in the street until the sun set."

Wendy threw out her arms. "AND YET—"

"And *yet*," Mrs. Darling said with incredible finality.

Wendy sighed and reached into the cage to give Nana a few pets before returning to the window.

"We know you're a good girl and your friend probably is, too," Mrs. Darling said. "It won't be forever, just until everyone gets settled and you get a bit more familiar with the city."

"I know, I know," Wendy said, defeated.

"Besides," Mrs. Darling continued, "it's harder to tell if something could be dangerous when you're not as familiar with your surroundings. You're smart and creative, but even smart and creative people can get caught off guard. Your father and I trust you—we just don't trust this situation. You understand that, right?"

"You sound like you're speaking from experience," Wendy said with a smirk, hoping to lighten the mood.

Instead, Mrs. Darling looked pensive. "When—when I was fourteen, a couple of friends and I went out to a party with some older teenagers and things got really out of hand."

"Is this another 'teen mom warning' story?" Wendy asked.

Mrs. Darling scowled. "I had you at sixteen, not fourteen, and no, it is not. Anyway, we went to a roller rink in a part of town that I had never been to before, and everything started out normally. One of my best friends met a cute boy who bought us sodas and fries. He was really glamorous in this . . . Billy Idol way: kind of punk rock but with a really sweet face. His friends were with him and they were also very cool and really nice to us. They paid for our arcade games, and the main guy even won my friend a stuffed animal. I remember thinking that he was amazing at Skee-Ball, could have gone pro if there was a market for that. Very light-fingered . . ."

Mrs. Darling looked out the window for a minute, then she gazed at the train car floor.

"After the roller rink closed, we were going to head home, but the boys wanted to hang out at this cemetery across the street. One of them had a bottle of wine and wanted to share it with the group. I remember thinking it was so funny because none of them were old enough to have gotten it from the store, but it just sort of appeared. It made me a little nervous. But mostly, I thought they were cool, and I'd never drank before, so we decided to follow them."

Wendy sat down across from her mom and leaned her head against the window as she listened.

"He took us all the way to the center of the cemetery," Mrs. Darling continued. "It was windy and dark, but they lit a small fire with some twigs, and we began passing the bottle around. I didn't drink much; I didn't want your grandfather to smell anything on me when I came back home.

"It wasn't late enough for him to get really mad; it was only around ten thirty. Up until that point I wasn't *really* doing anything I wasn't allowed to do yet, and I wanted to keep it that way.

"Eventually, someone suggested that we tell scary stories. I remember . . . listening to stories told by some of the other boys, but losing track of where the leader was for a while. We were having such a good time that I didn't really notice he was gone until my best friend complained that she was cold without him next to her. One of the boys shrugged and said that the leader liked to wander off and that maybe he'd gone to the bathroom or something. It sounded feasible, so we accepted the explanation and kept going. The story we had been listening to was building to a crescendo and we were all really invested.

"Suddenly, right before the story was going to end, one of the boys threw dirt over the fire and the entire cemetery went dark."

"What happened?" Wendy asked quietly.

Mrs. Darling shook her head and pressed her lips into a tight line. "We were kids and we were scared, so we started running. Not just us, the boys, too, and they were yelling for—I'm sorry, Wendy, it was years ago, and I don't remember his name anymore. I'm sure you're probably tired of hearing me call him *the leader*, but that's what it seemed like he was. Anyway, we were running, and I spotted the cemetery gate. All I had left to do was jump over it and head for the bus stop, when suddenly there was a bunch of screaming. Not yelling like we had all been doing, but horrible, frightened screaming. Shrill, like you only hear in movies. Then it was quiet."

Mrs. Darling put her hand in Nana's cage and smoothed it over the dog's fur gently for a second before continuing.

"I didn't look back. I jumped over that fence and ran so hard and fast. I ran past the bus stop and got on the train instead because I didn't want to wait on the sidewalk. When I got home, I went straight to bed and didn't talk to anyone until the next day.

"When I went to school, I found out that the rest of my

friends had made it home safely, so I started to relax. Then two weeks later, Grandpa was watching the news while I was in the kitchen finishing dinner. There was this story on about a body having been found in the cemetery in an open grave. It said there were bruises shaped like fingers around the neck and that one of the victim's thigh bones had been broken like someone had kicked it with all their might. When they showed a picture of the deceased, it was one of the boys we'd been with that night. One of the quieter ones, who had held my hand as we skated for a whole song when he'd noticed that I wasn't as steady on my feet."

"Did Grandpa know?"

"I refused to talk to him about it, but he could tell that I was getting depressed and was a bit jumpy. I got over it after some time, of course. But when Grandpa got an opportunity to work in the suburbs, he leaped at the chance and moved us all out of the city."

Wendy tapped her foot on the ground. "Whatever happened to the leader? Do you think maybe whoever killed that boy killed him, too?"

Mrs. Darling shook her head. "I don't know, Wendy; we didn't even know them. We'd only met them that night at the roller rink. We never saw any of those boys again."

"Oh."

Mrs. Darling sighed. "Our stop is next, so get ready to carry."

Nana woofed softly and sniffed at the cage door, then

settled primly with her giant head on her paws, waiting for Wendy and Mrs. Darling to pick her up.

Wendy watched the back of her mother's head as they carried Nana down the stairs and out of the train station. She couldn't imagine her mother being fourteen at all, much less a part of the chaotic story she'd just heard. But it was rare that Mrs. Darling lied to her. The entire concept of her mother being defenseless and running in the night filled her with dread.

As soon as they made it out of the train station, they put Nana's crate on the ground and opened its little door. Nana shook herself all over and walked delicately out of the kennel. The Saint Bernard looked back at Wendy—who was struggling to pick up the giant kennel in her thin arms—as if to say, *You could try being more dignified*, and waited patiently for Mrs. Darling to attach her leash.

The walk back to their new house was quiet and tense.

Wendy could tell Mrs. Darling was lost in thought and not quite in the mood to talk anymore, so she trailed unhappily behind her in silence.

When they reached the front door, Mr. Darling threw it open before Mrs. Darling even managed to get her key in the lock. "I see the duchess has come to grace our home with her presence!" He hurled himself to his knees before Nana, who sprung up with delight and lavished his face with slobber. "How have you been, you old girl?"

"I see you're home early. Well, she was as poised as ever

on the train, decadent being carried in her kennel, and lovely as we strolled down the block," Wendy said, dumping the kennel in the front hallway.

"Of course she was! Of course she was!" Mr. Darling cooed. "Let's get Nana some lunch."

"And *us* some lunch?" Mrs. Darling asked, hanging up Nana's leash on the hook by the front door.

"There's pizza on the counter." Mr. Darling practically carried the ecstatic Nana to the kitchen and poured her a bowl of dog food.

"So you unpacked the dog supplies, but not the pots and pans," Mrs. Darling said, sitting down at the table and opening up a box.

"Only the best for Nana," Mr. Darling replied chipperly. "So how was the ride over?"

"Nice," Wendy interjected before Mrs. Darling could say anything. "Mom showed me how the train system works, and we made it past the front kiosk without any issues because Nana was so well-behaved."

"That's good to hear." Mr. Darling leaned over and kissed Mrs. Darling on the top of her head. "And for you, my love, I *did* do the pots, pans, silverware, plates, and cleaning supplies. We'll leave the rest for the movers, but for now, my best ladies won't have to eat off paper and plastic."

Mrs. Darling covered his hand with hers. "You want to take some pizza up to your room? You can if you want," she said to Wendy.

Wendy leaped at the chance. She snatched a plate from the cabinet, grabbed a few slices, and scampered up the stairs.

Her window had cracked itself open yet again, and the wind had blown on one of the books so violently that its cover was thrown wide and the pages were fluttering. Wendy pulled the book back, slammed the window down again, and shoved the stack closer to the window, pinning it shut. Then she flopped down on her bed and pulled out her phone.

Eleanor was getting ready for church and probably couldn't talk, so Wendy decided to look up some places for them to visit when she was finally free to travel around on her own.

Eleanor loved museums, so they'd have to hit those first, starting with the Art Institute of Chicago and working their way backward toward the Field Museum and Adler Planetarium, ending with the Shedd Aquarium, which would probably be Wendy's favorite. Then they could get lunch and head to a bookstore or something. There were a couple of local ones not too far from downtown that seemed promising. Wendy knew that Eleanor preferred comic book shops to bookstores, but Wendy had left a decent amount of books back in the suburbs, and her collection was looking a bit thin.

She was about to begin working on a decent itinerary for next week when she heard Nana barking, louder and angrier than she had in a while. Wendy froze, listening.

When Mr. Darling's shouting began to accompany Nana's barks, Wendy jumped up from her bed and flew down the stairs, nearly colliding with Mrs. Darling.

"What's happening?" she asked.

"Nana caught someone trying to hop over the back fence in the yard," Mrs. Darling said. "She scared him off, but I think she might have bitten him and torn some of his clothes."

"She got a piece of his jacket!" Mr. Darling crowed triumphantly, holding up a scrap.

Wendy eyed the dusty gray denim sleeve in her father's hands warily.

"Do you think this will become a regular occurrence?" Mrs. Darling asked, concerned. "Maybe we should get an alarm system . . ."

"We should definitely get an alarm system," Mr. Darling agreed. "But for now, Nana's all we've got, and she's doing a wonderful job."

"My window is broken, and people are hopping our fence. Are you sure this is a 'good neighborhood'?" Wendy asked sarcastically, parroting Mrs. Darling from earlier.

"Oh, our property tax practically guarantees it," Mr. Darling replied. "But this house was empty for a while before it was rehabbed and went on the market. "Maybe people are just surprised to find that now it's occupied."

"Okay, great," Wendy said. "Maybe instead of staying here alone when you and Mom go to your work party tomorrow night, I could go and sleep over at Eleanor's house that has two whole parents in it."

"You're pushing it, Wendy," Mr. Darling said.

"I don't even— They're literally at church right now," Wendy muttered. "They go to Friday church, for fuck's sake."

"One last chance," Mr. Darling warned.

Wendy exploded. "But what if the guy who tried to break in comes back? Is it really that much worse for me to be with people you don't know than be in an unsupervised house with no alarm system, broken windows, and a burglar Nana barely foiled?!"

"That's it!" Mrs. Darling shouted. "Upstairs, now! You're grounded for a week, and don't you dare think of leaving that room until next Friday!"

Wendy stared at her parents in horror and outrage, but she didn't say another word. Instead she marched upstairs and gently closed her door.

CHAPTER 3

Wendy didn't have many fights with her parents, so she always felt dark and ugly whenever she did. She'd known her mother's nerves were frayed and that her father was probably rattled from the break-in, but this safety protocol was an objective reality that she simply didn't agree upon. Mr. Darling was stubborn, so Wendy always tried to be immovable, too, if she could manage it. If her parents didn't want her to leave her room until next Friday, then Friday it would be. She saved pizza from yesterday and ate it in the morning, resolutely refusing to come downstairs when she was called for breakfast.

Wendy lay on her bed reading for the whole day and texting sporadically with Eleanor—who was not thrilled to hear the news that there was no hope for having any plans this Sunday. Wendy figured that when Mr. and Mrs. Darling headed off to the party at her father's new job, she could run across the street to the nearby 7-Eleven and stock up on snacks so she could really lean in to camping out in her room.

She slipped into a hungry, fitful nap as the sun set and missed Mr. Darling coming into her room with a plate of chicken and some rice. He placed the plate on her nightstand and lovingly tucked the Saran wrap around it. He picked her pizza plate up from the floor next to her bed and let himself out of her room, closing the door quietly behind him.

In fact, Wendy missed Mr. and Mrs. Darling getting ready, feeding Nana, and locking her up for the night. She slept straight through Mrs. Darling's gentle, apologetic knock on her door, her whispered good night, and the sound of her parents slipping out to the party.

But what Wendy *didn't* miss was all the books in front of her window crashing to the floor. She startled groggily and tried to make sense of what she was seeing. Long arms thrust their way through the open window, followed by a head of wavy, tousled hair. The intruder pulled himself silently into the room and slid along the wall toward the door.

Wendy sat up and turned on the bedside light. "Who the fuck are you, and what in God's name are you doing in my room?"

The man turned to look at her, and Wendy's breath caught in her throat. He wasn't a man; he was a boy. More specifically, a boy her age. Even more specifically, an incredibly attractive boy her age.

They stared at each other in mutual horror.

Wendy took in his long dark eyelashes, his smattering of freckles, the way his nose turned up at the tip, and the impossible whorls of his auburn hair. He was golden-eyed like a lion and looked just as hungry, but his mouth was soft, pink, and generous. She followed the lean lines of his body—broad-shouldered with sharp, slim hips in excruciatingly tight jeans—to land on his faded T-shirt and gray jean jacket that was missing a sleeve.

"Your dog ripped my jacket," the boy said in a soft voice. "I'm just getting what's owed."

"You're . . . robbing me?" Wendy asked in quiet disbelief.

"Don't flatter yourself," he drawled. "I'm only taking enough to resell and replace what was destroyed. Didn't even know you were here. This place used to be empty."

Wendy scowled. "It's not empty anymore, and you need to leave or I'm calling the police."

While she'd been talking, the boy had inched closer to the door and grasped the handle, but when Wendy mentioned the cops, he froze.

"That's not fair. I haven't even taken anything just yet," he said, scandalized. "And you're the one whose dog ripped up my jacket, so technically you're the one who's done something to me first."

"What do y— You know what, I'm not arguing with a burglar." Wendy sprung up from the bed and began rooting through the covers for her cell phone, but the boy was faster.

He snatched it off the corner of her quilt and held it up. "You bring me something that covers the cost of my damages and I give you your precious phone back and disappear."

"Dude, we just freakin' moved here," Wendy snapped loudly, done whispering. "All of our stuff is still packed. Even if I wanted to give you something, everything is in boxes."

"Then you have a problem on your hands, don't you?" the boy asked, tossing the phone up and catching it.

Wendy stared at him and thought for a minute.

He was clearly very fast, so if he wanted to hurt or even kill her, he probably could have done it by now. Plus, he hadn't said that he wanted to steal all their valuables, just recoup the cost of replacing the jacket. But even if she knew how much the jacket cost, he could just lie to her to make a profit and take off with their TV. And much more terrifyingly, just as she had warned her parents, there was a stranger in their home, and she had no real way to escape him or contact the authorities.

The boy relaxed against the wall and pushed his hair back from his face, cradling Wendy's phone in his slim fingers. He raised an eyebrow at her impatiently.

Wendy gritted her teeth. "Will you. Accept. A trade of labor? As you can see, everything is packed except for my room. I have sewing materials here, and I'm pretty sure your entire sleeve is downstairs, lying on the kitchen table. If I sew your sleeve back on, will you get out of my house and never come back?"

The boy gaped at her. "You . . . what? You'd do that for me?"

"Not for *you*, you weirdo. I'm doing it so you'll leave!" Wendy shouted.

"No one has ever . . . yes. Please sew my sleeve back on. This jacket means a lot to me and I just . . . yes." He sat down on the floor to wait.

Wendy went out of her room and dashed down the stairs. The sleeve was indeed lying on the kitchen table, and she grabbed it. The landline phone caught her eye and a thrill of triumph quickened her heart for a moment, but when she picked it up, she realized the connection hadn't been set up yet, which meant any lifelines were still out of reach. Her stomach fell in disappointment and fear, and she made her way back up the stairs.

The boy was sitting there patiently, leaning against the wall. He had her phone perched in the well between his long thighs and was doing a cat's cradle with some yarn. He looked up when she came back into the room, and his eyes laser-focused on the sleeve.

Wendy sat on her bed and pulled the sewing kit from underneath her mattress. She threaded a needle with thick button thread and waited.

"I can't actually sew the sleeve on without the jacket," she said icily.

The boy scrambled out of his jacket and held it out to her, his eyes round with anticipation.

Wendy snatched it from him, turned it inside out, and began to pin the sleeve back on. "You know, you could have just come to the front door during the daytime, apologized to my parents about the misunderstanding, politely asked for the sleeve, and sewed it back on yourself."

The boy let out a snort of laughter and then covered his mouth like he was surprised it had found its way out.

"I don't know how to sew," he admitted sheepishly. "And I doubt that would have worked, anyway."

"Why does this jacket mean so much to you that you'd trespass just to fix it?" Wendy asked. "It's only a jean jacket. You can get one just like it at H&M."

The boy hummed low in his throat and leaned the long line of his neck back to rest his head against the wall. "I've had this jacket for a very long time. It used to belong to a friend of mine—the very first friend I ever had. I've kept it safe for him for ages. I know the circumstances of our meeting tonight aren't exactly . . . cordial. But I do really appreciate you fixing it for me. I hope you know that," he said softly.

Wendy glanced over at him in spite of herself. The boy was gazing back at her through lowered eyelids, half closed but still sharp and observant in the light of her bedside lamp. He was studying her, she realized.

"You're very pretty," he said. "I don't mean that in a selfish way. I just thought you should know."

"Thanks," Wendy muttered and tugged the thread extra tight.

"So, you said you just moved here? From where?"

"I'm not telling you," Wendy said immediately.

"Why?" the boy asked, as if it was the simplest thing in the world.

"Because we don't even know each other!"

"We could." The boy climbed to his feet and crossed the

room in quick strides. He placed her phone on the corner of her bed and held up his hands, backing away, when she snatched it.

"Please don't call them. You're almost done," he said softly.

Up close, Wendy could see that he had been crying. Eyes rubbed red around the rim; nose still puffy from wiping it.

"I'm Peter," he said, sniffing. "Peter Pan."

"Wendy Darling." She felt the words leave her mouth helplessly.

Peter gave her a watery smile. "Nice to meet you, Darling."

He turned around and looked out the window and down into the alley below. "We're not strangers anymore, I don't think. Acquaintances, now, I guess." He turned back to her. "I'll wear your stitches with pride, of course. They'll just make the jacket more magic."

"The jacket magic . . . ?" Wendy echoed.

"Sure," Peter replied, shrugging. "It definitely helps."

Wendy tied a double knot at the end of the row and pulled it tight, then she turned the jacket right side out and held it out to him. Peter shimmied into the jacket quickly, then he held his arms around himself and took a deep, grateful breath. His eyes fluttered closed and he shivered a bit.

When he opened them, they twinkled with mischief.

"Would you like to see some magic now?" he asked excitedly.

Wendy opened her mouth to say, *No, and also get out of my*

house, but before she could, Peter flashed his fingers behind her left ear and pulled out an acorn, then darted his other hand behind her right ear and pulled out another piece of yarn. Then, quicker than felt safe, Peter whipped a blade from his pocket and slit the acorn stem down the middle, scratched the side of the acorn a bit, and strung it along the yarn like a necklace.

"If you give me more time, I'll make something prettier," he said bashfully, presenting it to her.

Wendy took the acorn from his hand and turned it around. Peter had carved her name and a small star into the side. The yarn itself was elegantly braided to keep the acorn in place. She hadn't seen him do that . . .

"It's like a shadow," he explained, gesturing at the jacket. "Hides what needs to be hidden for just long enough."

Wendy didn't know what to say. She looked at the acorn, then back at Peter. He backed away from her bed and opened her window again.

"So, I'm off. As promised," Peter said with a wry smile. "Thank you for your time, your kindness, and the pleasure of your company. Welcome to Chicago, Darling."

He slipped beneath the windowsill and into the night.

Wendy looked down at the acorn necklace for a minute, then strung it around her neck. It was warm on her skin, as if Peter had been holding it against his own skin for hours.

She was just about to get out of bed and make sure all

the doors in the house were truly locked when Peter popped his head back up and into her room.

"Sorry to startle you," Peter said, "and forgive me if this is a bit too forward, but do you want to come to a party?"

"Do I . . . what?!" Wendy clutched her chest and willed her heart to stop racing.

Peter grimaced. "It's . . . kind of an open invitation sort of thing, and you *did* mention you were new to the city, and your parents clearly aren't home. Do you want to come out and see the sights with me? I promise I'll get you back before morning."

"I'm not going anywhere alone with some strange boy I just met. Are you high?"

Peter looked over his shoulder at the two-story plunge below him and chuckled. "Well. Yeah. But I'm not alone. Tink's here. We could all go together."

Wendy got out of bed, went to the window, and peered down into the alley.

Leaning against the wall was a very short and very angry-looking girl. She had her blond hair entirely shaved except for two patches by her ears, and long bangs she had swept to the side. She was wearing a forest green velvet minidress and leather jacket, and her tights were ripped practically to shreds. She had a wooden pipe in her hand and was smoking out of it with a stiffness and unapproachability that nearly equaled Peter's graceful and attractive sprawl against the side of Wendy's house. The girl glared up at the window at Wendy and Peter but didn't say a word.

"She's a girl, too, which helps, I think," Peter explained. "I wouldn't have asked if I didn't think you'd be more comfortable with other people here."

"Has she been down there this whole time?" Wendy asked. "When I was sewing your jacket and everything? That was like a half hour!"

Peter shrugged. "I brought her for safety. Climbing houses is hard and I'm good at it, but old Tink here won't let me go anywhere without a spotter. She's a stickler for rules."

Wendy frowned and turned back into her room to think. She looked down at her pajamas, around the room she had been intending to stay in for a whole week, then back at Peter. Beautiful, magical Peter, who had cried in her room over torn fabric and was leaning dangerously against the trellis, waiting for her answer.

"I . . . uh . . . I have to call a friend," Wendy said.

"For permission?" Peter asked interestedly.

Wendy began dialing Eleanor's number. "Something like that."

CHAPTER 4

"Is he still at your house?!" Eleanor whisper-shrieked into the receiver.

"Yes," Wendy hissed back. "He's balanced on the trellis, and I need you to calm down. If he wanted to murder me, he would have done it thirty minutes ago."

"Oh *God*, I am calling the cops," Eleanor said. "I am going to call the police, and I *know* how you feel about that. What kind of question is that? 'Should I go to a party with him?' WHAT? Do you even hear yourself talking?" Wendy could hear Eleanor shaking her head, her curls bounding wildly.

"I know, I know, but Eleanor! It's just a party. I've been to plenty of those. And if anything was to go wrong, I could just hop on a train or a bus. Worse comes to worst, I can just Google Maps a police station and get an Uber there. I have some money, and he has another girl with him, so it's not like I'm going out with him alone—"

"You shouldn't be going with him at all! There is a huge difference between going out with me and going out with some strange man to God knows where."

Wendy glanced over at Peter, who had swung his legs back inside the windowsill and was picking through her copy of *Paradise Lost*. He held it awkwardly, like he'd never read a book in his life and didn't quite know why anyone would want to own such a thing. When he looked up and saw Wendy watching him, he shoved the book back in the pile with the others and shrunk away from them self-consciously.

"I'm going to do this, so we need to compromise," Wendy said.

Eleanor was silent for a while. "If you straight up get murdered, what's going to happen?" she asked quietly.

Wendy sighed. "I promise. I promise you that I'll be okay."

Eleanor let Wendy's words sink into the night for a full minute before responding. "Okay. Turn your location on and FaceTime or text me every half hour. If I don't hear from you ten minutes after the hour, I'm going to call the cops and send them your location. Take a picture of this guy and his friend when they're not looking so we can have at least some record of who fucking kidnapped you. Also—and I swear to God—if you die, I'm going to your funeral and I'm going to yell at your corpse in front of your entire grieving extended family, do you hear me?"

"Yes, Mom." Wendy laughed dryly.

"Wear a sweater and bring a little umbrella in case it rains. Don't forget your charger, and wear shoes good for running."

"Mmkay." Wendy unzipped the suitcase of clothes near her bed and started rummaging for her sweater.

"Don't drink any alcohol or do any drugs, and I swear to fuck if you get anything else to drink at all, watch it for the entire time you're drinking it, and don't leave it with anyone.

Not even any girls. You don't know these people, and they don't love you like I do."

"Gayyy," Wendy teased.

"You know it," Eleanor said quietly. "Don't forget to take pictures and send them to me."

"I won't. It will be okay. I'll be back by midnight."

"You had better," Eleanor snapped.

Wendy hung up and grabbed her purse.

"So. You coming or . . . ?" Peter asked, raising a slim eyebrow.

"Yeah. I just need to find an umbrella . . ." Wendy bent down to look under her bed.

"You don't need it," Peter said calmly.

"What if it rains? I'd rather be safe than—" Wendy started, but Peter interrupted her.

"If you need anything out there, I'll get it for you."

"You couldn't even afford to get your jacket fixed," Wendy declared.

Peter hopped down into her room and crossed his arms. Wendy instinctively backed away toward the bed. He dragged his golden eyes from her tennis shoes up past the sweatpants she'd been sleeping in, the sweater she'd hastily thrown on over the T-shirt from her old school's gym uniform, and let them settle on her face. "If you're going out with me, I won't let you get wet, Wendy Darling," he said seriously. "If you're going out there with me . . . I'll get you whatever you want."

"Oh," Wendy said.

Peter grinned.

"So," he said brightly, "are we going down the trellis, or are we going out the front door? Tink's not a patient girl, so we've got to make a choice quickly."

"I . . . I don't have a key to lock the door yet," Wendy stammered.

"Okay, then on my back you go. You don't look like you scale a lot of walls. I'd rather actually make it to the party than take you to the emergency room." Peter turned around and crouched low so Wendy could climb on his back.

Wendy swallowed, tightened her resolve, and wrapped her arms around Peter's neck. His hair was terribly soft against her cheek. He smelled like smoke, metal, and—strangely—flowers. Fresh in a way that she'd never known boys to smell. Like maybe he used floral shampoo or something. She could already feel his wiry muscles beneath his jacket, but it still startled her when he curved his hands beneath her thighs and lifted her properly onto his back with a small hop. Peter was much stronger than he looked, she realized dizzily.

"Curl your legs around my waist, Darling. I need my hands for climbing. I can't hold you." His cheek inadvertently brushed against hers as he spoke.

Wendy was too beyond words to reply, but she dug her ankles deeper into his hip bones like he requested.

Then, before she could really process all the sensory information about being this close, he was out the window and scaling down the side of her house. The wind blew hard, whipping her hair around his face. Wendy apologized anxiously, but Peter tossed his head to get it out of his eyes and laughed, bright and sweet.

"It feels like flying doesn't it?" he asked. "It's better when you're climbing higher up."

"How high do you usually go?" Wendy clenched her eyes shut in terror as Peter stretched to put his toe on the top of the downstairs kitchen window.

"Higher than this."

He held on to the edge of the trellis with his fingertips for a second before swinging down to the kitchen windowsill. Wendy shrieked, even as Peter clamped onto the top of the kitchen window without falling. His boots landed solidly on the slim strip sticking out of the siding, where Mrs. Darling had wanted to put a flowerpot so she could look at marigolds while she washed the dishes.

Peter tightened his grip on the ledge and paused. He shifted Wendy's weight on his back so he could reach behind and cup the side of her head reassuringly. "We're okay. We're almost down."

Peter stretched a leg from the sill to the grass below and eased them into the alley. Then he leaned back gracefully so that Wendy could unwind her legs from around his waist and release her iron grip around his throat.

"You didn't have to hold him so closely."

Wendy turned around.

The girl, Tink, was scowling at her. Her arms were tight against the side of her body and her hands were clenched into fists.

"You could have just held him normally," Tink said.

Peter sighed like this was an old argument. "She *was* holding me normally."

"Who is she, anyway?" Tink spat. "And why did you bring her with?"

"He asked me to a party," Wendy replied blandly. She wasn't going to be intimidated by someone who thought crushed velvet was an okay fabric to wear in the twenty-first century.

"I wasn't talking to you," Tink growled. "I was talking to him. You have no idea what you're doing, and your opinion is meaningless to me."

"I mean . . . you don't have to come with us, if you don't want to," Peter said with a sharp grin. He flicked a spike on the shoulder of Tink's leather jacket. "I'm sure Darling and I will have a nice time without you."

Darling? Tink mouthed in disgust.

Peter's grin grew wider.

Wendy stuck out her hand to be shaken, boldly. "Wendy Darling. Nice to meet you."

Tink looked at Wendy's hand and turned away from it with a wave of her own. "Whatever."

"This is Tinkerbelle," Peter said. "My ex-girlfriend."

"Ex-something," Tinkerbelle muttered.

"Tinkerbelle is an interesting name," Wendy remarked as Peter began leading them down the alley and toward the street. "Is it a nickname?"

Tinkerbelle ignored her, opting to glare at the ground and trudge beside Peter in silence.

Peter shook his head and answered for her. "It's a nickname. She's good at metalworking and fixing electronics, so I used to call her Tinker. After a little while, I added the 'belle.'" He grinned. "I mean, look at her . . . it fits."

"That's actually kind of cool," Wendy said conversationally. "We had a program for engineering at my old school where you could transition straight into the community college and get your associate degree six months quicker."

"Well, lucky you," Tinkerbelle snarled.

"Okay." Wendy stopped walking and put her hands on her hips and turned to face Tinkerbelle. "Will you calm down?"

"You should go home and just leave us alone. No one wants you here!" Tinkerbelle shouted, throwing her arms out wildly.

"Wow! I just might!" Wendy exclaimed, turning on her heel. "It was nice to fuckin' meet you, Peter—"

"I want her here," Peter interrupted in a voice as unamused and dry as the leaves blowing down the street.

Tinkerbelle seemed to shrink instantly. Her big blue eyes snapped to the asphalt, and her mouth twisted tightly as she clenched her teeth. Peter put his hand on Tinkerbelle's shoulder and leaned in close to her. "Wendy is our guest. She's new to the city, and I wanted to show her a good time. She's been so brave tonight already, what with finding me in her home and climbing down the trellis. She deserves this. Can you make some room for her?"

"I really don't have to go, if she's that upset," Wendy said. She glanced over her shoulder. She could still see her bedroom window.

"No, please," Peter said gently. "Stay."

Tinkerbelle closed her eyes like something was hurting her immensely, then her shoulders sagged. "Fine. I'm just— It's . . ." She took a breath and started again. "It's been a long day. I didn't expect to have to look after someone tonight, and I really just wanted to relax with my friends."

"It's all right." Wendy shrugged. "You don't have to look after me. I can look after myself."

"I'll look after you, too," Peter said firmly. "I'm the one who needs to make sure you get home safe."

Wendy could feel her cheeks burning and steadfastly willed her heart to stop racing whenever Peter said things like that. When she looked over, Tinkerbelle was watching her.

Now that the tension was dissipating, Wendy took the time to actually look back at her. Tinkerbelle was staggeringly pretty. Also, now that she was seeing Peter and Tinkerbelle next to each other, she could picture how well they would have looked together when they were still dating. They even moved like they had grown used to being close.

Peter towered over Tinkerbelle, who was clearly irritated by that, but he still had his shoulder turned toward her protectively. Tinkerbelle had her arms wrapped tightly around herself, but she swayed toward Peter like she couldn't help it.

Her clothes went well together, but they looked worse for wear in the same way that Peter's did. Like they'd been washed too many times or worn for too long. The crushed velvet green dress had a few patches where the fabric had been stripped completely bald. Her jacket was a size or so too big for her. Not big enough to have been chosen that way as a cool "boyfriend" aesthetic, but more like she had either lost a massive amount of weight, or it had belonged to someone else before her. She had dark blue eyeliner crusted in the corners of her eyes like she had applied it the night before and just applied more on top of what was left. Her tights were practically strings left over from a pair of pantyhose, and the Vans she wore had duct tape holding them together.

Despite all this, both still looked dazzling—Peter, tall, auburn-haired, and golden-eyed, and Tinkerbelle, blond and with a gaze as deep as the sea. Wendy's hand itched to whip out her phone and take a photograph of both of them as they stood stock-still in the middle of the alley, looking like a freakin' editorial. Eleanor would lose her goddamn mind at how cool they looked, but Wendy couldn't do it while they were both staring right at her.

"Look," Wendy said. "If things get out of hand, or if I get

lost or something, I'll figure myself out. I have my phone, and I'm not an idiot. You don't have to worry about me. Let's just pretend that none of this ever happened and start from scratch. It's nice to meet you, Tinkerbelle, I'm sorry you had a hard day, and I won't cling to your ex-boyfriend. Now. Where the fuck are we going?"

Peter laughed, threw an arm over Tinkerbelle's shoulders, and led them to the end of the alley. "We're going to a few places, actually. First, we have to go home and pick up a few friends. Then, we're getting dinner at a place called the Mermaid's Lagoon. Afterward, we're heading south to the warehouse, where the party is."

"That's a lot of traveling," Wendy remarked.

Peter nodded in the direction of the train station up the street. "The night is young." That smile was plastered back on his face. "And what sort of adventure would this be without a bit of travel?"

CHAPTER 5

Wendy texted Eleanor while Peter and Tinkerbelle were busy fiddling with the train ticket machine. She opened the camera on her phone, zoomed in on one of the train platform's round security mirrors, and got a decent snapshot of Peter's and Tinkerbelle's faces without either of them noticing.

> **Eleanor:** Oh wow, he looks like a model. Your idiocy from earlier in the night is beginning to make sense to me.
> **Wendy:** He's really nice, too. He's buying my train ticket and everything.
> **Eleanor:** Train tickets are $2.50, do not sell your dignity to men for $2.50.

Wendy chose to ignore that.

> **Wendy:** I'm surprised you don't have anything to say about his friend? She's a knockout.
> **Eleanor:** She's ok. She's not my type. I like brunettes. 👀
> **Wendy:** Valid. She's also kind of a bitch. Apparently, she and Peter used to date??? Peter helped me get outside and I guess we were standing too close and she was HEATED.
> **Eleanor:** lmao

Wendy: She was like "get away from him" and we hadn't even properly said hi. It's like b I don't want your boy

Eleanor: u do tho

Wendy: I DO THO 👀 👀

Eleanor: MESSY

"Come on, we don't have all day," Tinkerbelle said, pushing Wendy's ticket into her hand. Peter scanned his card but then hopped the turnstile just for the fun of it. Tinkerbelle pushed Wendy through behind him, and they both followed him up the stairs to the platform.

The train stop felt much stranger at night than when Wendy had come here with her mom. There was a completely different kind of population this late. None of the chipper stay-at-home moms in Lululemon with designer strollers were out anymore. It was just tired, late-shift workers, people in their thirties going out to have a good time, and a few college students. From this high up, the streetlights glittered in the distance, and the city looked like a movie set. Like real people weren't living in all those buildings; they were just put up to complete a skyline for a postcard view. There was such a large difference between seeing places like this on TV and standing in the middle of them in real life. She turned to say something about this, but Peter was looking off into the night, his pretty face stony and expressionless.

What's wrong? Wendy almost asked, but to her surprise,

Tinkerbelle tugged the sleeve of her sweater and then shook her head urgently. Wendy paused. Peter stood like that for almost a minute, so still it was eerie. People coming up the stairs to wait for the train gave the three of them a wide berth. Peter's eyes shifted back and forth rapidly, like he was thinking very fast. Then he closed them, paused, and seemed to breathe life back into his body all at once. When he finally turned back to Wendy and Tinkerbelle, it was as if all that had never happened.

"The train's coming," he said. "We're heading up to Wilson."

"How many of the boys are coming with us?" Tinkerbelle asked.

"Only a few of the older ones," Peter replied. "Since we'll be out late."

The train came into the station fast enough to blow everyone's hair back before slowing to a stop with the doors directly in front of them.

"THIS IS FULLERTON. TRANSFER TO BROWN- AND PURPLE-LINE TRAINS AT FULLERTON," the train blared loudly, and the doors slid open with a soft bang.

To Wendy's surprise, the train was already very crowded. Peter pushed through the throng and held the metal bar above the seats so that there was an alcove of space beneath his arms for Tinkerbelle and Wendy to stand in. Tinkerbelle ducked underneath and wrapped an arm around the back of his waist. Wendy, thinking about what happened the last time she was wrapped around Peter, reached up and grabbed the bar above them instead. She tried not to inhale the smoke-and-flowers scent radiating from Peter's body.

The doors closed and the train lurched forward.

"So, how far is Wilson?" Wendy asked.

"Not far," Tinkerbelle replied. "It's a decent walk from your place, but it's walkable if you don't have train fare. Maybe thirty minutes?"

"Do you do a lot of walking around here? Is the area safe at night?"

Tinkerbelle snorted. "Nowhere is safe at night. Especially not when you've got a face like yours."

Wendy thought they were done with the rude part of the evening. She scowled and opened her mouth to snap back, but Tinkerbelle clarified, "You know. Sweet and a bit stubborn, like mine. Plus, you're a girl, and you know how that goes."

"I'd never let anyone do anything to you," Peter said a bit absentmindedly. "The boys are always out there watching."

The corner of Tinkerbelle's mouth ticked up, but it couldn't really be called a smile yet.

"There *is* that," she said fondly. "But they only watch out for me."

She turned to Wendy. "*You* should be careful if you're thinking about night jogging."

"I'll keep that in mind," Wendy said.

Tinkerbelle looked out at the city as it whizzed by. "I think you'll like the boys. They like tough girls. Smart girls."

"What are they like?"

Tinkerbelle bit her lip while she thought. "They're kind, but a bit rough."

"They're resourceful," Peter said.

"They're family," Tinkerbelle insisted.

Peter huffed gently. "Yeah, that, too. No one else but family can be such a hassle."

"Ignore him," Tinkerbelle said. "He loves them. Or, well . . . as much as he can, I guess."

That remark didn't settle well into the atmosphere between them, and the air seemed a bit colder.

"So," Peter said brightly, changing the subject. "Tell us a bit about you?"

"Well," Wendy started, "I moved here from Hinsdale, like, four days ago. I'm a senior, but I haven't started back at school yet."

"Why did you move?" Tinkerbelle interrupted.

Wendy shrugged. She might as well use this to help her prepare for this conversation, because she was sure she'd be having it at school over and over again in a couple of days.

"My dad got a new job, and my mom wants to adopt a few more kids. They figured that living in the city would be better than having my dad drive all the way out here every day. Also, probably make it a bit easier to showcase that we're stable enough to take in new children. Plus, they're looking for older ones because they have lower chances of getting adopted or something. It's a good time, too, because I'm probably going to college out of state, and they can go back to being parents again instead of being empty nesters in their mid-thirties."

Peter and Tinkerbelle spoke at the same time.

"What kind of kids are they looking for?" Tinkerbelle asked urgently.

"Your parents are in their thirties?" Peter blurted in disbelief.

Wendy went with Tinkerbelle's question first. "They're looking for someone around twelve to fourteen, probably boys."

Tinkerbelle's face did something unexpected when she received that news, but Wendy didn't know her well enough to figure out what it meant. Wendy looked up at Peter instead. "Yeah, my mom is, like, thirty-three, and my dad is thirty-eight. She had me young, and they met afterward while she was in graduate school. It's not a big deal, but I can see why they would want to have more kids after I leave. This way they can do the whole thing over again and actually be able to afford to take them on real vacations this time around."

"Hmm," Peter said.

"Which," Wendy continued, "the new kids would *also* deserve, since I'm sure the foster system isn't a picnic."

"It's not," Tinkerbelle said.

Oh.

Before Wendy could process her social faux pas, Peter pulled his arms down and whispered, "We need to change train cars."

"We're not even at the next stop," Tinkerbelle started to complain. "Wilson is only two more—"

Peter looked over his shoulder quickly and grabbed Tinkerbelle by the back of her collar, pushing her toward the door. "Go. Now," he said roughly.

Wendy followed his gaze and landed on a police officer near the back of the train car. He wasn't facing them, but he was close to the train doors, and if he shifted a bit, they would definitely be within his line of sight. When she turned back around, Peter and Tinkerbelle were nearly through the crowd. At the last second, Tinkerbelle reached a hand out and firmly grabbed Wendy's, pulling her toward the door.

"Those doors are for the train conductors only!" Wendy hissed.

"Just come on," Tinkerbelle whispered back. "Don't look down and you won't fall."

"But—"

"I won't let you fall," Tinkerbelle clarified fiercely.

Peter ducked low and wrenched the door open. The noise from the tracks was deafening as they hurtled through the night. The train car in front of them swayed ominously back and forth. The platform between the two cars was only a half-moon of space, about a foot across. There were no handles to help Wendy keep her balance, just chains that connected the two cars, draped slack. Peter charged forward unflinchingly and yanked open the back of the next train car. He slipped across the space gracefully and made it into the next car without a hitch. Then he stuck his foot in the door to hold it open.

Tinkerbelle went next, but instead of hopping into the next car, she stretched her feet across both small platforms and held her arms out across them. Then she leaned against the chains and stared back at Wendy expectantly, using her own body as a railing between the cars.

"You can do this," she said firmly. The wind whipped her words clean out of her mouth and flung them far beyond Wendy's ears.

Wendy took a breath and stepped out of the train car. She grabbed Tinkerbelle's arm for balance and saw Tinkerbelle clench her teeth. The platforms between cars felt a lot sturdier than she'd imagined, and the swaying that seemed so chaotic on the inside of the train was absorbed by her body now that she was outside. She transferred smoothly between the cars, stumbling into the following car just in time for them to make it to the next stop. Tinkerbelle pushed Wendy forward as she stepped in behind her and closed the train door.

"Why couldn't we have just changed train cars when we got to the next stop?" Wendy asked breathlessly.

"He would have seen us running. There's just enough

time between stops where you can get on the train," Peter explained. "The distance between one car door and another is farther than you think. If you don't hurry, they'll close before you make it."

"He wasn't looking at us yet," Wendy said, collapsing against the door to catch her breath. There was a small, closed-off seat in the back of the train car by the doors, and Tinkerbelle tossed herself into it, annoyed.

Peter blocked off the archway to the rest of the car with his lanky body and gave Wendy a dry glance. "I don't know how much you know about city cops, but they're nothing like whatever you experienced back in Hinsdale."

"What do you mean?" Wendy settled down next to Tinkerbelle, who shifted away toward the window in response.

Peter thought for a bit before he continued. "You went to school, so this comparison might work for you: You know how individual ships in the British Navy would defect to piracy when they realized that they could? They would have their own pirate flag, but also the union jack. Then, depending on whether the circumstances required, they would raise one flag and lower another?"

Wendy had no idea what he was talking about, but she nodded anyway.

"They had the ability to reap the benefits of piracy and also had the power to prosecute pirates and enforce British maritime law. So, of course they just went everywhere drunk with power, fucking shit up, and no one could tell them to stop, or had the ability to stop them . . . because they were who you would go to when you needed to stop pirates."

Wendy nodded.

"It's like that. But cops."

"Uh."

"Yeah, it's not great," Peter snapped.

Wendy wasn't sure what her face was doing, but whatever it was made Tinkerbelle smile.

"You regret coming out with us yet?" she asked in a suspiciously sweet voice.

"No," Wendy said bullishly.

"Good." Tinkerbelle's smile grew wider. "Do you want to hear a story?"

"A story about what? Cops?" Wendy grimaced. She did not.

"A story about our Peter and why we have to run when we see police."

Wendy looked up at Peter, who shrugged and nodded as if to say, *Indulge her*.

"Uh. Okay." Wendy felt her back pocket to make sure her phone was still there.

Tinkerbelle scooted closer to Wendy and began, "A while back, closer to when Peter and I first met, we had been hanging out by the train graveyard—the place where the train cars go to sit when the station closes down for the night. We were having a small party. Pried open one of the train's doors so it was like one big room. Some of the kids from down south had come up to be there. It was a really great night. I don't know exactly what happened, but somehow the cops knew we were there and decided to come out full force to shut the party down."

Tinkerbelle leaned back and kicked her legs up against the train car wall.

"I scampered off, of course. I'm good with hiding and running, but we had some younger boys with us that needed to be watched, protected, and led back home. They were new, you know."

"Slightly and Curly," Peter filled in. "Thirteen and fourteen at the time."

"Indeed," Tinkerbelle said. "Just babies, really. And this wasn't your everyday raid; the police had the clubs and gear out in full force. No tear gas, but shields and all of that—who knows why they thought they needed it. None of us are ever armed. Also, this night in particular, the detective was out and heading the raid."

Peter hummed, eyes twinkling as he listened.

"Detective Hook himself," Tinkerbelle said the name proudly, like it meant something.

"Detective?" Wendy echoed.

Tinkerbelle nodded. "The worst of the lot of them. Anyway, we needed a distraction to get them away from our boys. Peter, bright as he is, had predicted we might have had trouble. He'd made a few fire starters and tossed them over the top of a few of the train cars to get attention. Then, while they were blazing hot and high, we made a run for it in the dark.

"Now, I've only heard this story secondhand, but from what I know, Detective Hook himself ran Peter and the boys down until the little ones couldn't run anymore. Then he lined them up against a train car and called for backup."

Tinkerbelle looked up at Peter, but he was gazing steadfastly at Wendy. He seemed amused by the way Tinkerbelle was telling the story. But Wendy was not amused; Wendy was horrified.

"Slightly started crying, so Hook tased him, which infuriated everyone, of course. Then when Hook turned his back for a second, Peter sprinted at him and wrestled him to the ground. He grabbed a rock and knocked the taser out of Hook's hand and then smashed both of them with the rock until he couldn't call for backup or use his pistol. Then Peter picked up Slightly, put him on his back, and carried him all the way back home."

"Oh my God," Wendy said.

"Yeah. A couple of months later, one of the boys saw Detective Hook coming out of a coffee shop. One of his hands was in a splint, but the other one had been amputated. So, chasing us down is now his personal vendetta."

Wendy gasped. "Oh my God, that's fucking crazy."

"It's not as bad as you think," Tinkerbelle said coolly, lowering her eyelids. "We just stay out of their way, and they stay out of ours."

Wendy didn't know what to say, so she didn't.

Tinkerbelle looked very pleased with herself. Wendy could feel the waves of Tinkerbelle's satisfaction rolling off her, and it pissed Wendy off.

Peter, on the other hand, was looking out the window contentedly, like beating someone with a rock until their entire hand had to be cut off was a completely normal and reasonable thing to do. The train rocked suddenly, and Peter caught himself against the side of the door. Wendy's eyes snapped to his arms. Arms that had carried her safely down the side of her house, had carried Slightly—whoever that was—all the way home after being tased. When she looked up, Peter was watching her.

"He tased a child, you know," Peter said quietly. "A little boy who was crying and scared." He shook his head. "It wasn't the best way to handle the situation, I know, but I said I would never let anybody hurt him."

Wendy could hear the unspoken *And I would never let anyone hurt you*. It was heavy in the air. He reached out and squeezed her shoulder. She could feel the heat of his big hand through her sweater, like a brand.

"THIS IS WILSON. TRANSFER TO PURPLE-LINE TRAINS AT WILSON," the train blared. Then the speaker crackled and the conductor took over. "THIS TRAIN WILL BE STANDING AT WILSON STATION FOR AT LEAST TWENTY MINUTES DUE TO A DISTURBANCE AT THE STATION. ALL PASSENGERS WHO NEED TO TRANSFER

MUST EXIT THE TRAIN. THERE ARE SHUTTLES THAT WILL TAKE YOU TO THE NEXT STOP."

Wendy looked up, alarmed. "Wh—"

Tinkerbelle shoved her out of the seat and toward the door. "Don't worry about it; this happens every so often. Just follow the crowd down the stairs. This is our stop, anyway."

Wendy was carried out of the train car and off to the platform by the people pushing behind her. She stumbled down the stairs and into the lobby, where it was immediately clear that something was wrong. At the front of the crowd, the station staff and several officers stood by the Wilson Station doors, shouting at passengers that they couldn't go onto the platform.

At the sight of the officers, Peter went ashen. "I'm finding a new way out. Take care of Wendy." He turned back against the press of the crowd.

"What?!" Tinkerbelle complained. "You said I wouldn't have to watch her!" But Peter was too far away to hear.

Tinkerbelle looked back at Wendy, then tightened her lips in resolve. "Fuck this." She scampered off after Peter.

Jesus Christ. Wendy continued making her way to the exit, but only because she had to. The people behind her wouldn't let her stop and regroup. They rushed her to the front of the lobby and pressed her forcefully out the door and into the street and a world of lights and noise.

There had to be at least thirty cop cars parked around the Wilson and Broadway intersection, and maybe a hundred police officers in the area. Everyone who had been on the train was shouting about being kicked off and asking about the shuttles they'd been promised. The train staff had bullhorns and were yelling at the riders about what street the shuttles would be picking up passengers. The actual police had the sirens on all their cars going full force. Their lights threw the street into a strobe of blue and red. There were officers at every intersection redirecting traffic and officers randomly demanding that people show identification.

Wendy pulled out her phone and immediately looked for a ride share, but the price for the area had spiked to nearly $60, and she only had $35 allowance left in her bank account. Her phone battery was also way lower than she felt comfortable with. She had fallen asleep without plugging it in to charge, and now it was at 16 percent. She turned back to the train station.

"I need to get back on the train platform. I don't care if I have to wait there for an hour. I just need to get back home," Wendy said to one of the train workers nearby.

He shook his head. "No one is getting on the train at this station. What shuttle do you need to be on?"

Overwhelmed, Wendy couldn't remember the name of the stop near her house.

"What neighborhood are you going to?" the train worker asked loudly, clearly losing patience.

Wendy wracked her brain but kept coming up empty, panic making memory difficult. The train worker grabbed her shoulder firmly, steered her back into the flow of the crowd, and returned to his job of denying people access into the station.

Wendy followed the crowd for half a block, then ducked into an alley and crouched down to catch her breath. Her phone's alarm broke her panic attack, reminding her it was time to text Eleanor.

Wendy: don't be mad at me but things are going BAD.

Eleanor: what are you lost or something

Wendy: lmao I wish!! I'm by the Wilson train stop and there's like fifty million cops everywhere and Peter and Tinkerbelle are like N O W H E R E to be found and I'm freaking out

Eleanor: Tinkerbelle???

Wendy: Peter's friend, the blond who you don't think is hot

Eleanor: that's a bad name. Do her parents even love her

Wendy: she has no parents!! Found that out too! But only after I said something weird about my family and why we came here. lmao kill me

Eleanor: ok coolcoolcoolcool alright you're by yourself. Well. You do have options.

Wendy: WHAT ARE THEY

Eleanor: you could just get back on the train and go home.

Wendy: train door's blocked by cops next option

Eleanor: you could call an Uber. Or hell, I'll call you an
Uber.

Wendy: the cops are blocking off the whole street and
are questioning ppl who try to leave next option

Eleanor: you're not gonna like this BUT you could walk
up to an officer and be like . . . pls take me home

Wendy: would they even do that?

Eleanor: probably not, but most city people don't just
t a l k to cops. If you do that, then you're clearly not
from around here, not scared of whatever's happening and not likely to be a suspect lmao. Just
babble about being from the suburbs and being
lost.

Wendy: I don't want to talk to cops Eleanor! I'm too
Black to just saunter up like "hello officers"

Eleanor: lmao STOP. I know I know. I'm just focused on
my best friend making it home safe and sound to
her family who loves her so we can have a nice and
reasonable parent supervised first meetup. Maybe
you'll get lucky??? Or something???? Please just get
this situation sorted

Wendy: FINE fine yeah, I'll do it.

Eleanor: you had Better

Wendy put her phone back in her pocket and took a deep
breath. Then she stood up and looked around for a cop who

didn't look intimidating. There was one across the street that seemed kind of mom-ish. Late fifties, short, and kind of pudgy. She seemed like a good bet. *Gambling with the police state, here we come.*

Wendy swung her leg out to start in that direction when a hand covered her mouth and several others pulled her backward. She tried to turn around to figure out who was grabbing her, but before she could, they wrapped a T-shirt over her head and shoved its fabric in her mouth.

Wendy screamed, but the cloth muffled it. The deafening noise of the police and the crowd drowned out everything else, anyway. The hands held her upper arms in a firm grip, dragging her down the alley and up too many stairs for her to count. Her assailants were silent and seemed organized. She could tell there were more than three of them, and they didn't seem to need to communicate to get things done. After a disorienting ride in what felt like an elevator and a few stomach-churning jaunts down and up flights of stairs, making sure she couldn't identify which direction she'd come from, Wendy was pushed down into a hard metal seat. Her arms and legs were tied to the chair firmly before her assailants ripped the T-shirt off her head and pushed it back into her mouth.

CHAPTER 6

The first thing Wendy noticed was the incredible mess. Or maybe *clutter* was the right word . . . Either way, she was in a kitchen. There was art tacked up all over the walls to the point where none of the original surface was in sight. The art was a mix of finger paintings, crayon drawings, and surprisingly high-quality pencil sketches, all together like a giant mural. A massive sculptural arrangement of glass bottles of many colors hung from the ceiling, twisting from the entryway into the kitchen and back out of the room. The bottles were tinkling lightly, and the street light coming in from the window was throwing specks of brightness off their glass. It was stunning, and Wendy wished she could look more closely, but only the bottoms of the bottles were visible from where she was sitting. There was a stack of dishes by the sink and crates of plants stacked in the corners. On one side of the room was a massive pile of cans sorted by type into jagged towers, like stalagmites. On the other side was a large table that looked handmade out of two doors stuck together, with at least ten chairs around it. There was so much stuff crowding the space, but all of it was neatly arranged. Not exactly organized, but delicately placed, almost like an art project, for the pleasure of the viewer.

The second thing Wendy noticed was the children. Or teenagers, to be specific.

There were seven of them, ranging in age from ten to

about seventeen, if she guessed correctly. The younger four children sat by her arms and legs, looking ready to grab her if she began to struggle. The three oldest were standing in front of her, having the strangest screaming match that Wendy had ever had the displeasure to witness.

"The boys were in the streets?" the first boy said angrily. "At this time of night and with the pirates swarming?" He looked like he might be the youngest of the three, but clearly too old for "grab her" duty. He was African American, with smooth dark skin and slender eyes. Unlike the others in the room, who were in varying levels of disarray, he was dressed in an expensive-looking black turtleneck and black jeans. He also had an apron on and a plastic soup ladle in his hand. His voice was soft and rich, but he was clearly just as angry as the other two.

The boy directly next to him reared back, scandalized. "Fuck you, Slightly, you didn't have to make that decision. What Peter says—" This boy, the loudest of the three, was much taller than both Slightly and the redheaded boy on the other side of him, and skinny. His pants were too small for him, and he'd tried to obscure that fact by rolling the legs up into partial capris. His skin was very pale, and he had curly dark hair that he'd braided into two long pigtails. In spite of the warm weather, he was wearing a sweater that had clearly been darned by a novice.

"Curly—" Slightly began plaintively, but the silent red-headed boy next to him shook his head sharply. This one was definitely the oldest. He stood placidly with his arms crossed. He had bright red hair, was wearing a hearing aid, and was a little short for his age. His arms were incredibly muscular and bulged intimidatingly. He'd clearly torn the sleeves off his shirt to show them off. He hadn't yet spoken, but every so often he would gesture crisply or shake his head in a particular way, which set the boy in front of him into hysterics. The darker the look on the redhead's face got, the louder Curly screamed.

"I can't just *not* listen when I'm given a direct order, Nibs!" Curly yelled, throwing his arms out dramatically. "I'm a fucking lieutenant! Not a captain, like you! I can't just waltz up to him all, 'Hey, Peter, I decided not to get the girl you wanted because it felt weird.' He would bash my head against the sidewalk!"

Slightly scoffed. "You could have gotten her on your own. You don't know what's out there tonight! We could have lost someone!"

"She's not a fucking baby, and I'm not a brute like Nibs," Curly remarked. "I'm not strong enough to drag someone around over hill and dale, like we're supposed to when we bring people here, all by myself."

Nibs grinned. "You could be," he said. His voice was startlingly deep, and hoarse to the point of softness. "If you cared to try."

"STOP CRITICIZING MY WORKOUT ROUTINE!" Curly howled.

Nibs ignored Curly's outburst very intentionally and instead nodded over at Wendy. The smallest boy near Wendy's left ankle tightened his grip and growled at her. "Either way, we took some liberties."

"Peter didn't say that he wanted her tied?" Slightly gasped. "Curly, then why did you—"

"IT WAS NIBS'S IDEA! GOD! Every deviation from Peter's rules isn't always me, *Slightly*." Curly spat Slightly's name, like saying it tasted horrible in his mouth.

Nibs raised an eyebrow and gestured quickly.

"Fuck you both. It's always 'Curly this' and 'Curly that.' For once this isn't my fault. I'm fuckin' done." Curly stomped out of the kitchen and down the hall.

Slightly and Nibs turned to look at Wendy, who wisely didn't try to say a word, before continuing their argument.

"I know she's one of them, not one of us, but if Peter just said to bring her over, he didn't really specify that she was our prisoner . . . ," Slightly said.

Nibs shrugged one shoulder and snapped his left hand, saying something so low and quiet that Wendy couldn't hear him.

Slightly sighed loudly. "It doesn't make sense, but you can't make those kinds of decisions without Peter's permission. Yes, we can't trust her, and yes, it's better to be safe than sorry, but none of us ever know what Peter wants unless he tells us. You're still on thin ice from the incident with the peaches. I just . . . Nibs, you've got to be more careful with—"

The front door of the apartment slammed open and Peter and Tinkerbelle walked in. Nibs and Slightly flinched. Slightly backed away toward the wall. But Nibs stood firm and held Peter's gaze defiantly.

Peter took in the scene with a tight look on his face. He surveyed the group of boys holding Wendy down, and Wendy herself with the T-shirt still stuck in her mouth, sitting very still in a veritable throne of limbs. He glanced at Slightly, who held up his hands defensively, as if to say, *It wasn't me*. His eyes tracked from the ladle in Slightly's right hand to the pot of still-steaming soup on the stovetop. Then his gaze landed firmly on Nibs.

Tinkerbelle opened her mouth to say something, but Curly pushed in from behind her and blurted, "I didn't do it."

"I know you didn't, Curly," Peter said, still staring at Nibs. "It's not your style."

Nibs's face was blazing red, but he stood stock-still, not bowing beneath the ferocity of Peter's stare. Tinkerbelle reached out a hand and put it on Nibs's arm.

Nibs kept his eyes on Peter but nodded over at Tinkerbelle.

"That wasn't your call to make," Peter said. "She is our guest. Untie her."

The younger boys jumped to follow Peter's order. Peter turned to Wendy and knelt at her feet.

"I am so, so sorry," Peter said quietly. "This was *never* meant to happen. When I got off the train, I texted Curly to meet you and take you to our house, but I was hoping he'd bring you by and introduce you to everyone, not take you hostage and scare the shit out of you."

The boys removed the T-shirt in her mouth last.

The instant Wendy's mouth was free, she began shouting. "Get off me, GET OFF ME!" She wrenched her arms out of the boys' grip and jumped up from the chair.

"Hey, *hey*," Peter said gently.

Wendy lurched forward to leave, but Peter caught her in his arms and held her fast. She hadn't been going for a hug at all, but she could see how he would have thought she was; in her panic, she hadn't even gotten to fully turn toward the door. Now that Peter had her in his arms, he held her close and rocked her back and forth. He murmured into her hair, cupping the back of her head tenderly, saying, "I'm so sorry, I'm so sorry" over and over again until Wendy's panic subsided. She could feel tears spring to her eyes. The other boys watched in silence. Wendy gazed at everyone over Peter's shoulder. Slightly dropped his hands and moved swiftly over to the overboiling pot to stir it. Tinkerbelle watched Peter hold Wendy for a moment contemplatively—not at all like she had when they'd come down the side of Wendy's house—then she turned and went deeper into the apartment. Curly looked incredibly sheepish and kept glancing over at Nibs. Nibs refused to look at Wendy, continuing to stare at the back of Peter's head angrily.

Peter didn't focus on any of that, opting instead to take the time to console Wendy. He gently rubbed her back, rocking them both side to side until she stopped shaking, and relaxed enough to bury her face into the curve of his neck.

"I'm sorry I failed you," he continued. "I'm sorry I left you. I'm sorry you were alone. I'm sorry you were lost. I'm sorry you were taken. I'm sorry they treated you roughly. I'm sorry, Darling, I'm so, so sorry."

"I'm sorry," one of the littlest boys echoed. Wendy pulled her head off Peter's shoulder to glance at who had spoken. He couldn't have been older than seven, looking earnest and on the verge of frightened tears.

"It's okay," Wendy heard herself saying, even though it wasn't. "It was just a misunderstanding."

Peter's grip gentled, and he stepped back to hold her hands in his. "This is quite possibly the worst way that I wanted you to meet my family, but would you please give this another try? It wasn't what I intended at all, and I still have friends who would love to meet you. I texted a bunch of people that you were coming to the party, and they're waiting for us . . ."

Wendy looked back and forth between Peter and the boys, then thought about her phone in her pocket. As long as she had it, she could find a charger. She still had control of the situation. She took a deep breath. Then she nodded and squeezed Peter's hands. "I forgive you," she said firmly.

Peter's shoulders immediately relaxed. He sighed in

relief, then grinned wide and sweet. "Let's start again!" he said brightly. "This is my home, and this is my family."

He brushed a hand through his rakish brown curls and sauntered over to Slightly, clapping a hand heavily on the boy's shoulder. "This is Slightly. The one by the doorway is Curly, and the one responsible for the circumstances of your capture is Nibs."

"Hi," Curly said in an anxious, high voice.

Slightly nodded at her. "Nice to meet you." He returned his attention to the boiling pot.

Nibs waved sharply and went back to folding his arms.

Peter crouched down by the boys still waiting by the chair. He brushed his hand over the hair of the one who had echoed his apology, then kissed him crisply on the cheek. "Line up and give the lady your names."

They scrambled to follow his instructions.

"Tootles," the boy who'd apologized said. He had messy dark hair and was wearing school uniform shorts.

The next boy had his head shaved and looked like he could be in seventh grade. Unlike Tootles, he didn't seem repentant at all and still eyed her with suspicion. "I'm First."

Another boy, who looked exactly the same as First but with hair, followed. His face was bright and curious, and unlike his twin, he seemed less suspicious and altogether friendlier. "I'm Second," he declared. Now Wendy was willing to suspend disbelief for Slightly, Curly, and Nibs, but those couldn't possibly be their real names. These all had to be nicknames.

The last boy, who had been holding her left leg, stood up and stuck out a hand for her to shake. He was the oldest of the younger boys, maybe fifteen or sixteen at most. "Nice to meet you. I'm Prentis. I . . . just got here a few months ago," he said, shaking her hand firmly before stepping into line with the others.

Peter sauntered to Wendy's side and put an arm over her shoulders. "And this, my friends . . . is *Darling*."

"Where did you find her, Peter?" Second asked excitedly.

"Well," Peter started, then paused for theatrical effect. "This evening I went out to mend a part of Shadow . . ."

The younger boys clambered closer to hear the story, sitting at Peter's feet. Slightly turned off the pot and leaned back against the counter to listen. Nibs glanced at Peter one last time, then wandered into the back of the apartment. Curly went to sit with the younger boys and looked up at Wendy. He smiled openly at her, and she couldn't help but spare him a quirk of the side of her mouth.

"I was sneaking into the abandoned cottage down by the grotto," Peter began. "I'd heard that new owners may be coming soon, and I wanted to get some copper wiring to sell. Gotta get Slightly a new pair of glasses, and Nibs—trouble as he is—needs a new retainer. I'd barely gotten my leg over the fence when a monster of a dog came growling and barking."

Peter crouched down and curled his hands into claws and

gnashed his teeth theatrically. Tootles giggled and curled his small hands into claws, too.

"I was hurrying back over the fence," Peter continued. "But she grabbed ahold of my pants and dragged me down into the yard. Then, when I was defenseless and beaten, she bared her mighty teeth and clenched the sleeve of Shadow in her fearsome jaws, and shook for all she was worth."

"How did you get free?" Tootles gasped, brown eyes wide and scared.

"Oh, your Peter is too clever to be taken down by a beast of that size," Peter said dramatically. "She pulled and I pulled, and the sleeve ripped free. I scrambled over the fence and waited on the other side, biding my time until the monster was fast asleep. Then, and only then, could I rescue Shadow's sleeve and slip away into the night."

"But your sleeve is attached," First remarked, furrowing his eyebrows.

Second elbowed him in the side. "Shut up, he's not done," he hissed.

"That's right," Peter said. "I'm not. This is the story of Darling, and she hasn't appeared yet, has she?" He put an undercurrent of warning in his voice.

First shook his head and looked sullenly at the linoleum. Curly reached over and squeezed First's shoulder to console him.

"So. With Tinkerbelle playing watchman and the sun three hours past bedtime, I snuck up the side of the building and slithered through the window." Peter glanced over his shoulder at Wendy before continuing. "It was dark, and warmer there than I ever remembered it being, and I heard breathing, so I crept even quieter. All of a sudden, the lights turned on, and there sat the prettiest and angriest girl I've seen in weeks." Peter put his hands on his hips and mock glared at Wendy.

Tootles giggled loudly, then covered his mouth with both hands.

"*'What are you doing in my house!'* she shouted—very bravely, I might add—as she was lying there quite weapon-lessly, in her pajamas. So I told her, honest and true, that I was there for Shadow's sleeve and anything else I could get my hands on. Instead of screaming or making a fuss, she jumped up and got Shadow's sleeve quick as a flash. Then she stitched it right back on, good as new." Peter bent down to show Wendy's handiwork.

The boys scrambled closer to see.

"Slightly's a better sewer," First said mulishly, after a glance.

"Slightly wasn't even there," Second snapped.

Wendy glanced over at Slightly, who shrugged apologetically. "I took a fashion class at After School Matters," he said. "First doesn't mean anything by it. He's just shy."

First scowled harder.

Peter wiggled his eyebrows at Wendy conspiratorially, his golden eyes twinkling.

"Then, for her faithful service," he continued, "I magicked her up a token. Do you mind showing them, Darling?"

Wendy dug in her shirt and pulled out the acorn necklace. Curly gasped and Tootles jumped to his feet.

"That's a good one, miss!" Tootles shouted.

Even Slightly looked surprised. First and Second, on the other hand, were having some kind of wordless argument and were entirely focused on each other.

"Pardon me for asking, but why . . . are you here?" Prentis said, fiddling with his glasses.

"Um. Peter invited me to a warehouse party," Wendy said.

"Oh." Prentis put his chin in his hands. "I've heard those are very nice to go to. I haven't been able to attend as of yet, but I'm sure when I'm a bit older I'll get to go."

"You definitely will," Peter said, then turned to Wendy. "We don't do super-underage drinking in this house. Gotta keep things on the level, you know?"

Wendy blurted what she'd been wondering since the minute she'd been untied: "Are you their dad?"

There was a long silence, and then everyone began to laugh. Curly doubled over and began wheezing alarmingly, and Second slapped him hard on the back.

Slightly shook his head, chuckling as he ladled his soup into some bowls. "I really hope not."

"He's more like our manager," Prentis answered earnestly. He was the only one not actively guffawing. "Or perhaps our squad leader."

79

"We have ranks, actually," Peter said, wiping his eyes. "When I find them on the streets, I bring them home, get them to fit in. I'm the commander, and everyone else is ranked in seniority by age, just so we have something concrete to go on when it comes to who makes the rules. But anyway, I take them in. Give them what they need and all that. The only one who has somewhere else to go is—"

"Tink," all the boys said in unison.

"I hear she has real parents out there somewhere," First said dreamily.

"If they were *really* parents, she wouldn't be here," Second replied, crossing his arms.

"Oh, speaking of which," Peter said, "Tink has some things you can change into. Proper party clothes. I'm sure she wouldn't mind if you borrowed something. Curly?"

Curly scrambled to his feet and stood waiting for instruction.

"Can you take Darling to Tink's room? Make sure she gets there safely?"

Wendy thought about Tinkerbelle's size and considered her own. Tinkerbelle was at least five inches shorter than her and maybe a size double zero, whereas Wendy was probably a size ten. There was no way *anything* that tiny person had in her closet would fit her.

"Peter, I don't think—" she started.

But Peter shook his head. "Don't worry about it—she won't mind. I'll call you for dinner in a bit." Peter slapped Curly on the shoulder, then crouched down to pick up Tootles, clearly considering this conversation over.

Curly and Wendy locked eyes.

"So. Uh . . . this way," he said, ducking beneath the doorway.

Wendy followed Curly into a living room just as exceptional and beautiful as the kitchen. There were crates adhered to the walls. Each one was either crammed with books or odds and ends, organized by color: white light bulbs with white figurines and white marbles together, yellow rulers and yellow pencils and yellow figurines in their own crate, and so forth. The glass bottles on the ceiling continued from the entryway into the living room. They gave way to light bulbs speckled between them, throwing brown and green light over the room like a stained-glass mobile. The bottles were close enough that any wind from open windows in the house made them clink together. She also noticed nails and washers at the bottom of some of them that made an even crisper twinkling, filling the space with constant industrial music. The bottles even matched the color of the decor in the rest of the apartment, and were arranged with an eye for design: lighter brown bottles fading to darker brown bottles, mixing with darkest green and fading out to lighter green bottles. They hung in lengths that varied in millimeters and produced a textural wave like an ocean made of glass. They had a television here as well, and to Wendy's surprise, a few game systems neatly arranged in crates.

There was a large old couch with haphazardly patched corduroy, and a few recliners that didn't match. Nibs was sitting in one by the window, focused very hard on finger-knitting what looked like a large blanket.

"Hi," Wendy said softly.

Nibs looked up, startled away from his work. He paused for a moment, as if to settle himself, and said, "I'm sorry. For scaring you earlier."

Wendy almost reflexively said, *It's okay*, but she thought again and instead replied, "Thank you for apologizing."

Nibs nodded and turned from her, returning to his knitting.

Curly explained. "Come on, I know this is a lot to look at, but Tink's room is just around the corner."

She followed him into a hallway with five bedrooms. The doors were all open, and she could tell whose belonged to who pretty quickly. The twins' room had doubles of everything; one half of the room was messy and the other was cluttered, but neat. Prentis's room was very tidy but didn't have many personal effects—which made sense, as she remembered him saying he was new. Curly shut the door to his room before she was able to see inside. Nibs's room had a few weights in it and a pull-up bar in the door-way. The last room had the door firmly shut, so Curly had to knock.

"Peter sent Darling to ask you about clothes or something, I don't know," Curly called through the door.

Tinkerbelle pulled the door open just enough for Wendy to slither inside, and then she shut it hard.

"I'm not really sure I want to go to this party anymore," Wendy said immediately.

Tinkerbelle scoffed and rolled her eyes. She opened her closet and started riffling through it. "Don't you think I know that?" she asked. "Something is going to happen tonight, and you really shouldn't be here. Not that you listened to my warning back at your house or anything. Too busy being dazzled by boy wonder out there."

"I wasn't dazzled," Wendy shot back.

Tinkerbelle stopped and turned around completely. "Yes, you were. I was, too. You're not special for pretending that he isn't sexy and interesting. He just is. And now he has you somewhere you didn't know you would wind up, doing something you don't really want to do, and it gets harder to remember that you don't want to do things when you're right there beside him. Come on, Darling, no one in this room is stupid. How the fuck do you think I got here?"

Tinkerbelle looked Wendy up and down. "Size ten or twelve?" she demanded.

"Ten, but wait, wait, go back. You said you were trying to warn me about something? Why didn't you just say what you meant?" Wendy asked shrilly.

"Keep your voice down," Tinkerbelle hissed. "And because he was *right there*. I promise you, the less you know, the happier you'll be."

Tinkerbelle threw a couple of dresses on her bed, then started rooting around at the bottom of her closet in her giant pile of shoes.

"Now. You had three chances to get out of this: first, when Peter asked; next, when I told you to leave; and last, when you got separated from us at the train station. You might have another couple opportunities before the night is over, and if you're clever or really lucky, you might be able to take them. But for now, let's just get you presentable and follow this to the end."

Tinkerbelle pulled a large trunk out from the back of her closet and pushed it over to the vanity she had set up against the wall.

"Then afterward," she continued, "you can go back home to Lincoln Park—and the life you were planning on having—and sincerely focus on being happy to never see any of us again."

Wendy looked at the pile of clothes, then back at Tinkerbelle. "I don't think they'll . . . ," she started.

"Dude, they're your size. Just pick something you like and try it on," Tinkerbelle said, sitting down at the vanity. She pulled out her cell phone and started typing.

Wendy looked around Tinkerbelle's room as she slowly pulled off her sweater. It was more normal in here than she would have expected. Tinkerbelle had a small twin-size bed, with a stuffed tiger and a few finger-knit quilts (courtesy of Nibs, most likely). There were band posters on the wall, surrounded by pictures of her and the boys, and she'd also tacked up concert and movie ticket stubs and cutouts from magazines. Her room had an overhead light, but instead of using it, she'd taped Christmas lights all around the perimeter of the ceiling and crisscrossed them overhead so the room was lit with a soft glow.

The dresses Tinkerbelle had picked out were indeed Wendy's size, but she felt weird about wearing someone else's clothes. She held a long-sleeved gold sequined minidress up to her nose and sniffed. It smelled freshly cleaned, if a bit dusty, like Tinkerbelle didn't wear it often. Or like the last time she'd worn it was ages ago, back when it probably fit. That was probably for the best, all things considered. The other two dresses were black and not exactly to her taste, so she shimmied into the gold dress and zipped up the back. Tinkerbelle had also laid tights out for her. Unlike the stringy beat-up tights Tinkerbelle was wearing, these were so new they still had the cardboard inside. They were also fleece-lined and warm. Wendy looked at the back of Tinkerbelle's head and thought about her long white arms gripping both sides of the train car, leaning back into the night so Wendy would feel secure as she crossed. She thought about Tinkerbelle pulling warm new tights out for someone that she just met.

She had never in her life known a girl like this.

"Hey," Wendy said when she'd finished dressing.

Tinkerbelle looked up. She pursed her lips and then shrugged one shoulder. "I liked that dress when it fit me. It looks good on you," she said brusquely. "When you go home, you don't have to worry about returning it."

"I don't think I would even have anywhere to wear this, after tonight," Wendy said, looking down at the clingy fabric.

Tinkerbelle snorted rudely. "Probably not. But it works well on you, just the same. Now, do you want anything done with your hair and makeup, or are you just leaving it like . . . that?"

Tinkerbelle didn't even have much hair, so Wendy wasn't confident in her skills regarding that at all. At least with the clothes, she could tell Tinkerbelle had a higher than average understanding of coordination.

"My hair is fine," Wendy said firmly. "And I don't wear makeup."

Tinkerbelle cocked her head to the side and considered Wendy's face. "You don't need it, either. But you might like to look less like *yourself* tonight," she said quietly. "Trust me on that."

Wendy realized that she'd been having a feeling off and on all night that she couldn't quite name, but was growing in urgency. It was like a brush of regular anxiety combined with the sort of thrill you get when something incredibly dangerous is about to happen. She'd felt a whisper of it in the alley, but she'd brushed it off as nerves from sneaking out. She'd felt it on the train platform, though it had gone nearly as quickly as it came. She'd also felt it the moment before Peter had held her in the kitchen, but the warmth of his body had chased it away. But all of those instances were spaced out. Now, Wendy had felt it twice in the five minutes she'd been alone in this room with Tinkerbelle, and that was significant.

Tinkerbelle had already said that Wendy wouldn't want to know what the source of that thrill was. Tinkerbelle also didn't seem like the type of person to rescind things she had already made a decision about, so maybe it wasn't the best idea to demand clarity on the situation.

Wendy looked down at her tights, then back up to Tinkerbelle's determined little face. Whether or not this person valued her or liked her was immaterial. Tinkerbelle had cared about her safety in a way that was important: If she wasn't allowed to know what was going on, perhaps Wendy could leverage the needs of the one person who wanted her to get home as much as she did.

"No one in this room is stupid," Wendy echoed Tinkerbelle's words from earlier. "So, I'd like to make you an offer and ask you some questions that I think you can answer without creating problems."

Tinkerbelle tilted her chin up in defiance. The ghost of a smile was back on her face.

"Something is happening tonight, and it's something that I am not supposed to be involved in," Wendy said. "You know what it is, and I don't, and . . . it is in both of our best interests to maintain that balance of information . . . correct?"

Tinkerbelle's expression didn't waver.

"But," Wendy continued, drawing on the negotiation skills from every police procedural she'd ever seen in her life, "if I'm not provided with good information that will allow me to make reasonable decisions, my actions—or inactions—might have negative consequences for both of us. Correct?"

Tinkerbelle's eyes sparkled.

"So it would benefit the both of us if I consider your suggestions a roadmap of how to eventually remove myself from what will be happening tonight," Wendy said tentatively. "And, in return, it would help if you don't do things that make me question whether or not you still care that I'm able to get the hell out of here."

Wendy finished that last line with a bit more threat in her voice than she'd originally intended. But she let it sit in the quiet of the room while Tinkerbelle thought about it.

"Ah. So, Wendy Darling wants to parlay," Tinkerbelle replied silkily, her eyes narrow and smile sharp as a serpent's.

"Should I let you do my makeup?" Wendy asked, this time with meaning, staring down at Tinkerbelle from her position at the foot of the bed.

"Yes," Tinkerbelle said resolutely. "But first, we have to shake on it."

She licked her palm and stuck it out. Wendy grimaced, but licked the center of her hand as well, trying not to think about all the things she'd touched in the train station. Tinkerbelle grasped her hand tight and shook.

CHAPTER 7

Tinkerbelle curled Wendy's already curly hair with a thin curling iron, then rolled each section on a foam roller to cool. Then she disinfected her makeup brushes and began working. First, she darkened Wendy's brown eyebrows to nearly pitch black and contoured her face until her cheeks were sharp and her nose was pointed. She painted a wide strip of dark blue almost a full inch wide across Wendy's face, over her eyes from ear to ear, lightening her touch until it faded perfectly into Wendy's skin. Under the band across her face, Tinkerbelle dusted dark pink blush over the apples of her cheeks and daubed just a bit of liquid lipstick in the center of her lips. She spread it to the edges, leaving the richest color in the center, as if Wendy had bitten her lips for hours.

"I look like something from *Blade Runner*," Wendy remarked, turning her face from side to side, letting the Christmas lights reflect off the shimmer.

Tinkerbelle laughed quietly. "You do. Just because you're covering your face doesn't mean you can't still look pretty. I know what it's like to feel nervous around police and strangers. I'm sorry my makeup doesn't quite match your complexion. But under the circumstances, it's the best we can do."

She began unwinding the curlers from Wendy's hair, gently pulling the ringlets loose. "Do you have your cell phone on you still?" she asked.

89

Wendy felt a spike of anxiety.

"You should keep it on airplane mode, so you don't waste battery," Tinkerbelle said. "You'll probably need it later on."

Wendy thought about the conversation they'd had fifteen minutes ago and resisted the urge to snap that she knew how phones worked. Instead, she pulled the phone out of her pocket to follow Tinkerbelle's instructions.

To her horror, now she only had 10 percent battery—and Eleanor's texts were the last thing she'd opened. Tinkerbelle gazed at them placidly over her shoulder as Wendy clicked out of the app as fast as she could.

"You should turn on your location, too," she said, to Wendy's surprise. "It still works when your phone is offline."

"You're serious about this," Wendy said.

Tinkerbelle hummed low in her throat and continued back-combing the crown of Wendy's head. "You'll thank me later," she said.

There was a knock at Tinkerbelle's door. She put down her comb, but before she could reach the door, it swung open.

"Tootles!" Tinkerbelle cried. "What have I said about knocking!"

Tootles immediately looked chastened. "You have to wait until after, when the person says come in . . ." He backed out of the room, clearly about to try the interaction again, but Tinkerbelle stopped him.

"No, no, no, don't go back outside, just do better next time. What do you want?"

"Peter says it's time for dinner," Tootles said, swaying back and forth in that fidgety way little kids often do. "It's time to wash up."

"Okay, fine, tell him we'll be there in a second," Tinkerbelle snapped. "And close the door on the way out."

Tootles did just that, and Tinkerbelle returned to Wendy's hair, giving it a few more floofs and spraying the whole thing with hairspray. "The bathroom is to the right at the end of the hallway. There's a window in there, but if you climb out of it, not only is there a thirty-foot drop, but I'm pretty sure Peter would chase you or be waiting for you at the bottom by the time you managed to climb down."

Wendy felt a thrill of fear, and it probably showed on her face because Tinkerbelle put a hand on her shoulder. "We spit-shook on it," she said seriously. "I promised that I'll protect you. I just . . . understand the temptation, and wanted to nip that idea in the bud before it occurred to you, too."

"Okay," Wendy said. "I'm uh . . . just gonna go. Thanks for the hair and makeup."

Tinkerbelle nodded and turned to work on her own makeup.

"And thanks for the advice," Wendy added.

Tinkerbelle rubbed at her eyeliner with a makeup remover wipe. "I like you, Wendy," she said bluntly.

Wendy had been halfway out the door, but she stopped and looked back.

"You're sharp and you don't let people push you around,"

Tinkerbelle continued. "I respect that. I just wanted you to know that I wouldn't put this effort in if I didn't think a girl like you deserved it."

Wendy didn't know what to say to that. She'd been bottling her emotions about the events of the past hour, and there had been so many of them that she couldn't process, so she just felt numb in the face of genuine kindness.

Tinkerbelle was lining her eyes with red eyeshadow, but when she realized Wendy was still standing there limply, she looked over her shoulder in irritation. "Go wash your hands. Peter is waiting."

Wendy backed out of the room.

The bathroom was right where Tinkerbelle said it was, and Wendy was quite frankly very surprised at its cleanliness considering how many boys there were in this house. She locked the door and shoved a towel at the bottom to help muffle any sound. Then she immediately video chatted Eleanor. It only rang once before her friend picked up.

"WHAT THE HELL IS GOING ON AND WHY DO YOU LOOK LIKE THAT?" Eleanor screeched.

Wendy jumped and turned the volume all the way down. "Please be quieter," she hissed.

"You look so scary right now, you have no fucking idea," Eleanor whispered.

Wendy laughed in mild hysteria and tried to keep from weeping. "I'm terrified and I don't have much time, so I need you to be quiet while I explain what's going on."

Eleanor nodded.

"So, I was about to talk to that cop when some people literally black-bagged me with a T-shirt and abducted me straight off the street. When they finally stopped dragging me around, they took the T-shirt off my head, and it was a bunch of teenage boys," Wendy said quickly.

What? Eleanor mouthed, her eyebrows knit in concern.

"Yeah-boi, and it's about to get worse!" Wendy whisper-screamed. "So, they immediately start arguing with each other about whose fault it was that they had to kidnap me, when Peter bursts into the room. He instantly gets really mad and instead of asking questions or whatever, he immediately starts apologizing and saying that it was a miscommunication?"

"Oh my God, Wendy . . . ," Eleanor says softly.

"Then he hugs me really hard and says sorry to me or whatever—like that would even help. Then he tells me that all the guys who kidnapped me are his family and that he lives in this house with them. He explained that he told them to find me and help walk me there after we got separated at the train station. But apparently they decided to kidnap me instead?"

"I am calling the cops," Eleanor said flatly.

"NO!" Wendy lowered her voice immediately. "No. Let me finish. So, after I get individually introduced to these kids—and by the way, one of them can't be any older than maybe seven—I get told that Peter provides for them, and they're basically all orphans or something? And Peter rehashes the story of how we met and, like, it's very clear that these really are just kids in a really bad situation. No—I see the look on your face, don't hang up and call the cops, Eleanor."

Wendy paused and breathed.

"So, one of the kids was making dinner—which, by the way, I am in the bathroom because I'm supposed to be washing my hands for it, and Peter was like, *Oh, we're still going to the party. Go to Tinkerbelle's room and change clothes so you can look cooler or something.*"

"I will kill this man," Eleanor said.

"Then," Wendy continued, "here is the wildest fucking part! So you know how I told you that Tinkerbelle was kind of a bitch? APPARENTLY, she was only being like that to try to get me not to come to the party because something really dramatic is going to happen tonight!"

"What could be more dramatic than this?" Eleanor hissed.

"Dude! I don't know! That's high-key the craziest part!" Wendy said hysterically. "Anyway, she's like, *You can't leave or you'll ruin everything. I'm gonna help you.* And she was so fucking serious about it. She did my makeup and hair because she thinks that will help make things safer for me? She's also started giving me survival tips, like . . . Eleanor. I think I walked into, like, a sting operation or something."

Eleanor was just shaking her head back and forth. "No. No, no, nope. Not at all, none of this at all for you," she said.

"You need police. You need your parents. You need to contact the FBI or something, but this shit needs to end right now."

"Don't you think I know that?!" Wendy asked. "I wouldn't be locked in a bathroom whispering at you if getting out of this situation was that fucking easy. I would already be sprinting home. Dude, and not only did Tinkerbelle start giving me a bunch of warnings, but she also saw that I was texting you and said that it was good and to turn on my location so someone can track where I am. This is so serious."

Eleanor put her head in her hands and gripped tight as she thought frantically. "So," she started, "there's a commotion outside that's distracting the cops from being able to effectively focus on you. You're outnumbered by enough people who have already proven they can physically constrain you. Peter has proven to be unreliable and has a temper, and you're trapped in his house in his neighborhood, so he knows the terrain better than you. Public transportation is out of the question, and I can't send an Uber to pick you up if they keep moving you. Peter also knows where you live, so if you don't figure out a way out of this situation, he could 100 percent just randomly show up at your house."

Wendy looked at the bathroom door and at the time on her phone. It had been almost five minutes, her phone was dying, and if she didn't want anyone to start looking for her, they needed to wrap this up. "Yes."

"It's only been, like, an hour. How does stuff like this even happen to you?" Eleanor groaned.

"I don't know, but I do know this: Tinkerbelle said she was going to help get me out of here permanently, and I believe her. Also, even if I didn't trust her, I trust that she doesn't want me to fuck up her plans badly enough that she'd actually help me, even though we aren't even friends. I swear to God, the instant I get a moment away, I'll run. But I need you to start monitoring my location."

"And regarding calling the authorities?" Eleanor asked, rubbing her temples in anguish.

"If you don't hear from me, and something seems wrong, I'm giving you permission to share my location detail with them. But, I have to go, now; I'm running out of time," Wendy said. She flushed the toilet and turned on the faucet.

"If you live, and we meet in person, I'm going to physically fight you for putting me through this," Eleanor said, scowling.

Wendy nodded seriously. "If I live, I'll let you. And just for the record, I want you to know you were right."

Eleanor nodded and clenched her eyes shut tight. "I love you," she said. "Please, please stay safe."

"I know," Wendy said. "I'll try."

She hung up and turned off the faucet. When she opened the door, Tootles was standing outside it.

"I have to go to the bathroom," he said accusatorily. "Why were you in there talking?"

Wendy opened her mouth to concoct an explanation, but Tinkerbelle came up behind Tootles and pushed him aside so Wendy could get out.

"She was reciting poetry, Tootles. Darling's an artist. Maybe if you're good, she'll do some for you later," Tinkerbelle said, giving Wendy a warning glance.

"Oh! Okay!" Tootles instantly accepted that explanation and closed the bathroom door.

Tootles isn't very bright, Wendy thought, *but at least that's convenient.*

She followed Tinkerbelle back into the kitchen. The other boys were sitting at the massive table made of two doors, waiting for them. The table was crammed with homemade candles in a way that made it look like a beautiful fire hazard. Slightly had filled all the bowls with the soup she'd seen him making earlier, and to Wendy's surprise, it smelled very good. In addition to the soup, there was a hunk of dried, smoked meat that Slightly was currently carving slivers of. There was also a giant, steaming loaf of bread that couldn't have come anywhere but straight out of the oven. Wendy suddenly realized how hungry she was, having gone to bed without eating.

Peter was at the head of the table, and he was doing some sort of magic trick for Second, opening his hands and showing a coin, then blowing on the coin and pulling it out of Second's ear. Then he clapped, making the coin disappear entirely. First had his chin in his hands. He glanced over at Wendy and Tinkerbelle reproachfully for making him wait to eat. Slightly, Nibs, and Curly were seated next to each other. Nibs looked less angry now, and more bored. Curly stirred his spoon in his soup, but like the rest of the table, he was waiting to eat. Prentis was sitting farthest away from Peter, near the empty spaces where Wendy and Tinkerbelle were clearly supposed to sit. He jumped up from his seat and pulled Wendy's and Tinkerbelle's chairs out for them as they approached.

"Thank you," Wendy said softly.

Prentis smiled, blushing gently, and settled down into his own chair.

"Tootles!" Peter shouted. Wendy jumped. Tinkerbelle pressed her hand to Wendy's leg under the table to settle her, but pointedly didn't look at her.

The toilet flushed down the hall, and Tootles ran into the room, flinging himself into his chair. "Sorry," he said sheepishly.

Everyone at the table bowed their heads, while Wendy watched suspiciously.

"We love our bread, we love our butter, but most of all, we love each other," they recited in unison instead of saying a traditional grace. When they finished, everyone began eating, talking loudly, and passing the plates around.

"You should try the bread," Prentis said. "Slightly is a great cook, but Curly is an amazing baker." He passed the plate to Wendy to take the first piece. When she tore off a piece, steam erupted from inside the loaf and filled the room with a yeasty aroma that literally made Wendy's mouth water. Tinkerbelle nudged the margarine over in Wendy's direction.

Wendy picked up her knife and slathered the steaming bread with a smear and took a bite. It wasn't in Wendy's repertoire to be particularly hyperbolic, but in the moment immediately after biting it, she swore she could see God. She could also see Tinkerbelle out of the corner of her eye, grinning. Curly was also watching her hopefully as she chewed.

When Wendy finally swallowed, she pointed at Curly. "I forgive you, specifically, for the kidnapping." She gratefully crammed more bread into her mouth.

Everyone at the table laughed. Curly pumped his fist in the air and went back to eating. The soup was amazing as well, Wendy noted. A thick, creamy broth with chunks of potatoes, carrots, onions, and corn; it was unexpectedly a little spicy, which elevated it immensely. It went well with the dry meat everyone was eating. She hadn't expected to like that dish at all, but it matched the rustic flavors of the bread and the soup in a way that was really satisfying.

Slightly beamed as he watched her wolf everything down.

When everyone seemed like they were close to being finished, Peter stood up. "So, Tinkerbelle, Nibs, Curly, and

I will be going out tonight and won't be back until late. First, Second, Tootles, and Prentis: Slightly is in charge, as always."

Slightly nodded. First put his head down on the table dramatically, so Second flicked him in the back of the neck and he sat back up.

"As you know," Peter continued, "the pirates are swarming the streets tonight. It's dangerous, and I'll have no one leave the house while we're gone. Is that clear?"

The boys nodded, but Curly raised his hand. "If . . . the pirates are out and it's dangerous, am I allowed to stay home? Nibs and I have been talking, and—"

Peter cut him off. "The answer is no. And we're meeting up with Omi and her team, so I figured you'd be excited."

Curly immediately went pink and slouched deeper into his chair. Nibs smirked and elbowed him hard in the side.

"Quit it." Curly lurched away from Nibs's elbow and focused very hard on his soup.

"Some kind of team?" Wendy asked quietly.

Prentis leaned over. "Some more of Peter's friends. They play football for Luther South High School." He glanced over at Peter—who was still talking—and said much quieter, "Curly has a crush on one of them, but we haven't been able to figure out who. There's a girl on the team this year, so it could be her, but that situation is . . . complicated."

Wendy looked over at Tinkerbelle for more explanation,

but to her surprise, Tinkerbelle was also a bit pink and was keeping her eyes firmly on the table.

Wendy turned back to Prentis, who said, "I would know more about it, but Peter won't let them come by the house, so we've never met. Slightly has met them, though, and he says they're nice, but—"

"Prentis, stop talking," Peter said loudly, having finally noticed their separate conversation.

Prentis shut his mouth immediately and turned away from Wendy.

"Anyway," Peter continued, "the Crocodile is also out tonight, which should be more incentive for some of you to stay inside. It's close to payday, and as you know, he is always a bit techy around then. Does anyone have any more questions?"

Wendy started to raise her hand, but Tinkerbelle pushed it back down.

"The Crocodile is a bounty hunter that Peter pays for protection," she said, answering Wendy's unspoken question brusquely and quietly. "We'll talk about it later."

Tootles raised his hand, hopping up and down in his seat.

"Tootles?"

"I finished all my soup, and I didn't spill anything. Tinkerbelle said that if I was good, Darling would tell me a poem," Tootles said proudly.

Peter locked eyes with Wendy from across the long table. "Oh?" he said.

"Yes," Tootles said. "I was waiting for the bathroom, and Darling—"

Tinkerbelle interrupted Tootles loudly. "Darling was taking too long and Tootles was upset, so we promised him a treat if he went to the bathroom and got to the table on time."

She squeezed Wendy's knee hard under the table as Wendy tried not to have a panic attack.

"I see." Peter's eyes were bright and intelligent as he looked between Wendy and Tinkerbelle. "Well, we should really be leaving, but I think we have room for a treat. Come on, Darling, share some of your poetry with me and the boys."

Wendy looked desperately at Tinkerbelle, whose frantic grip was beginning to pinch. Then she looked back at Peter, who was staring at her wolfishly, and wondered how on earth she had thought a person like this was vulnerable when he was in her home. She couldn't even remember what he looked like crying, even though that had happened less than two hours ago.

The entire table was staring at her now, and from the feel of Tinkerbelle's hand, she was running out of time. "Um." Wendy was stalling. "Are you sure you all want to hear it? It's not very good. I could just—"

"Yes," Peter said firmly.

Wendy wracked her brain for something to say. Her

mouth felt unbearably dry even though she had just finished eating.

"Give us a poem about anything," Peter said challengingly. "Your favorite flower, your favorite food. One of your dreams. Come on, Darling."

"Come on, Darling!" Tootles echoed excitedly, completely oblivious to the mounting tension at the table.

Wendy closed her eyes and, by the grace of God, snatched on a memory of something her mom had sung to her as a kid. Hopefully it was good enough.

"I wish I had a pretty house,
The littlest ever seen,
With funny little red walls
And roof of mossy green."

Tinkerbelle loosened her death grip on Wendy's knee and looked so relieved that she seemed like she was about to faint.

"Next I guess, I think I'll have
Gay windows all about,
With roses peeping in, you know,
And babies peeping out."

None of the older boys looked particularly impressed with this poem, but Tootles seemed enchanted. Wendy paused and looked at Prentis, who seemed just as relieved as Tinkerbelle that Wendy had come up with something.

"One more line," Peter said quietly. He stared at her unblinkingly from across the table, his hands steepled in front of his mouth. "For Tootles."

"Um . . ." Wendy wracked her brain desperately.

"I'll have a chimney big and tall
With black smoke at the top
To share the warm hearth with you all
And . . . I would like to stop."

Peter burst into laughter at her last line, tossing his head back winningly—reminding Wendy, with startling clarity, just how distractingly beautiful he was when he smiled. When Peter finished laughing, he looked at her differently: cheeks gently flushed and golden eyes hazy. Closer to the way he'd looked at her when he was inside her house. "Darling, you really are something else, aren't you?" he said, his voice rough and warm. Familiar.

Tinkerbelle reached under the table and squeezed Wendy's hand tenderly. This had clearly been some sort of test, Wendy realized, and she had just barely passed.

The cool tension had lifted from the table, and Curly stood and began picking up everyone's plates to bring them to the sink.

"Grab your stuff. We're heading out," Peter announced. "Those football meatheads are downstairs, and I don't like to keep them waiting. Curly, change out of those pants and into something else. They don't fit, and you look ridiculous."

Curly scowled, but headed off in the direction of his room.

Slightly leaned over. "I'm not sure if I'll see you again after this, Darling, but I just wanted to say that it was nice to meet you."

Slightly and Prentis were so different from the other boys. Prentis reminded her of someone who could easily have gone to her old school, or maybe even somewhere fancier. Slightly, on the other hand, acted much more like an actual adult than anyone his age she'd ever met, and seemed like he had his life way more in order than even Peter. Prentis said he had just arrived, so that sort of made sense. Slightly, on the other hand, had been the one who was tased in Peter's train story. So he had to have been living here for at least three years.

Wendy stuck out her hand to Slightly. "It was nice to meet you, too. You're an amazing cook, and I really hope you . . . do well."

Slightly smiled warmly, his dark cheekbones sharp in the candlelight. "Me too," he replied.

Prentis stood to pull Wendy's chair out again. "You look really nice," he said. "I hope you have a good time at the party."

"Thank you."

Prentis looked over her shoulder at Peter, who was putting a few things in a messenger bag across the room.

"I hope you have a *safe* time at the party," Prentis said, so quiet that Wendy could barely hear him.

"Same," she replied, just as quiet. "See you around."

CHAPTER 8

Wendy didn't recognize the area she was in at all when they got downstairs. It made sense, because she'd had a T-shirt over her head, but it was disconcerting to realize that she really and truly did not know where she was. Nibs and Curly had changed quickly before they'd left. Curly had braided red ribbon into his pigtails and was wearing a pair of torn black jeans that looked suspiciously like they were Peter's. He was also wearing a blue denim jacket with some patches sewn to it and what appeared to be hand-stitched embroidery.

Nibs had thrown on a leather jacket that had white bones painted on the arms. He'd pulled his chin-length red hair into a half ponytail and was wearing a bandanna over his mouth to obscure his face.

Now that they were in the street, Wendy noticed that Nibs and Curly liked to be shoulder to shoulder and walked in lockstep with each other. She wondered how the two boys had met, and if they had been friends—or "brothers"—for long.

Peter was walking in front. He'd put on sunglasses, even though it was night, and wore the black messenger bag she'd seen him messing with in the kitchen. Wendy watched the backs of the three boys in front of her and thought about how Tinkerbelle said they roamed the streets watching out for her, and understood how that would make her feel safe.

In the house, in the comfort of family, they had looked young and a bit playful. But lit only by streetlights and the moon, Peter, Nibs, and Curly looked strong, coordinated, and threatening.

They turned at the end of the block, and the neighborhood started to look more familiar to Wendy. They actually weren't far from the train station. They were coming at it from behind and from the opposite direction that she'd left it, but she had an extremely rough idea of where she was now. Not enough to run off on her own, but maybe enough to consider trying.

As they drew closer to the train station, police sirens got louder and louder.

Wendy hadn't exactly expected that whole ordeal to be over, but she figured things should have calmed down at least a little bit, and it was kind of alarming to be wrong.

They turned down the street, and Curly glanced over his shoulder at Tinkerbelle and Wendy. "You guys should get in between us and Peter," he said. "That way we can guard your backs." He reached over to curl his arm around Tinkerbelle's shoulders and gently guide her forward.

Nibs moved aside to let Wendy get ahead of him, then he slung his arm over her and squeezed her shoulders reassuringly. "I've got you," he said, hoarse like smoke.

Wendy's heart ached at the gesture in a way that she couldn't describe, and she silently forgave him, too, for the incidental kidnapping. When they turned the corner, out of the residential area and onto the main street, they were plunged back into the chaos Wendy had gratefully left earlier.

There were fewer police, but there was much more activity: The train station doors had orange cones around them and signs about redirection were posted to the door. All the station attendees had left the area, and there were only police now. Wendy couldn't tell exactly what was going on, but she did see a few people lying on the ground with their arms behind their backs as an officer stood over them, barking questions. There were a few other people being detained, and the whole thing seemed like it was escalating terribly. Wendy assumed Peter would turn at the sight of the police and take them all in another direction. She was surprised to hear him swear and start jogging toward the scene. She was just about to ask what was going on when Tinkerbelle made a noise that sounded like a cross between a gasp and a scream.

She pushed past Peter and started running at a full sprint toward a car at the edge of the commotion. Curly and Nibs started running, too, so Wendy followed their lead. Peter wasn't far ahead of them, and she watched him pull his scarf up over his face and take what looked like a firework out of his messenger bag.

"Omi! Omi!" Tinkerbelle shrieked, smacking at a police car window. Immediately the nearest police officer shouted at her to get away from the car, but she refused to stop screaming and banging on the window. Behind the glass was a dark-skinned girl with long black hair. She looked exhausted and significantly less hysterical than Tinkerbelle, but she had her palms pressed against the window from the inside.

Peter whooped, so high and loud that Wendy flinched and almost stopped running entirely. Peter twisted, deadly fast, and snatched something else out of his bag and chucked it at Nibs. The metal pinwheeled through the air like a boomerang, but Nibs leaped up and caught it squarely. It looked like the mixture of a crowbar and doorstop, with a wedge on one end.

Peter whistled sharply and with a rhythm that made Wendy realize he was communicating with the boys wordlessly. At the noise, everyone looked up—cops and people being arrested, alike. The other kids on the ground began curling their legs underneath them as if preparing to get up and run, despite the angry shouting from the officer who had been handling them. The officer dealing with Tinkerbelle gave up on talking her away from the car and decided to bodily haul her off. He had barely lifted her up from the ground when his head snapped back violently, and he fell like a stone. Wendy looked over, terrified, and saw sweet baker Curly with a bandanna over his face and what looked like a military grade slingshot in his hand.

Peter whistled again, and Nibs tossed the metal bar to Curly and picked up speed, leaving Curly and Wendy behind, following Peter in the opposite direction of the police car.

"There he is!" one of the officers shouted.

Immediately all their attention was on Peter and Nibs. Peter had duct-taped the firework, which was now lit, to what looked to Wendy like a crudely constructed Molotov cocktail—if the war films she'd watched had any accuracy to them. Peter threw it directly into a car window.

A lot of things happened at once.

Curly pushed Wendy violently forward, hard enough that she ran even faster, stumbling into Tinkerbelle, who was still clawing at the police car door. Then Curly yanked both girls down to the ground at once and covered them with his body.

Wendy made eye contact with the girl in the police car, Tinkerbelle's "Omi," and saw her brown eyes widen with terror as she turned in slow motion to what Curly was protecting Tinkerbelle and Wendy from.

The car exploded in the brightest red Wendy had ever seen. The Molotov cocktail provided ten times the incendiary a firework needed, so what should have been a slowly burning display in the sky instead filled the area with a light so bright that it looked almost like dawn as it went off all at once. As well as a noise so loud, it made her eardrums ache. Thousands of brilliant sparkles went in every direction, and burned significantly longer than Wendy assumed they would.

Curly leaped off Wendy and Tinkerbelle the instant the noise faded, then spun the crowbar-type thing in his hand expertly, jammed it in the crack between the cop car and its door, and began wrenching at it.

Wendy spared a moment from watching Curly try to break into the car to witness the aftermath of the most dramatic act of crime she'd seen in real life. All the law enforcement that had previously been focused on detaining the kids on the ground had adjusted their level of alarm to calling for backup, screaming into their walkie talkies, and peeling off in their cars or running toward the explosion on foot. As curious people began making their way over to see what was making all the light and noise, only to start screaming and coughing from the smoke, the remaining police began to focus on crowd control.

Wendy realized that Curly was tugging on her sleeve.

"Cut their zip ties off," he said.

"What?" Wendy asked dazedly. She realized the people who had been lying on the ground in the throes of being arrested were crouched on the same side of the cop car as they were. They were about high school–aged and looked as terrified as Wendy felt.

Curly handed her a wicked-looking pair of gardening shears. "Come on! We don't have much time. They're minors and they didn't do anything."

"We don't know that!" Wendy cried, but Curly was no longer listening to her. He had backed up about ten feet from the cop car, then without warning, sprinted back at it, leaping at the last minute. He flew at a horizontal angle, slamming the bottoms of his feet against the bar wedged in the door with breathtaking athleticism and accuracy. The car door gave a groan of protest before hanging at a looser angle, but still firmly shut. Curly landed hard on the pavement. He groaned in pain, but scraped himself up off the ground, anyway. Then he grabbed the bar tight in his fists and wrenched again, this time with all his might. The bandanna over his mouth and nose had fallen and revealed his face, still soft with baby fat, teeth clenched in a grimace of effort, eyes pressed shut. He pulled so hard an involuntary screech escaped his throat.

Then with a noise quieter than Wendy would have thought, the police car door cracked open, and the girl inside flew out and right into Tinkerbelle's arms. They pressed foreheads together, Omi cupping Tinkerbelle's jaw in both hands, an inch away from a kiss. Tinkerbelle swooned against her, sobbing something Wendy couldn't hear, looking more tender than Wendy could ever have imagined the icy girl who had painted her face and shouted at her in the street could look.

"Oh my God, dude, please!" one of the guys behind Wendy begged, his eyes wide with terror. "I just got a college scholarship, and all we did was walk out of the train station, and they said we were witnesses or something. I can't get arrested. My parents will kill me. Please. Please!" He looked like he was on the verge of tears, so Wendy numbly started working on cutting his zip ties off.

Curly was standing there, looking at Tinkerbelle and Omi with the gentlest expression. He put his arms around the pair and held them as they rocked back and forth in relief. He kissed Omi on the top of her head and curved his arm up so he could cup the back of Tinkerbelle's skull in his hand.

"This nice, but we need to leave from here," one of the boys on the ground said in a heavy Russian accent when Wendy finally got to him last. The instant his hands were freed, he leaned over and smacked Curly on the back, hard. "Focus," he said firmly.

Curly pulled away from Omi and Tinkerbelle, looking a bit dazed for a moment, and then his vision sharpened. He tilted his head to listen, then started walking away from the car.

"Don't run," the Russian said to Wendy in a conversational tone. "Draws attention."

Wendy looked over her shoulder, and the other boys were following at the same pace, occasionally glancing over at Curly like he was their savior and a demon at the same time. They blended in with the crowd that had come to watch the explosion, as they walked up Broadway to Lawrence Avenue. Wendy tried not to look around too desperately, thinking hard about how she looked and wishing she hadn't let Tinkerbelle decorate her face so ostentatiously. Behind them, over the sounds of people yelling and cop car sirens and fire truck sirens, there was the flash of green light and the boom of another explosion that followed as Peter presumably threw another Molotov firework. Wendy flinched, and Curly reached back and pulled her in front of him, protectively.

The instant they turned the corner, Curly started picking up speed until he was jogging.

"He's going for the bus!" one of the boys exclaimed, and they all ran behind him. Curly smacked the side of a bus with a flat hand, and the doors that had been on the verge of closing reopened. Curly jumped inside, then stuck his hand out, waving for them to follow quickly. Wendy thanked God and also Jesus that she'd worn tennis shoes and forced her aching legs to continue churning until she was safely clinging to the pole just inside the bus's front door. Curly pulled his wallet out of his jacket and slid two twenties into the meter.

The bus driver, a rotund and serious-looking Black man, eyed the group of children warily. His eyes slid from Wendy's garish makeup to the welts on the other kids' wrists to Tinkerbelle and Omi holding hands tightly, landing at last on the tool with which Curly had wrenched open the cop car door. A tool which, in the hand of a teenager and not a locksmith, was clearly only to be used for mayhem. Then, with a sigh, he decided to mind his business and close the door. The bus pulled away from the street.

Wendy's heart felt like it was about to slam right out of her chest. She needed to sit down, and she needed to sit down now. She pushed through the group, made her way to the back of the bus, and collapsed into an empty seat. She closed her eyes and tipped her head back, covered her face with her arm, and focused on breathing hard enough to get oxygen back into her tired muscles. There were so many horrifying things happening that her thoughts were reduced to only the most banal, probably as a psychological shield to protect her from going completely to pieces. Currently she was thinking about how she needed to start working out more. She'd probably done what was equal only to about a mile of running and walking, but physically, she felt like she was about to die.

Fabric brushed her leg and Wendy cracked her eyes open. The rest of the group had settled around her, completely filling the seats in the back, Curly and the Russian on her left side, Tinkerbelle and Omi on her right, and three other boys split between the two forward-facing seats right in front.

Now that Wendy was finally catching her breath, she did some inventory of the people she'd released from police custody.

Omi was gazing at her with a lot more concern than someone who had only recently been in a cop car should have for someone else. She, like the rest of the group, looked about seventeen years old. She was wearing black skinny jeans and a black T-shirt with a matching blazer over it, the sleeves pushed up to her elbows. Her black hair was parted down the center, and she had one side braid tied off with a thin red ribbon. She looked like she was on her way to an art gallery, not like she'd left the house specifically to run around in the streets.

In fact, all the kids were dressed nicely.

The Russian boy was in actual dress pants, although he had a T-shirt on and no jacket. To Wendy's amusement, his blond hair was combed back into a pompadour. He was clearly trying to look charmingly vintage, and if Wendy was honest with herself, it was working. He was also the tallest of them and seemed the most laid-back about what had happened, his legs propped up on the chair in front of him as he gazed out the window.

The least laid-back about what had happened had to be the boy who had begged her to cut off his zip ties. He was openly weeping into the shoulder of the boy sitting next to him. He, too, was dressed fashionably in a slender-cut denim button-up shirt, with chinos rolled up at the bottom. He was African American, and like the rest of them, he was very muscular and stocky.

His friend, an Asian boy who seemed quietly shaken, had on a white dress shirt and dark jeans. He looked self-conscious about comforting his friend and was pointedly looking away, but he kept his arm firmly wrapped around his crying friend's shoulder.

The last boy looked a little bit like Omi and was curled completely into a tight ball, knees under his chin. Only his dark eyes and eyebrows and short dark hair were visible above them. He looked a little bit younger than everyone else and a little less muscular, but still athletic.

"Are you the football people? Peter said we might be meeting up with you?" Wendy guessed.

Omi's expression immediately changed, her face shuttering closed like a slammed door.

"Is she one of Peter's friends?" Omi asked in quite literally the prettiest voice Wendy had ever heard.

"Don't call them that," Curly said quickly. "Peter only does because no one can stop him."

Tinkerbelle shook her head at Omi and put a gentle hand on Omi's knee. "No, she's not Peter's friend. Peter kidnapped her from her house, and now she's coming with us to the party."

Omi frowned harder. "You should go home," she said firmly to Wendy.

"She can't," Tinkerbelle said with a sigh. "Peter has been looking at her with that face that means he's focused on her and will be until something more interesting comes along. If she runs without reason . . ."

The silence on the bus was deafening until the Russian boy tapped the unlit cigarette he was holding against the seat in front of him and glanced at the girls. "He hunts you down," he said with a crisp nod before turning back to the window.

"What? Seriously?" Wendy asked. They had to be joking.

Omi stared at her blankly, clearly not kidding at all.

"How much does she know?" Omi asked Tinkerbelle, her brown eyes not leaving Wendy's face.

"Nothing important," Tinkerbelle replied. "Enough to follow instructions."

"Let's keep it that way," Omi said, and it sounded like a promise.

She reached a hand over to Wendy. "I'm Ominotago; only Tinkerbelle is allowed to call me Omi."

Wendy shook her hand lightly.

Ominotago pointed over at the boy who looked like her. "This is Waatese, my little brother. He's a sophomore."

"Nice to meet you," Wendy said. Waatese buried his face deeper into his arms until Wendy could only see tufts of his hair.

"Fyodor is the one pretending he's not scared," Ominotago said, pointing at the boy with the Russian accent.

Fyodor raised a hand in a combination of a wave and a dismissal. "Your hair," he said to Wendy, with a smile tucked in the corner of his mouth. "Beautiful."

Wendy thought about the fried curly mess, which, after all this running, must be sticking straight out from her head. "Uh. Thanks," she said, not believing him at all.

"He flirts with everyone; don't pay attention to him," Ominotago said tersely.

"I'm Minsu," the slightly shaken Asian American boy

said from across the bus, giving Wendy a peace sign with the hand currently wrapped around his crying friend. "And this is Charles. Give him a minute."

Charles covered his face with both hands and continued crying.

Ominotago gazed at him fondly. "He's one of our linebackers."

Curly reached across the seats and smacked Charles comfortingly on the back.

"Yo, don't hit him. He doesn't like to be hit," Minsu said sternly.

Curly immediately shifted to a firm squeeze before leaning back into his seat. Wendy stared out the front of the bus window blankly for nearly a mile. Curly typed into an old phone while Tinkerbelle and Ominotago sweetly whispered to each other. The rest of the boys sat in complete silence, like they were riding home after an extremely tense day of school.

Wendy looked over at Curly and thought about what Prentis had said. She wondered which of these people Curly had a crush on. He wasn't acting sheepish like he'd been at the dinner table, so it was extremely hard to tell.

Wendy glanced over at the blond, Fyodor. He could be an option if Wendy stretched her imagination a bit. Ominotago had said Fyodor was a flirt, but she didn't say it was just with girls.

Waatese, Ominotago's brother, seemed a bit young for

Curly, but Wendy wasn't sure how old Curly was, either, so that wasn't a guarantee.

Minsu, who was still comforting Charles, was a maybe. But he had just snapped at Curly, and Curly didn't react at all the way someone would if their crush snapped at them. He'd hardly reacted at all.

Charles was adorable, and so far he was Wendy's best guess. Charles was clearly emotional, but probably the most physically impressive of the entire group. She was surprised he hadn't just ripped the zip ties off with sheer force. He looked like he could give Nibs some tips, and Nibs was no slouch in the biceps department.

"So," Wendy said to Curly, getting ready to start fishing for hints, "how did you all meet?"

Curly didn't even look up from his phone. "Ominotago and Waatese are my cousins."

Ominotago perked up at the sound of her name and Tinkerbelle turned to Wendy, but Wendy was busy staring at Curly. He looked absolutely nothing like Ominotago and Waatese. The only feature they shared was dark hair, but Ominotago's and Waatese's were jet black and straight, and Curly's was very dark brown and, well, curly.

"My mom was Irish, but my dad was Ojibwe," he said, continuing to type.

"He's what?" Wendy asked.

"Chippewa," Ominotago clarified. She scowled when Wendy's face still didn't dawn with comprehension.

121

"American Indian," Fyodor explained from far away, striking a match and lighting his cigarette.

"Oh, cool," Wendy said. Well, that canceled out Ominotago and Waatese. "Prentis said he thought you—"

But before Wendy could finish, Curly groaned loudly and slouched dramatically in anguish against the bus wall. "Prentis doesn't know we're cousins, and neither does Peter. But I fought Peter after we introduced him to Ominotago, and now he thinks she's my girlfriend. It's so embarrassing."

Ominotago grinned. "I'm too cool to be your girlfriend, even if you weren't my cousin."

"Truth," Minsu called, nodding. Charles had stopped crying, but it looked like he'd cried himself right to sleep. Minsu had moved his arm from cradling what was clearly his best friend, to resting it over the top of the seat while Charles's head lolled on his shoulder. It was cute, but Wendy still had questions.

"Why did fighting Peter make Prentis think Ominotago was your girlfriend? And what about—" Wendy nodded over at Tinkerbelle and Ominotago, who had refocused themselves on their private conversation.

Curly looked just as embarrassed as he had at the dinner table. "Peter gave Ominotago a nickname, but she didn't like it and asked me to make him quit calling her that. So, I asked him to stop, but like always, he didn't want to. Instead he bothered me all week until I just snapped and pushed him to the ground to beat some respect into him. He won the fight, of course, since he's bigger than me, and he also punished me for trying. But he did stop. Now he rarely refers to her directly unless she's physically in front of him. He calls her 'Omi' now, which is annoying because only Tinkerbelle is allowed to call her that and everyone else respects this, except him.

"He doesn't ever own up to his mistakes or apologize when he's rude," Curly continued, bitterly. "He just stops doing whatever he's doing or pretends he doesn't remember when he hurts your feelings."

Christ. "Why do you live with him?" Wendy asked quietly. "You don't have to tell me if you don't want to, but . . ." She shrugged.

Curly looked stricken. His dark eyebrows pinched, and the corners of his mouth twitched up and down like he was trying to force himself to smile but failing. He gazed out the window for a bit and dragged a hand down one of his braids anxiously before answering. "I was . . . different back before I met him. I was really angry, getting into trouble at school and just doing whatever I wanted all the time. I wore out the people who were taking care of me, and then I wore out my extended family, and only a few of them will talk to me now." Curly's eyes flicked over to Ominotago.

"I mean, I'm sure if I went back to them now it would be different," he continued. "I could do school; I have the patience for it now, and I would do so much better. But I was really, really bad. Just, breaking things and . . ."

Curly was talking so quietly now that Wendy had to lean close to hear him. She could see Fyodor over Curly's shoulder, watching them both as he smoked.

"Anyway, I didn't have anywhere else to go," Curly said firmly. "Slightly was already there and seemed so overburdened with taking care of the littler ones. I couldn't just leave him there alone, working so hard like that. He was the only one who had real skills, you know? My parents never taught me how to do the things Slightly knows how to do, but he taught Nibs and me quickly, even though we're older. His birth family was really strict, I think.

"It's been three years since I moved in, and I'm almost eighteen, so I'll be free to do what I want soon," Curly said hopefully. "I'm going to go back to my family and apologize and get all my real paperwork, and I'll get a job and go back to study. Maybe go to a trade school or something."

"You could do this now," Fyodor said lowly. "Nothing to stop you."

Curly frowned. "The timing isn't right yet. You don't know what I did, Fyodor. Just take my word for it."

Fyodor turned around to face them both, his heavy-lidded eyes serious. With the cigarette in his hand, he gestured at Curly's pocket and at the prying tool he had on his back. "You make slingshot, you make that. You weld. You could get apprenticeship, easy. Anyone can see. You need to come out from pretty cave you made and choose real world. You are ready."

"Bro, I don't think we're allowed to smoke on the bus," Charles interrupted, looking over his shoulder at the cloud of smoke surrounding Fyodor.

"You are ready," Fyodor said firmly, ignoring Charles. "Seventeen? Anywhere else, you are a man."

Curly seemed very cross suddenly and opened his mouth to argue, but Fyodor kept going.

"You can keep that secret?" He nodded over at Ominotago. "You can keep secret of your freedom. I know this." Fyodor reached over and squeezed Curly's shoulder. Then he leaned back and grinned mischievously. "If not, would be easy finding women to take care of you. You make . . . pretty things."

Curly's entire face went pink immediately, his mouth a small *o* of shocked pleasure. Wendy watched in exhilarated surprise as Fyodor raked his eyes up and down Curly with astonishing heat and Curly covered his blazing cheeks with both hands. Apparently she'd guessed correctly about Fyodor's flirting habits.

"Leave Curly alone!" Ominotago shouted across the bus, noticing instantly.

Fyodor barked out a peal of laughter, before winking at Ominotago and clicking loudly out of the side of his mouth in dismissal. He refocused his attention on Wendy and continued. "He make . . . what is it called? The hmm . . . display on the ceiling and walls in Peter's house. Very talented."

Wendy remembered the incredible bottle installation

and understood Fyodor's struggle to come up with a word to describe it. It was probably the best piece of art she'd ever seen in her life. There had to have been thousands of bottles, and it had to have taken Curly months or even years to build.

She also remembered the crates and the intricate placement of household objects by color. Then her gaze tracked back to the embroidery on Curly's denim jacket.

"You're incredible, Curly," she gasped.

"It's not a big deal," Curly mumbled, clearly embarrassed by all the attention. "My mom was an artist."

"*You* are an artist," Fyodor replied lowly. He tilted his head back and let the smoke leak out of his mouth, sultry and smooth like a 1930s film star.

"FYODOR," Ominotago cried, slamming a hand down on the seat sharply.

"Okay," Fyodor said firmly, putting his cigarette out on the back of the seat in front of him. "I do not stop. She make us run drills," he remarked to Wendy, rolling his eyes.

"We're almost there." Curly stood up suddenly, leaned over Fyodor, and pulled the cord on the window to let the driver know to stop the bus. Then he stumbled down the stairs to the side door, like he was relieved for a reason to escape the conversation.

Wendy turned anxiously to Tinkerbelle. She had been so tired from all the running, and distracted from meeting so many people in such a short amount of time, she'd forgotten they were going anywhere at all. She assumed they'd just hopped onto the bus to escape.

Tinkerbelle nodded out the window as everyone got to their feet. "The Mermaid's Lagoon," she said to Wendy. "We're getting in through the back."

"I bet you Peter is already there," Ominotago said to Tinkerbelle as they stepped onto the pavement outside. "That son of a bitch can wiggle out of anything."

Tinkerbelle made a little hum in agreement as Wendy followed her into the street. The bus door snapped shut behind Wendy, and she jumped anxiously. Unthinkingly she reached out to Tinkerbelle, then realized what she was doing and dropped her arms to her sides.

Ominotago caught the gesture and paused. She dropped Tinkerbelle's hand and turned, catching both of Wendy's hands in hers. Then Ominotago breathed in deeply and let the breath out slowly.

The lights of the Mermaid's Lagoon glowed rainbows across the sidewalk behind Ominotago, and the streetlamp threw her face into shadow, like the center of a halo. Wendy glanced over Ominotago's shoulder at Tinkerbelle, who crowded close to them both until they were in a small triangle.

"Breathe with me," Ominotago demanded in a way that brokered no argument.

Wendy tried to calm her racing heart, but it wasn't quite

working. She was breathing entirely too fast. Distantly, outside herself, she felt stupid and childish. She had been fine on the bus, seconds ago, and she'd held it together for the majority of the night, but somehow now she wanted to curl inside herself until she was small enough to disappear.

Ominotago squeezed Wendy's hands hard enough that it shocked her out of her own head and back into the warm brown of Ominotago's gaze. Wendy focused on this stranger's face as she mimicked the speed of her breaths. Ominotago's eyebrows, black and graceful like they had been painted on with ink; her nose that spread seamlessly into her cheekbones; the stubborn jut of her chin and the girlish curve of her mouth; her blue-and-purple-and-pink blush, blending like watercolors, lovely like nothing Wendy had ever seen.

Tinkerbelle's beautiful girlfriend, broad-shouldered and strong, taking her time teaching Wendy how to breathe in the middle of the street, was wasting valuable time with someone she'd just met as the boys disappeared into an alley around the corner. Ominotago's hands were warm. Wendy could feel how they were calloused from playing sports and thought about Tinkerbelle's small, impossibly soft hands. Wendy broke Ominotago's gaze to look over at the other girl. Tinkerbelle's head was bowed as she matched Ominotago's breaths, the glow of the streetlights reflected dramatically off the gold glitter she'd applied around her eyes. Wendy looked back at Ominotago and realized she was breathing at the same pace as Ominotago, Wendy's shoulders naturally having fallen from being pinched around her ears.

Ominotago nodded slightly and loosened her grip on Wendy's hands until she was holding them as sweetly as if they'd been friends for years.

"Tinkerbelle told me what happened," she said seriously. "You have had a very long night."

"Y-yeah." Wendy's voice broke and she cleared her throat. "Yeah, I have. I really just want to go home now."

Ominotago nodded. "I know. I'm sorry. But the night is going to get a bit longer."

Now that Wendy was relaxed enough to stop hyperventilating, she was too unguarded to stop tears from springing to her eyes at hearing that.

"Tinkerbelle told me you just arrived in the city and that you haven't even started school yet. You shouldn't be here; you should be at home," Ominotago said, firm and resolute. "You didn't deserve to be lured outside, to be pressured into changing train cars, to be kidnapped, or to be held in that man's home. You also didn't deserve to be around explosions or be in a position to make a decision about how to handle police in a community where you know no one, and trust very few of the people around you."

Something wild and anguished opened up like a flower in Wendy's chest, and suddenly she found herself crying in the middle of the street. She didn't deserve any of this at all, and it was so refreshing to hear anyone in this group of people admit that out loud. Nothing on earth could have prepared her for what had happened in the past three hours. Even though she was extremely aware that making the decision to leave home was entirely her own horrible choice, Ominotago seemed like a normal person with a normal perspective, so it was validating to hear her describe the entire night so bluntly.

Ominotago let go of Wendy's hands and gripped her by the shoulders instead. "You don't deserve any of those things, but tonight is important to everyone here. Curly has been waiting for this night for a year, Nibs has been waiting for three. Even my friends have been waiting for months. Now, I don't know you, Wendy." Ominotago tilted up her chin in challenge. "But from what Tinkerbelle has told me, I know that you're daring, I know that you're clever, and I know that you are strong, otherwise you wouldn't be here. However, you intruded on something we have been working on, and we need you to keep it together. For the rest of us."

Wendy looked over at Tinkerbelle, who nodded back at her firmly.

"Wendy promised," Tinkerbelle said. "And she spit-shook."

Wendy remembered having to touch Tinkerbelle's saliva-covered hand, and it was ridiculous enough to make her stop crying as she wondered at the intensity with which Tinkerbelle and Ominotago took such a gesture seriously.

"Enough people have been hurt over this whole thing,

and we're not adding outsiders to that tally," Ominotago said resolutely. "If Tinkerbelle can't get you home safely, I will. If I'm otherwise occupied, any one of the boys will handle it. I understand if you're worried about going somewhere with a boy you just met, but I promise you, you're safe with them. Fyodor is here on a visa and can only stay if he continues his education. Minsu is literally a Boy Scout. Charles would die before touching you any way you did not want him to. Waatese is a boxer in addition to playing football, and he's family. You're safest with him. My friends and I have parents who care where we are at night, and we are supposed to be home by two a.m."

Ominotago dropped her hands from Wendy's shoulders. "That's four hours from now," she said simply. "You should be home before then."

"What about Fyodor? You were yelling at him on the train," Wendy said. She wasn't scared of him in particular; it just seemed strange Ominotago would warn Fyodor away from Curly so aggressively if she thought he was so safe for Wendy to be around.

Ominotago scoffed and rolled her eyes. "Despite his dramatics, Fyodor is asexual—he won't touch you. But for Curly? He can do better. Fyodor flirts with everyone, and Curly hasn't ever dated anyone before. He's vulnerable. He doesn't need a playboy boyfriend . . . or girlfriend. He needs stability."

Tinkerbelle brushed her shoulder against Wendy's playfully and smiled more openly than Wendy had seen her that night. "Fyodor would be good for *you*, though. Since you're the type of girl who likes bad boys who feel dangerous," Tinkerbelle teased. "Fyodor's got that appeal, but on the inside he's actually a good person. Fyodor would never kidnap anyone."

Ominotago nodded. "All bark and no bite. Good kisser, but nothing else." She opened her arms to give Wendy a brusque side hug. "Are you going to be all right?" she asked.

Wendy closed her eyes and took another deep breath. She had made it this far; she could make it to the end of the night. She rolled her shoulders, bent down, and tightened her shoelaces. She pulled her phone out of her pocket to check the time and battery: 11:03 p.m., 8 percent battery, and a single text from Eleanor that said: Called the police and gave them your deets. FaceTime me when you're alone and DON'T GET MURDERED BEFORE THEN.

Will do. Ty she sent back while Tinkerbelle read over her shoulder and nodded in approval.

"I'm all right. I'm ready," Wendy said.

Tinkerbelle took her hand and led her into the Mermaid's Lagoon.

CHAPTER 9

Now the Mermaid's Lagoon had large front windows and was lit up as bright as Christmas so everyone could see inside from the street. There was a garish, giant sculpture of a woman with a tray of beer and hamburgers smack in front of the main entrance. The sign on the outside said CABARET AND DRAG SHOWS in blinding lights.

Wendy felt pretty confident she was prepared for what she was about to walk into. In fact, she was already thinking about bringing Eleanor to this place. Wendy could hear pulsing showtune music from outside the restaurant. Plus, even though she was still full of Slightly's soup and Curly's amazing bread, she wouldn't mind snacking on some bar food. Having a full-scale panic attack and running at top speed was a metabolism booster.

But when Ominotago pulled open the side door and guided Tinkerbelle and Wendy inside, Wendy found herself once again lost at sea. First, the side door led directly into a dressing room. It was roughly the size of Peter's living room, which is to say it wasn't nearly large enough. The walls were fully covered with posters and magazine clippings of stage shows and divas: Marilyn Monroe, Judy Garland, *Chicago*, *Kinky Boots*, Aretha Franklin, the Supremes, *Hairspray*, *My Fair Lady*, and what appeared to be an actual shrine to Dolly Parton complete with candles underneath and flowers glued around the poster. The farthest wall had a giant mirror encrusted with light bulbs, and the table beneath it extended from one end of the room to the other. The corner nearest to the girls was a huge wardrobe of clothes racks and shelves crammed with wigs, jewelry, gloves, scarves, gowns, and boots of incredible colors and heights. A large shared vanity was crowded with makeup, tubs of cold cream, wig glue, rollers, curling irons, flat irons, blow dryers, bows, clips, giant fake flowers, and even a glue gun. The drag queen nearest the door was nearly completely dressed, except for a strip of eyelashes that lay limp in her hand as she stared at the three girls. The queen next to the first one had a full face of makeup on, lashes and all, but was only dressed from the waist down. Her muscular chest contrasted interestingly with a gingham skirt and tights, while the rest of her costume hung on a hanger hooked to the back of her chair. There was a queen next to the wardrobe, in the throes of gluing feathers to the sides of her face with wig glue. She was in a full flesh-colored unitard with padding beneath it. Her tights were absolutely stunning, dotted with iridescent feathers starting mid-thigh and fading to tight clusters at her ankles, which were tucked neatly beneath the table. There were also queens wearing what looked like the restaurant's waitress uniform, getting undressed and putting their street clothes back on.

Charles, Fyodor, Minsu, Waatese, Curly, Nibs, and Peter were all crowded in the center of the dressing room, having a dramatic conversation while the drag queens watched in irritation.

As the three girls joined the boys, the drag queen in the gingham dress hissed, "Oh great, more children. This isn't a day care center!"

Peter, who looked a little worse for wear, with ashes on his cheeks and his bright eyes shining with manic energy, was saying, "You'll have to stay here until they leave."

Ominotago, not nearly as starstruck as Wendy, pushed through the boys until she was standing directly in front of Peter and staring him down fiercely. "Tell me what's going on. Now," she demanded.

Peter narrowed his eyes to slits and didn't answer her. Instead, his eyes trailed over Tinkerbelle and landed on Wendy. "Nice to know you made it, Darling. I see you've met my other ex, Ominotago."

Unlike Tinkerbelle, Ominotago didn't even flinch. Her hands were already curled into fists, and her body was angled to keep Tinkerbelle and Wendy behind her protectively. Charles, Waatese, and Minsu, who were standing behind Peter, looked at him in open disgust.

"Detective Hook is here," Curly answered Ominotago, breaking the tension. "He's asking for permission to search the restaurant, but management isn't letting him ruin their dinner service without a warrant."

"Sounds like a problem, but you're not staying in here," the queen in the gingham dress snapped. "You're lucky Bella even opened the door for you."

Peter said nothing, but turned around and snatched a

box of makeup wipes off the vanity. He began briskly rubbing the ash off his face, arms, and hands.

"Those were mine, but you're welcome to them," the queen who was holding her lashes said sarcastically as Peter nearly emptied the entire box.

When Peter was finished, he grabbed a comb from the vanity and began fixing his hair. "Detective Hook can't get in for a search, but if he buys something, he can get in as a customer and he *will* walk around. So. Everyone who wasn't detained by police can come into the restaurant and sit at my table." He painstakingly put himself to rights. "Everyone else, find somewhere else to hide. I'm friends with the head chef, so you guys can probably slip into the kitchen."

Peter did something bafflingly swift with his hand without reaching into his jacket at all, and suddenly he was holding a business card. He gave it to Fyodor, who took it gingerly from Peter like it was a cursed object.

"The chef's name is Joe," Peter said. "Give him this, and he'll let you go into the pantry."

"How do you know this man?" Fyodor asked suspiciously.

Peter grinned at the opportunity to show off. "I know everyone who is worth knowing in this city." Wendy noticed, for the very first time, how sharp his eyeteeth were. Peter turned his back on Fyodor, clearly finished speaking to him. Fyodor joined Charles, Minsu, and Waatese in looking at

Peter's back in disgust, but he, Waatese, Charles, and Minsu left the dressing room.

Now it was just the queens, Peter, Nibs, Curly, Ominotago, Tinkerbelle, and Wendy. Ominotago watched, arms crossed, as Peter picked up a compact, daubed a fingertip in some concealer—also belonging to the queen holding her eyelashes—and patted it beneath his eyes until he looked as fresh as when Wendy had met him.

"Tinkerbelle," Peter said, "you can come with me, Nibs, and Curly if you want. Om—"

Ominotago interrupted him. "You don't give me orders anymore."

"Fine," Peter snapped, finally addressing her directly. "Do what you want. Just keep Darling safe and hidden. So fucking stubborn." He tossed the compact back on the vanity as all the drag queens watched in scandalized silence.

Peter pointed at the door. Curly reached over and patted Wendy on the shoulder one last time and then followed Nibs out into the restaurant. Tinkerbelle squeezed Ominotago's hand and glanced up at Peter with a blank look that Wendy finally understood was fear, before following his instructions, as well.

Peter pulled another card out of thin air and handed it to the queen whose makeup he'd taken. "Thank you for letting me use your things, sweetheart. I'm sorry for not asking beforehand," he said in the gentle voice Wendy hadn't heard since he was hugging her after her kidnapping. "If you bring this to Elim Wig and Beauty and hand it to the cashier, he'll let you take one thing from the store for free. Any price, any grade of hair, all for you."

Just like Wendy had, the queen melted, and then she took the card from Peter.

"He's good for it, too," the queen wearing the feathered tights said as she ringed her eyes in iridescent green-and-blue shadow. She had spent the entire interaction focused on her costume, while the other drag queens had been watching the children hash out the details of avoiding the detective.

Peter wove in between the other queens to reach the corner where the queen in feathered tights was sitting. He pressed a quick kiss to the side of her face, over the feathers she had glued down. "Good luck tonight, Bella. I'll be watching you," he said sweetly.

Peter spared one more irritated glance at Ominotago before following Nibs, Curly, and Tinkerbelle out into the restaurant.

The instant he was out of the room, one of the waitresses who had stripped down entirely to street clothes crammed a baseball cap over his short hair and declared, "I do not like him at all."

"I don't, either, girl," the drag queen in gingham scoffed. "He gives me the creeps."

"He's not all bad," the queen named Bella said. "He tips crazy well, and if you're nice to him, he brings you gifts."

"I don't need gifts from that man," the waitress replied, raising an eyebrow and cocking his hip. "I buy my own shit. See you bitches tomorrow." He slung his backpack over his shoulder, rolled up one leg of his pants, and clipped it so it wouldn't get in the way of his bike chain. "Your makeup is fucked up," he said to Wendy on his way out the door. "Dorothy will give you a hand."

Wendy looked over to the vanity.

The drag queen in gingham—Dorothy—waved a hand, so Wendy went to go sit next to her.

Ominotago pulled out a chair and settled into it, looking at her watch. "I'm giving this about twenty minutes before I check on the other guys. I'm not leaving them in some stranger's kitchen."

"Were you crying, darling?" Dorothy asked, with a generous amount of sarcasm.

Wendy started for a moment before realizing "darling" was just being used as an endearment; this person didn't know Peter's nickname for her or that it was her last name.

"I've had a hard night," Wendy said quietly. "You don't have to help me with this or anything. I don't want to get in the way of you getting ready."

Dorothy threw her head back and laughed, showing a gold tooth in the back of her mouth. "Oh, I like this one. She's polite."

Up close Wendy could see the cracks in the plaster. Dorothy was older than Wendy had thought, and her makeup was significantly complex. Her face was pulled back with what looked like tape or pins of some kind and tucked into her wig cap. Her chin had to have been waxed to be this smooth this late at night. She had obvious highlighter dusted onto her cheekbones, but a much more subtle, expensive looking highlighter smoothed over the bridge of her nose, onto the sides of her jaw, and over her clavicle. Her lipstick was three different shades from the same color family layered from dark to light, creating the illusion of much fuller lips. It was like seeing a pointillism painting from a distance and knowing it was made up of dots, then leaning in close and realizing the dots were actually Rubik's Cubes, painstakingly arranged to form a much larger picture. Wendy was impressed.

"I like this one better," said the drag queen by the door, who had finally put her other lash on, while waving a hand at Ominotago. "*Her* makeup actually looks good."

Ominotago was busy doing something on her phone and didn't acknowledge the compliment. Wendy had only known Ominotago for approximately thirty minutes, but she already felt safer with her than she had with Tinkerbelle. Ominotago was much more serious, and she hadn't backed down to Peter at all, hadn't given him a single inch. Whatever fight she and Peter had before Wendy arrived had already been won, and it was extremely clear that Peter was the loser. Wendy wasn't stupid enough to ask about the whole Peter/Tinkerbelle/Ominotago dating time line, but she was curious about it. Who was first? Tinkerbelle? Ominotago? How did he even manage to get Ominotago to like him? That alone seemed like a monstrous feat. Had he treated Ominotago as aggressively as he seemed to treat Tinkerbelle? Ominotago wasn't scared of Peter, that was obvious, but she did seem to dislike him a lot. And where did Curly fit into this? Did he fight Peter over giving Ominotago a nickname before or after Peter and Ominotago dated? What happened when Ominotago and Tinkerbelle started dating? They hadn't stated it out loud but they were clearly very much together. She couldn't imagine *that* reveal going over very well. She hadn't known Peter for particularly long, but there was no way that a boy who had spoken to Nibs the way he did in the kitchen without waiting for an explanation wouldn't have gone ballistic to hear that both of his ex-girlfriends had started seeing each other.

Especially because of how besotted Tinkerbelle clearly was with Ominotago. Wendy remembered how Tinkerbelle had beat her hands against the police car window in hysterics, and the relief with which she'd clutched Ominotago when the other girl was finally free. It was almost embarrassing how romantic it was to watch. If there hadn't been explosions and sirens accompanied by the sounds of Charles's sobs, Wendy would have felt extremely awkward. Almost like she'd stumbled into the climax of a movie set where the main characters were finally making out, accompanied by the soaring strings of the score.

"Hey, kid, look, do you want me to do this shit or not?" Dorothy was saying.

Wendy snapped out of her thoughts to see Dorothy holding a makeup wipe in her hand and looking impatient.

"Ground control to Major Tom," Dorothy said. "Either give me an answer or get out of the chair."

"Yes," Wendy said quickly.

Dorothy sighed in irritation and began roughly wiping the makeup off Wendy's face. "Okay, here we go."

"How do you get it to look like that?" The drag queen who had complimented Ominotago's makeup asked.

Ominotago finally looked up from her phone for a second. "I do it with my fingers. I just picked a bunch of colors that went together and kept at it until it looked okay." She returned to texting. She clearly didn't care.

The queen leaned back in her chair. "You are much more talented than you give yourself credit for, girl. That shit looks like a J. M. W. Turner painting. Dorothy, you see this baby doing yellow under her eyes and fading that to blue and pink, purple in the shadows?" The queen sucked her teeth and nodded. "Opulence."

Dorothy looked over Wendy's shoulder at Ominotago, who seemed irritated at the attention. "You can't teach that," Dorothy said.

Dorothy finished polishing all of Tinkerbelle's work clean off Wendy's face. "You want the same thing or something different?"

"Tink—uh, my friend did my makeup like this because she wanted me to look different. Not like myself," Wendy answered.

"Like a disguise?" Dorothy asked, raising a slim eyebrow. "What kind of mess have you gotten yourself into?"

Bella snorted, and Wendy turned to her, but Dorothy wrenched her chin forward.

"You sound too timid to be one of Peter's girls," Bella said softly. "He likes them spicy. You're too white bread and tap water."

"Too berries and cream," Dorothy echoed.

"Too Ann Sather's," the drag queen by the door said. "What are you doing with that wild-ass boy?"

"She's new," Ominotago remarked, not looking up from her phone.

"Oh, honey, you need to go home," Bella said in a deeply apologetic tone.

"I know," Wendy said firmly. "I'm working on it."

"Oh, never mind. There's that attitude!" Dorothy screeched, laughing again. "I should have known you wouldn't be here if you didn't have it."

Wendy wanted to frown, embarrassed that everyone knew Peter had a type and she apparently fit it. But Dorothy's fingers were too tight, and her grip was too strong for Wendy to feel comfortable offending her.

"The best disguise is subtle," Dorothy continued, squinting at Wendy's face. "If you try to look different, everyone knows you're trying, and they'll seek out similarities to what they're looking for anyway. You've got to change the little things."

Dorothy handed Wendy a hand mirror and started working. She darkened Wendy's eyebrows with mascara and eyeliner, then contoured her nose to look pointier at the tip and flatter at the bridge. She buffed blush on Wendy's hand to match to her skin tone, then purposely chose a brighter color and applied it lower on her cheeks than Wendy would have thought would look nice. Dorothy leaned back so Bella could get a look. Bella pursed her lips and nodded, so Dorothy continued.

She wiped the heavy mascara off Wendy's lashes and replaced it with a set of natural brown false lashes glued farther out from Wendy's lid than the corner of her eye actually went. Then Dorothy filled the excess space with brown liner with a bit of pink in the corners, like Wendy had seen on ballerinas up close. She contoured underneath Wendy's chin with brown shadow and dusted only the tops of her cheekbones with a pink-based highlighter. When Wendy looked into the hand mirror Dorothy gave her, she found that she looked almost like a doll, or like someone from a silent film. Dorothy was rough and kept wrenching Wendy's head around, but she was incredibly talented. Wendy doubted she'd ever look this good again.

"Do you want to keep the hair, or do you want something different?" Dorothy asked, raising an eyebrow.

"The hair looks good," Ominotago interjected unexpectedly. "Suits her."

Dorothy laughed. "Oh, sweetheart, you don't have to say that. She won't take your girl. This one is as straight as—"

That was enough. "You don't have to talk about me like I'm not here," Wendy said crossly.

Dorothy paused and leaned back. "Honey, I don't have to do anything." She lowered her eyelids in warning. "The only reason your little behind is in this chair and not out there in the middle of that cop-infested restaurant is because I will it to be so. Do you hear me?"

Bella clicked her tongue.

"And the only reason I will it to be so," Dorothy continued, crossing her legs, "is because it's not my way to leave children out where the wolves can get them. Do you understand?"

Wendy glared and gritted her teeth but answered, "Yes, ma'am."

"Now, you are out of your depth and out of your territory, and you are receiving a service far more expensive than you could ever afford. So when I ask you whether you want something done with your hair, you say yes, ma'am, or no, ma'am. Are we clear?"

"Yes, ma'am," Wendy said. Her cheeks were burning, but thankfully Bella was looking politely away.

"So," Dorothy snapped, "are we gonna brush out this nest into something worth wearing, or are you too stubborn to take kind unless it's wrapped up like a Christmas present?"

Wendy took a deep breath and tried her best not to sound sassy. "May you please do my hair as well, Ms. Dorothy?" she asked evenly. Eleanor would have been proud.

Dorothy clapped once very loudly and smiled wide. "Of course, I will!" she said. "But you have to close your eyes."

Wendy sat still in the chair, eyes clenched, for the next twenty minutes. At first she sat in muted rage from the talking-to she'd just received, then later to keep the tears of pain inside from Dorothy's rough brushing and the jabbing of pins. She promised herself that she wasn't going to do anything elaborate with her hair and makeup for at least a year. She didn't care if Eleanor's hot friend Montana would think she looked gross. Two makeovers in one night was two makeovers too many. She swore Dorothy had wiped her makeup off with pure rubbing alcohol, and Tinkerbelle's backcombing had probably given her a lifetime's worth of split ends. She also kept hearing the other queens making commentary, but Ominotago hadn't said a word since Wendy had closed her eyes. She was almost afraid the other girl had left—but she hadn't heard the dressing room door open and close. Wendy heard a crinkling noise and felt hard presses from Dorothy's fingers, then she received a spray of something that smelled floral in a fresh and expensive way, and then Dorothy patted her shoulder hard.

"You can open your eyes," Dorothy said.

Wendy swiveled in her chair to face the mirror.

Dorothy had brushed the crunchy ringlets Tinkerbelle had given her into soft, cinematic, fluffy waves that framed Wendy's face prettily. She had gathered the top half of the back into two loose braids by Wendy's ears and pinned it so that the hair fell back over her shoulders, curling playfully at the ends. Even though Dorothy was white, it was immediately clear that she had worked with Black hair before, and the difference in skill between her work and Tinkerbelle's was dramatic. Then, ever the master of detail, Dorothy had tucked sprays of baby's breath and dried leaves in a crown, through the braids and over the top of Wendy's head, a touch so delicate and tasteful that it was immediately clear to Wendy that Dorothy had spent her life learning this: the art of beauty. Wendy gasped softly and finally saw a genuine smile bloom on Dorothy's face like a morning glory. Wendy reached up to touch her hair in disbelief, but Dorothy smacked the back of her hand softly.

"Oh, Dorothy." The queen by the door swooned. "She looks like a wedding in the spring."

"She does, doesn't she?" Dorothy said gently. "Like Aida Overton Walker. Look her up when you get home, dear."

Ominotago looked impressed, as well. She put her phone down and rested her chin in her hands to watch Wendy watch herself.

"I didn't know I could look like this," Wendy admitted. She wished her mom could see her like this, just as hard as she wished her mom would never find out what she'd gone through to make it to this chair in the back of this restaurant.

Dorothy sucked her teeth loudly and put both hands on Wendy's shoulders. "You don't have to look like this every day," Dorothy said. "Sometimes it's enough to know that this is in there. You can reach for it whenever you like, because this look is a part of you. But it is always your choice whether you want to put in the work. There is power in *not* doing this, just as much as there is power in knowing how to do it."

Wendy didn't know what to say.

"You should say thank you," Ominotago suggested when the silence got to be a bit too long and the moment began to fade.

Wendy turned around to face Dorothy. "Thank you."

Dorothy snorted and waved a hand modestly.

"I really mean it," Wendy said earnestly. "You're so good at this."

Dorothy folded her arms and beamed back at Wendy with her hard-won, morning glory face. "Darling," Dorothy said softly. "I'm the best."

"Now, I wouldn't go as far as—" the queen by the door began, but the door burst open, and Curly shoved his head inside.

"Peter says we can come—Whoa, you look good." He paused to stare.

"*Aanii*, Curly, what does Peter want?" Ominotago asked urgently, waving a hand to block Wendy from Curly's line of view.

Curly went on his tiptoes to avoid her arm and continue gaping at Wendy. "Peter said we can come out, but the Crocodile and Detective Hook are sitting at a table. They're not doing anything, though. They look mad."

"Oh, great." Ominotago sighed.

"The Crocodile looks madder, if that's any consolation," Curly said.

Ominotago turned to Wendy and shrugged. "You ready?"

Wendy nodded and followed Ominotago and Curly out the door.

Compared to the dressing room, the rest of the restaurant was much less stressful. The mermaid motif was strong in the dining area. The walls were painted turquoise and purple, the tables were draped with gauzy blue-green ombre tablecloths, and at the center of each table was a white seashell with a candle in the middle. The tables were arranged in a semicircle around a small stage that was packed richly with fake seagrass and green tinsel. There was a machine pumping bubbles out into the restaurant from backstage, and the speakers played a light gurgling underneath the jazzy restaurant music. The waitresses, just as Wendy had guessed from backstage, were all drag queens. Their uniform was a crop top T-shirt and sequined miniskirt, and beehive wig in matching monochrome. They had white seashells glued over their chest to their T-shirts, mermaid style.

Peter, Nibs, Tinkerbelle, Charles, Curly, Fyodor, Waatese, and Minsu were sitting at the large table closest to the stage. Ominotago's friends were clustered together and had saved a seat for her between Waatese and Tinkerbelle. Nibs had his arm over the back of the chair next to him, which was Curly's. There was only one seat left and it was next to Peter.

Peter tapped the seat and looked at Wendy pointedly. She turned to plead with Curly to switch, but Curly's expression shuttered closed and he shook his head quickly. Whatever argument the table had about where Wendy was supposed to sit had clearly already been firmly decided.

Wendy made her way across the room and reluctantly settled into the seat next to Peter. He put his arm over the top of the seat behind her—not touching her, but close enough that Wendy could feel the warmth of his body and take in his smoky floral scent.

He leaned over to whisper in her ear. "You look incredible. But you looked better in your room, dressed like yourself. Full of fire and anger, with sleep in your eyes." He settled back so he could gaze at her in the low candlelight. "The Real Wendy Darling," he finished.

"Why?" Wendy asked.

Peter tossed his hair back and chuckled prettily. He paused to pick a glass of red wine off the recently vacated table next to them and took a sip. He swirled the liquid around his mouth for a second and swallowed languidly before looking over at her. "You know why," he said quietly.

Wendy did not. She decided to wait him out. She didn't look at his wine-red lips or his angel curls or his eyes like heated amber; she looked through him.

"Because . . . ," Peter said, after some time, still gazing at her. "The Real Wendy Darling is capable of anything."

His words struck something deep inside her that pooled low and hot in her belly, and she instantly remembered the wind in her hair as they'd climbed together down the trellis. Peter slouched lower in his chair and spread his legs, and Wendy thought helplessly about his muscles under her thighs as she'd clung to his waist and the firm full-body gentleness of his grip as he'd held her in the kitchen. The scent of him was overpowering: the smoke, crisp like night air; and the flowers, green, making her skin itch to roll in grass, soft and tender beneath her fingertips. As if following the path of her thoughts, Peter scraped his nails over the fabric behind her chair, in a slow smooth rhythm that was almost hypnotizing. Wendy suddenly understood very clearly how a boy like this had captured a girl as smart as Tinkerbelle and a girl as proud as Ominotago.

It was too much.

Wendy turned away from him and toward the table closest to the door just to catch her breath as she was immediately faced with the other part of Curly's message: the Crocodile and Detective Hook.

The difference between the two men was immediate and jarring to the point of near hilarity. The Crocodile was massive in height and as wide as two average-height people put together. He was wearing an outfit that would have been funny on anyone else, but just served to make him look scarier. He had on a brown floppy hat, and a brown vest that bulged ominously like it was crammed full of tools. The sleeves of his black button-up shirt were rolled to the elbows, and his bulging, hairy forearms swelled out. He had a massive watch on one wrist and what looked to be a house arrest monitor on the other arm. His eyebrows were furrowed so far down over his eyes that Wendy would have been concerned about his ability to see if they weren't glittering so brightly in the candlelight. The other alarming thing was that he had the man next to him—who was clearly Detective Hook—gripped tightly by the wrist.

Detective Hook himself looked very normal in comparison to the Crocodile, aside from the near-demonic expression of fury twisting his features. He had black hair with silver temples, and that rectangular sort of mustache that cops seem to favor. His nose looked like it had been broken at least twice, and he had more stubble than one would consider professional. He was wearing a surprisingly nice blue suit and shirt, with a maroon overcoat draped on his chair. Every single molecule in his body was focused on Peter, to the point where Wendy felt like she could feel him cooking the air between them with his rage. Also, of course, he had the prosthetic hand replacement. It was more delicate than Wendy had imagined a hook to be, clearly functional as opposed to decorative, but it was still beautiful.

However, noticing it made Wendy think about Slightly's sweet face, and reminded her that this man, Hook, had seen a younger version of Slightly and decided it was okay to hurt him. This made her dislike him on the spot.

The Crocodile saw her, but his eyes slipped off her disinterestedly, focusing on Peter. Detective Hook had a different reaction. Barely seconds after Wendy had turned in his direction to escape Peter's magnetism, Detective Hook's expression changed.

When Wendy and the detective locked eyes, he switched rapidly from a tight grimace of anger to confusion, then surprise, then to an anger ten times more potent. He wrestled his hand out of the Crocodile's grip and lunged to his feet so aggressively that the table they were sharing jerked loudly, screeching against the floor.

"Get away from her!" the detective roared. All the diners stopped eating and looked over at the spectacle. Even the waitresses stopped and didn't make a sound.

Peter was unfazed. He smiled at the detective and waved chipperly.

The Crocodile immediately rose, as if receiving an order, clamped Detective Hook's shoulder in his monstrous grip, and hauled him toward the exit. Detective Hook struggled against the Crocodile's strength, his face nearly purple as his anger choked him.

"That's enough!" the Crocodile said loudly, sharply, and in an accent way more Australian than Wendy would have guessed, and he heaved the detective through the door. There was an audible struggle outside as the two men grappled with each other. The diners watched their shadows through the window curtains in scandalized silence. After a while, Detective Hook got the upper hand, took a valiant leap in Peter's direction, and managed to get his head back inside the restaurant.

"I swear, I will see you in chains," Detective Hook promised darkly before the Crocodile overpowered him and pulled the door firmly shut after them both.

Peter shook his head. "Pirates don't like the Molotov fireworks. It's a *lot* of paperwork."

Wendy took stock of the expressions at the table. Nibs and Curly looked carefully blank. Minsu's and Charles's eyes were as big as dinner plates. Fyodor was looking away from the table in the same way he had on the bus, what Ominotago had described as "pretending he's not scared." Waatese, on the other hand, was looking at Ominotago, openly terrified.

Ominotago and Tinkerbelle were as blank-faced as Nibs and Curly, but they were holding hands tightly.

"Go home, little brother," Ominotago said quietly. "It is too dangerous for you."

Waatese immediately stood up.

"You heading out?" Charles asked warily.

"Yeah." His voice was higher than Wendy thought it would be, and she wondered again just how young he was. "It's getting late. I . . . have some homework to finish."

That sounded very obviously like a lie, but no one challenged it, and Waatese made his way to the door. Minsu and Charles gazed longingly at Waatese's back as he was allowed to leave what was clearly a situation they yearned to escape from. Wendy wondered why they didn't leave, too, but then saw how they crowded even closer to Ominotago protectively, and understood at once.

The detective's outburst had been dramatic, but it wasn't enough to keep the crowded restaurant quiet for long. The waitresses returned to bussing the tables, and the rest of the diners went back to talking, but Peter's table stayed deathly quiet, even while a waitress dropped off a few plates of fries and refilled all the drinks. Aside from Peter, they might as well have been wax carvings. Even Nibs seemed a bit shaken.

Peter rolled his shoulders contentedly and looked at his phone. "It's almost time for the show."

Like magic the ceiling lights grew dimmer, and the stage lights brightened.

"Oh, great," Wendy heard Fyodor say behind her, and it took all the discipline she had not to laugh in hysteria.

The music shifted from background jazz to a swelling

classical score, and a long, slender leg covered in feathers slowly peeked out from between strands of the tinsel seagrass curtain. The leg wiggled a familiar foot, then coyly snatched itself back behind the curtain. Then two feathered legs split the tinsel, wide and suggestive, before tucking back behind the glimmering strings.

Peter leaned back over to Wendy. "This is Bella's dance, the 'Never Bird.' She's been doing it at this place for fifteen years, I've heard. That's why it's so busy. Generally, on the nights she's scheduled, this place is booked out for weeks." He smiled softly. "I promised I'd show you something special, so I pulled a few strings."

The curtains pulled slowly back to reveal Bella, the drag queen who had sat behind Wendy in the dressing room. Bella was obscured by two giant iridescent blue and green fans made of ostrich feathers, and was wearing a towering headdress, nearly two feet tall, with plumes of even more feathers. Her fans were so large, Wendy couldn't see any of her body besides her long-lashed eyes and her downy legs. She looked incredible.

Wendy heard a groan and knew it came from Fyodor, who evidently wasn't prepared to enjoy this at all.

Bella fluffed her fans delicately in their table's direction and began dancing. It was surprisingly adorable. When the base thumped, she bumped her hip to the side, showing the tiniest sliver of the bodysuit Wendy knew she was wearing. When the tambourines clashed, she fluttered the fans around, changing their position. The gusts from the fans blew the bubbles delicately and made the seagrass billow realistically as Bella moved. Suddenly she moved the fan she was holding lower so the audience could see her red-painted lips, but only for a second before she snatched the view away, fluttering her feathers flirtatiously. Wendy surprised herself by laughing in delight.

Peter's eyes snapped back to Wendy, and he beamed at her.

Bella seemed to notice Peter's attention shift, and she sashayed across the stage until she was directly across from their table. Then she fluffed her fans hard, and two great gusts of wind blew over their table. Peter turned back to watch her, and Bella's eyes crinkled in triumph.

She twisted until she was at the very edge of the stage, then turned around and leaned, fans positioned at her front and her back until she was completely bent over in such a way that only Peter, Wendy, Curly, and possibly Charles and Minsu at the back of the table could see her whole face.

"Hello, old friend," Peter said, grinning sharply.

"Old friend," Bella echoed. "Better get going; the night isn't as young as we are."

Peter laughed loudly and slipped a hand under Bella's waist to help her back up and out of her contortions.

"I'll see you later, dove," he said quietly.

Nibs and Curly were already starting to rise when Peter turned to the table.

"All right, let's go," Peter declared. "We have places to be."

Wendy half expected both the Crocodile and Detective Hook to be lurking outside waiting for them, but the detective had left. The Crocodile was leaning against the side of the building, smoking, so out of the way and silent that Wendy didn't spot him until he reached out a meaty arm and grabbed Peter by the wrist.

To Wendy's surprise, Peter laughed in the Crocodile's face and snatched his arm back. "You don't have to get so testy," he said. "I've never been late."

Wendy looked frantically at Ominotago, but the other girl didn't seem alarmed, just tired. Fyodor looked mildly disgusted, but also unsurprised, which made Wendy feel safer. Peter flipped open his messenger bag, handed the Crocodile an envelope, and turned away.

"More," the Crocodile said to the back of Peter's head with a voice that sounded like two boulders rubbing together. "Tonight you're a hassle."

Peter scowled and whipped back around. "*You're* always a hassle," he snapped. Then he rummaged in his bag for his wallet and gave the Crocodile what looked like at least a hundred dollars.

"What the fuck?" Wendy started to say quietly, but Tinkerbelle tapped her and shook her head sharply. The Crocodile's beady eyes snapped over to Wendy, jolting her enough for her to take a step backward. The bounty hunter looked them all up and down one by one before moving his grizzled head back to focus on Peter.

"See you next month," the Crocodile rumbled. He flicked his cigarette, then pushed himself off the wall next to the restaurant and slunk back inside.

Peter took a steadying breath and turned back to Wendy. "Protection," he explained. "Keeps the coppers off our backs."

"That's normal?" Wendy couldn't help herself. She could make excuses in her head to rationalize a lot of things that had happened tonight, but this wasn't one of them.

"It is for me," Peter replied with a grin that didn't reach his eyes. "Let's go."

CHAPTER 10

After Detective Hook's outburst, it was a bit easier to see the dynamic of the group as a whole. Everyone was on edge and not doing a great job of hiding their emotions. Everyone but Peter, it seemed.

Wendy watched from the back of the group as they made their way toward the train station. Minsu and Charles were doing the least to disguise their hatred and disgust toward Peter, only changing their expressions when Peter looked at them directly. Now that Charles had properly cried out his terror from nearly being arrested, he seemed more serious and way more focused on using his large body to physically block Ominotago from view. Charles looked at Peter the way one would look at a sleeping lion: wary and ready to defend himself. Fyodor refused to look at Peter at all unless directly addressed. So aggressive was his refusal to participate and determination to stay faced away that Peter loudly began pointing out when they were turning, as if he thought Fyodor was about to walk in the wrong direction.

By contrast, Nibs and Curly looked at Peter often, as if waiting for orders he hadn't given yet. They leaned toward him the same way Tinkerbelle had leaned toward Peter in the alley when they'd first met. Nibs and Curly also moved in lockstep with Peter, like a pack, with Peter at the front. Tinkerbelle and Ominotago walked at the rear of the group. Peter seemed incredibly agitated by Ominotago's presence, but was putting up with her for reasons Wendy didn't yet understand. Unlike the rest of the people Wendy had met tonight, Ominotago didn't seem afraid of Peter at all. Now that she thought about it, Ominotago was also the only person who had seriously disobeyed him and gotten away with it.

I don't take orders from him, she'd said. Ominotago had stated that like a fact, as resolutely as Wendy would say that there were fifty states in America.

Tinkerbelle, she realized, was mimicking that. Her shouting in the alley was less impactful than Ominotago's conversational tone. Her rebellion was always followed immediately by cowering and silence. She was fighting back without the right weapons and without durable armor.

The air around the group was thick with tension. Nine different people walking together, wrestling with Peter's gravitational pull in their own ways while the boy himself gave off nothing at all. No fear, no guilt, no concern. Strolling down the street like the entire neighborhood was the inside of his house. Like it was midday instead of 11:33 p.m.

Wendy noticed that while his right arm swung beside him carelessly, his left hand was dipped into his messenger bag, where she knew he kept his bombs. He seemed nonchalant, but Peter was always ready.

The mood got even more anxious the longer the group walked in silence. It was beginning to feel dangerous, so Wendy decided to throw herself into the fray to ease the tension.

"So, what kind of party is this?" she asked.

To her surprise, Minsu was the one who answered. "It's a warehouse party out in Skokie. Ominotago, Curly, and Waatese throw it once a year. It's like a big . . . uh . . . like a show? There's local DJs and stuff." Minsu turned around and began walking backward. "Also, what's your name again?"

"Wendy Darling." Wendy stuck out her hand, remembering that Minsu had been extremely busy comforting Charles during the "get to know you" part of the bus ride.

Minsu fist-bumped Wendy's outstretched hand chaotically instead of shaking it. "Wendy like Wendy's™? Yikes. I'm sorry."

Charles did a double take, but then shook his head like he was already tired of dealing with Minsu's antics.

Minsu himself was unrepentant. He stopped walking backward but slowed down a bit so he and Wendy were walking next to each other. "I'm not sure if house music is your thing, because it's barely mine, but pretty much everyone in CPS who is cool enough to get an invite goes to this. It's, like, the biggest party of the year."

"CPS?" Wendy asked. "Is that the school you go to?"

"Chicago Public School," Ominotago, Charles, and Minsu answered in unison.

"We go to Luther South," Minsu elaborated. "You from out of town?"

Wendy nodded. "Hinsdale."

"Oh, so this is a *party* party for you," Minsu said

knowingly. "You responsible for this, Peter?" he called to the front of the group.

"Always," Peter tossed over his shoulder. "You treat her nice, now."

Out of Peter's view, Minsu made an incredulous face. "He doesn't know how to treat anybody," Minsu muttered under his breath.

"I'm beginning to notice," Wendy replied, just as quiet.

Minsu smiled at that, and it felt like the sun was burning off Wendy's whole face to look at him directly. Did Peter have a sexy-only policy? Who was responsible for gathering this many attractive people in such a small space? Did Minsu brush his teeth with literal bleach? Were you not allowed to go to public school unless you were a model? Not that Minsu looked like a model; he was entirely too beefy for that. *Which*, Wendy thought, *isn't actually a drawback.*

"Anyway, here's the rules," Minsu said. "One: Don't take any drugs, if anyone gives them to you. You don't seem like the drug-taking type, but I mean not even a mint or a hit of someone's vape, because one of my friends did once and it, uh . . . was not vape juice. Liquid. Crystals. Whatever, just don't do it." Minsu was counting on his fingers. "Two: Find a buddy and keep your eyes on them. Charlie is my buddy, right babe?" he asked sweetly.

"Everyday, everyday," Charles agreed, giving Minsu a solid low five.

"So you gotta find someone else," Minsu continued. "I recommend Fyodor, but he dances like a scarecrow in a wind tunnel, so you might wanna stay outside his arm-span."

Fyodor gave Minsu the finger without turning around.

"Rule three? Know all your exits. Basic theater policy. Last year there was a tornado warning, and a bunch of people rushed the same exit and got trampled. It's clear skies tonight, but anything could happen. Know how to get the fuck out.

"Rule four: Drink water. Always stay hydrated. It's also a basic life tip, but when you're dancing and drinking, it's doubly important.

"Rule five?" Minsu locked his fingers behind his head casually as they strolled into the train station. "Have fun and be yourself. Don't do anything you wouldn't want to wake up regretting in the morning."

"That's hypocritical, Minsu," Ominotago teased from behind Wendy.

"These rules are for *her*, not for me," Minsu said, smirking as he swiped his card at the turnstile. "I wore handcuffs today. Let me live a little, dang."

Somehow, Wendy felt a little better after listening to him. Minsu reminded her of Eleanor. In fact, Minsu, Charles, Fyodor, and Ominotago all reminded her much more of people she would have known at school than Tinkerbelle, Curly, or Nibs did. Weirdly enough, also knowing that they all had a specific time they were supposed to be home made her feel way more comfortable. It was strange how quickly being

164

in situations out of your control made you crave parental restrictions. Wendy was fairly sure that if her parents decided to ground her for a whole month, she wouldn't care at all because at this point it would feel like a vacation.

Tinkerbelle swiped her card twice so Wendy could get through the turnstile and pressed close behind her on the escalator up to the train platform. "You're doing great," she whispered. "Just stay nearby."

Wendy reached down and took the hand that Ominotago wasn't holding. Tinkerbelle looked surprised, her big blue eyes widening, but she squeezed Wendy's hand reassuringly.

"Stop," Ominotago murmured. Wendy dropped Tinkerbelle's hand like it burned. Ominotago shook her head almost imperceptivity and spoke so quietly that Wendy had to strain to hear. "We'll look like we're in cahoots. He's always watching."

Before she could control herself, Wendy turned to look at Peter, who was indeed watching them from the top of the escalator, nearly fifteen feet away. He had the same expression on his face when Wendy had been reciting poetry at the dinner table.

"Hurry up, lovebirds," he said with false cheer. "The train isn't going to wait forever."

Wendy, Ominotago, and Tinkerbelle scampered up the last few escalator steps and in through the train doors. Charles had been holding them open with his body. He stepped inside behind them, with Peter at his back.

The train car was way emptier at 11:45 p.m. than it was earlier. There were only three other people riding with them: an elderly woman with one of those foldable grocery carts, crammed tightly with bags; a sleeping homeless man at the far end of the car; and another younger man in a hoodie, who seemed close to college age and with headphones on, his eyes closed.

Charles and Minsu were seated next to each other by the door, Tinkerbelle and Ominotago across from them. Curly and Nibs each took a whole two seats to themselves, spreading their legs over the chairs rudely. Wendy joined Fyodor in holding on to the pole next to the door near Tinkerbelle. Peter stood in the middle of the aisle and held the metal bars on the back of Curly's and Nibs's seats, one in each hand. From where he was standing, he could see everyone in the train car, except for the homeless man sleeping behind him.

Nibs said something low to Curly, who flicked his eyes up at Peter without moving his head, and Curly said something back quietly.

The rest of the group watched their conversation in curious silence until Nibs got self-conscious. He snapped loudly and flicked his hand at all of them hard, as if to tell them to mind their business.

"So," Wendy said pointedly, "what else do you guys do for fun?"

Nibs nodded a thank-you to her before turning back to continue talking privately with Curly.

"What kind of question is that?" Minsu asked, scrunching up his nose. "Just normal things. Going to the movies, football, house parties. I'm not sure what kind of answer you're looking for here."

Charles bumped Minsu with his shoulder. "Would you give her a break, man?"

"Absolutely not," Minsu replied crisply with another blinding smile.

"I MEAN," Wendy said loudly, "are there any cool places you guys hang out? I have a friend who I already know here, and I want to bring her somewhere cool. Kind of impress her or something."

"Like an online friend?" Minsu asked.

"Yeah," Wendy said, ready to be defensive about it.

Instead of taking the easy bait, Charles and Minsu just looked contemplative.

"There aren't a lot of cool places that someone who has lived here their entire life wouldn't know about . . . ," Charles said. "What kind of stuff are they into?"

Wendy thought for a minute. "She likes . . . anime, nature hikes, and girls."

"Is it a date?" Minsu asked seriously.

"Absolutely not," Wendy echoed his words from earlier, winning herself yet another swoon-worthy smile.

"You could take her down to the Adler Planetarium," Ominotago offered. "There's this area right next to it that's kind of like a huge nature preserve, but instead of trees it's a field."

"There's a beach area next to it, too—" Tinkerbelle tacked on.

"Northerly Island!" Minsu exclaimed. "You should look it up when you get home. It's a good date place, but it's good for other stuff, too. I had to go there with my school for a biology field trip focused on, like . . . wild birds or something." He said the words *wild birds* like the birds had personally offended him.

Wendy giggled.

Fyodor snorted and rolled his eyes. "Always easy for this one," he said to Wendy, gesturing at Minsu. "So charming and 'funny.'"

Minsu looked mock-offended. "Yeah, whatever, Fyodor. You say that like you don't have a whole fan club of freshmen wandering around in love with you. All *Oh. His accent is so sexy*," Minsu said, ratcheting his voice up into falsetto. "Let me make girls laugh in peace."

Fyodor cocked his hip and leaned against the door divider, lowering his eyelids suggestively. "Is sexy," he said, smirking. "I cannot help this."

Minsu threw his arms out dramatically. "No, it's not! It's just Russian!"

"You are both sexy," Charles said loudly, putting his

hands on either side of his face to block out both of his team-mates. "Do not make us listen to this argument again."

Ominotago leaned forward to capture Wendy's full attention as Minsu and Fyodor began to bicker in earnest. "The Abercrombie store on Michigan Avenue has been hiring them both but alternating who they pick each summer," she explained. "This year was Minsu, and Fyodor won't let it go."

"Hired . . . to stand shirtless in front of the store?" Wendy asked, beginning to blush.

Fyodor took a moment away from Minsu to turn to Wendy. "Is windy, but good for portfolio if football does not work out. Plus, the visa is . . . different. I can stay if—"

"NEXT STOP IS GRANVILLE," the train speakers blared, interrupting Fyodor as the doors swung open. "DOORS CLOSING." The young man at the end of the train car yanked the headphones out of his ears and stood up fast. He seemed panicked as he squinted out the windows to see what stop they were at while the train pulled away from the platform.

As they passed a sign, he looked relieved and was about to sit back down when Curly shouted, "James?!"

The young man pulled the headphones back out of his ears and looked up. When he made eye contact with Curly, he went pale so fast he looked like he was about to faint.

"James . . ." Curly sounded incredibly hurt underneath his shock. "I thought you left town . . ."

James fumbled with his bag like a character in a horror film, trying to shove his phone and headphones inside too quickly as he staggered to his feet. Eyes wild, he attempted to make his escape.

He did not succeed.

Peter shoved past Curly and strode forward with that alarming speed he had coiled inside him, silent and radiating anger.

He grabbed James's upper arm in a punishing grip and wrenched him forward toward the dividers between the train cars.

"No! No, please," James gasped, clawing back toward the center of the car, but Peter was relentless.

"We need to talk," Peter said in a voice Wendy had never heard come out of him before. Peter forced James out of the train car and into the divider and closed the door firmly behind them.

The silence in his wake was deafening.

Nibs was the first to move. He lunged forward, eyes locked on the space where James had been standing, but Curly snatched him back. Nibs tried to shrug Curly off, but to Wendy's surprise, Curly slammed Nibs back to the seat and hissed, "Stop. He can see us through that window. James is gone, Nibs. He was gone to us before, when we thought Peter had gotten to him, and he's gone now." Wendy looked out the window on the dividing doors, but it was barely half the width of a man, and Peter's back currently covered the entirety of it. She couldn't even hear them outside with the noise from the tracks. She turned back to the group.

Curly shook Nibs hard by the shoulder just once before letting go. "We can't think about him. Not right now. We can't go after him, and you know why we can't. He is *gone*."

Nibs leaned his head against the window and squeezed his eyes tight in pain. "We lost him and now we have him and we're losing him again," he choked out, like the words were costing him.

"I know," Curly said, much gentler. "But we can't. I'm not losing you to him, too."

Nibs scrubbed his hands over his face and let out what Wendy could only describe as a whimper. She tore her eyes away from him.

Ominotago let go of Tinkerbelle's hand so she could curl her own into angry fists on her thighs.

"What—" Wendy started, but Minsu waved a hand in a quick "don't even bother" gesture. He was weak and pale now, like a puppet with his strings cut, all the class-clown energy stripped from him completely. The entire group was having some sort of extreme reaction that Wendy didn't have the context for, and it was scaring her badly.

Fyodor was visibly furious. "We couldn't even have five whole minutes of happiness," he spat. "He ruins everything. We almost made it relaxed for her and—"

He folded his arms around himself, too angry to continue talking, and glared out the train window. Wendy hadn't realized that Fyodor and Minsu's friendly bickering and the dramatic shift of mood that followed had been for her benefit alone. She felt a surge of tenderness.

Now that she was looking for it, Wendy could see the half-moons on the inside of Fyodor's palms from him clenching his hands into fists.

Charles had his arm around Minsu again, a gesture Wendy realized was actually for Charles's own reassurance.

Minsu had the sort of bags under his eyes that people only get from prolonged dread. They were harder to see when he was smiling. Perhaps that's why he'd been doing it so often.

Tinkerbelle, who Wendy already knew wasn't a quiet person, had been quieter than *ever* since seeing Ominotago in the police car, so it was clear that she was shaken.

Poor Nibs was in the middle of some sort of breakdown. Curly, jaw clenched, held Nibs close and rocked him in a way that made it clear that they had done this together many times before.

Ominotago was letting off a steady sort of anger, like she expected these circumstances but could not do anything to avoid them. Everyone was looking away from the doorway where Peter and James had gone.

"Nibs," Ominotago said suddenly. "He cannot see you like this. Not tonight."

Nibs let out a soft whimper of a sigh, and Curly shook him one last time before letting go. Eyes closed, Nibs pulled himself upright and breathed hard, forcing himself to relax. He clenched his hands into fists, then he rolled his shoulders. Nibs's face, which had been red enough to nearly match his hair, was beginning to fade back to normal. When his eyes fluttered back open, they were still a bit wet, but his face was bone-dry, and somehow that was worse to witness.

Tinkerbelle reached over and put a small hand on Curly's knee. Curly threaded his fingers between hers.

"Okay. You all need to tell me what is going on right now," Wendy demanded quietly.

Ominotago turned to Tinkerbelle. Tinkerbelle glanced up at Wendy and nodded. Then Ominotago looked at everyone in the group individually, from Curly and Nibs to Charles and Minsu, and up to Fyodor, and waited for them all to give their silent agreement. Then Ominotago closed her eyes and took a deep breath. She looked up at Wendy and opened her mouth, but before she could say anything, Fyodor interrupted.

"And maybe you should consider that next time, da?" Fyodor said.

"Yeah, whatever," Minsu replied sassily. "You don't control me."

Charles, Tinkerbelle, Ominotago, and Curly laughed loudly just as Peter pushed the train divider door open. Wendy realized instantly that Fyodor had seen Peter coming and faked being in the middle of a conversation. Hearing the other kids laughing, fake and loud, made Wendy feel like she was about to pass out. People don't get good at doing things like that unless they needed to. Unless they've done it often and for their own protection.

"Anyway," Curly added to the phony conversation, looking alarmingly fresh-eyed, "when we get there, both of you are buying me drinks."

"Fine," Fyodor said, rolling his eyes. "So spoiled."

Wendy could feel Peter watching them, even though she wasn't looking at him. She knew that if she looked up, his eyes would be shiny and piercing again.

Fyodor was the first to face him. He had another unlit cigarette in his hand. "Peter. You have light?" he asked.

To Wendy's surprise, Peter's eyes actually looked a little glazed, like he'd just woken up or something. The boy shook his head for a second as if to snap it out of something. "No . . . ," he said finally. "And you should stop smoking. You too, Tinkerbelle, and yes, a pipe counts."

Tinkerbelle stuck her tongue out at him cheekily, but Wendy could see her hand shaking in Curly's grip.

"Hey, Darling," Peter said, body still half outside the train car. "Can I talk to you for a minute?"

The tension in the train car spiked. Wendy saw Tinkerbelle's head twitch in her direction, but Tinkerbelle successfully kept herself from turning all the way. Instead she laughed and slapped Curly's knee, and Curly mocked being hurt by the gesture. Charles, the farthest from Peter, was openly staring at Wendy, so horrified that Wendy could see the whites around his brown doe-eyes. Minsu said something about drinks being expensive, but dug his fingers into the side of Charles's leg in panic. Charles snapped out of it and jumped back into the fake conversation, promising to buy Curly's drink on Minsu's behalf.

Wendy had never been more terrified in her life.

"Go," Ominotago whispered. She was blocked from Peter's view by the divider by the door, her lips barely moving. "You have to."

Wendy forced a smile onto her face. "I'll be right back," she said to the group.

"Don't get lost," Curly teased with an answering grin, his eyes haunted like he was never going to see her again.

"I won't," Wendy replied flirtingly, and made her legs carry her across the train car.

Peter was waiting for her patiently. As she got closer, Wendy could see that his cheeks were red and his nose was a bit pink, as if he'd been crying. Unlike last time, she still saw the ghost of Charles's terror, and her heart did not move.

CHAPTER 11

Peter held the door open for her, forcing their proximity as she ducked under his arm into the space between the train cars. To her surprise, James wasn't there, and she couldn't see him in the other car, either, though it was hard to see through the dirt encrusted windows.

The train was going significantly slower than it had earlier in the evening and it was quieter, but that didn't make Wendy feel any safer.

Peter leaned against the door and pushed his hair back from his face with a shaking hand. "Things haven't been going very well tonight, have they?" he asked quietly, not meeting her gaze.

Wendy wasn't sure of the safest way to answer that question. She wrapped both hands around the railing chains and squared her feet for better balance, then she shrugged. "Things could have gone worse," she said finally.

To her great relief, Peter laughed. "They definitely could have."

He mirrored her gesture, curling his hands around the chains and sighed. "I didn't want any of this to happen. I had been hoping to just show you a good time." The moonlight illuminated his handsome face in a soft glow. "I was thinking that you and Tinkerbelle would become fast friends because you seemed so similar. I was going to introduce you to Slightly and Curly and Nibs, and show off the art Curly had made in our space. Then we were going to go to the Mermaid's Lagoon together, and Bella was going to dance for you. She'd been practicing for weeks . . . She's an icon and I was so excited to show it to you."

Peter looked genuinely sad, and it was hard for Wendy to focus on remembering how scared and upset the others had been only minutes ago, but she was trying. Peter was so very talented at this. She couldn't even put her finger on exactly what he did to create these situations. It was some combination of forcing you to feel his body heat through proximity, projecting insecurity, and shifting the way he used his voice. No hard edges; instead, all vulnerability and open body language. Letting Wendy control how close they were, physically cowering like she was the thing he should be afraid of—not the other way around. And then there was his beauty. If Minsu and Fyodor were pretty, Peter Pan was radiant. He literally looked like an angel as the wind blew his curls around his face and the starlight made his clear skin gleam.

As if he could tell she was appraising him, Peter tucked his bottom lip under his straight white teeth and let his auburn lashes flutter down to his freckled cheeks. "All I wanted," he said in a very small voice, "was to make sure you had a nice time. I didn't know my brothers would freak out and drag you to our house. I couldn't predict the police would be harassing my friends. And the Crocodile . . . and Detective Hook?" Peter shook his head. "You should never have had to see them at all. That's not anything you should ever have to deal with. Those are my problems, not yours."

Peter rubbed at one of his eyes and looked out toward the moon. "I'm not having the best night, either," he said sadly.

As if he were a victim of these circumstances and not at all the source of them.

Then he dug around in his bag and pulled out some sort of stick. "I hope you don't mind, but it's a bit too dark for me to see," he said sheepishly as he dug out a lighter and lit the tip of the stick.

Wendy flinched as it burst into light, throwing sparks in every direction. Peter held the sparkler in between them, the golden light illuminating the leftover dampness beneath his eyes and the soft blush on his cheeks.

"You don't have to forgive me," Peter said firmly.

Wendy thought about how Tinkerbelle had looked hours ago, right after they'd first met, when Peter had spoken harshly to her and she'd clammed up as if Peter had been about to hit her.

"You're right," Wendy lied. "No one could have predicted that. Don't worry about it. We're almost to the party, and from what Minsu and Fyodor were saying, it sounds like it's going to be a great time."

She let go of one of the chains and wrapped her hand around the sparkler. Peter let go of it, something in him relaxing at Wendy's words. Wendy took the sparkler in her own hand and held it up high, so the sparks didn't ignite their clothing.

"Thank you," Peter said. "God, I'm so sorry about everything. Thank you for giving this another chance." He slumped against the door and looked out toward the moon again. "I don't want to unload on you or anything, but doing this is so hard."

"Doing what?" Wendy asked.

"This. All of it. Looking after Curly, Nibs, and the rest. Making sure everyone is okay. I know they talk about me behind my back and that they think I'm mean and stuff, but somebody has to be in charge. Somebody has to make the hard choices and sacrifices even if it makes them the bad guy, you know? I never wanted to be a dad; I just wanted to have fun with my friends." Peter looked absolutely crestfallen.

He covered his face again and sniffed. "And then James shows up like it's no big deal, and—"

Peter was crying again.

It was incredible how he cried like he was starring in a film. His face didn't get puffy, snot didn't drip from his nose, and his voice didn't get all squeaky. He just naturally wept, his eyelashes clumping in wet spikes with just enough tears to drip delicately down his chiseled cheeks and angled jaw.

"James used to live with us," Peter explained, his voice rough with anguish. "But he left. As soon as he grew up, he left and never came to visit any of us again. He was our family, and he just stopped visiting, and no one knew what happened to him. The twins cried for weeks. I . . . didn't even know what to tell them."

Wendy also didn't know what to think. She watched as Peter wiped stubbornly at his face, as if he were embarrassed to be crying but unable to stop.

"And Curly thinks I drove him away, and I don't know how to tell him that I didn't," Peter sobbed.

He rubbed his eyes harder. "I shouldn't." He took a moment to take a deep breath. "I shouldn't be bothering you with all of this. You don't even know any of us that well."

"I—I'm sorry," Wendy stammered, still at a loss for what to say.

The sparkler was getting low, spitting out its last bits of light.

"What do you even do when someone treats you like that, you know?" Peter asked, golden eyes wide. "We loved him, and he didn't even say goodbye. And just now, he just left the train . . . Left us all, again."

Wendy remembered Nibs's moan of horror and the clench of Tinkerbelle's hand and thought quickly. "Sometimes people just change as they get older, and they do things they might regret later. I'm sure if he knew just how much he meant to you all, he wouldn't have left so suddenly."

Peter was looking at the ground, at the train tracks rushing beneath them. Then he wiped his face again and took a few moments to compose himself. "I hate growing up," he said to Wendy quietly. "I don't want to change into someone who doesn't care about my family. I just want things to stay the same."

He pulled his gray jacket closer around himself and shivered. "You're a really nice girl," he said, incredibly heartfelt, and for the first time in more than an hour, Wendy didn't feel like he was lying.

The sparkler she was holding breathed its last and went cold, plunging them back into darkness. Wendy looked at the burnt tip for a second, then tossed the sparkler down into the rushing steel below.

Peter's eyes tracked the motion, then dropped. "When you go home," Peter began quietly, "and you start living your life. When you go to school and have fun with your parents and get taller and bigger and smarter. When you have the whole world ahead of you and all the opportunities there are to offer in your hands. When you're old enough to have your own daughter who wants to go on adventures and wants to see the world, will you remember us? Me and Tink and Curly and Nibs? Because when people grow up, they forget how . . ."

Peter was still gazing forlornly at the ground, so Wendy looked past him and into the train car beyond. She could see everyone's faces staring through the grime of the door. Tinkerbelle was half out of her seat and leaning forward to make sure Wendy was okay. Curly and Nibs were leaning into the aisle, doing the same.

Wendy looked back at Peter, then cupped his cheek. Peter allowed his face to be tilted upward until it was completely reillumined by the moonlight. This close, Wendy could see his imperfections, the sheen of makeup covering his dark circles, the turn in his nose that told her it had been broken at least once, the salt encrusted at the corners of his eyes, and the stubble that pricked at her fingertips.

"I will *never* forget this," Wendy promised.

Peter turned his head and kissed the swell of her palm—so gently it felt like a brush of a feather, but with too much heat and stickiness.

"Thank you," he said, voice rough, "for being so nice to me."

Peter straightened himself to his full height and stretched, leaning against the train car door as the wind blew his curls around riotously. The train was now going so fast and the wind blowing so hard that one of the flowers Dorothy had pinned in Wendy's hair finally flew off. Peter reached out and caught it, plucking it from the air like he was picking it off a tree, rather than grabbing something flying at God knows how many miles per hour past him, and Wendy was once again sobered by how dangerous this boy was.

He didn't try to put the flower back into her hair—though Wendy could see the thought occurring in his eyes for a moment. Instead he tucked the sprig of baby's breath into his own hair and smiled bashfully back at her, looking ten times sweeter and more innocent than Wendy knew he was.

"Are you ready to go back in?" he asked. "I'm sure the others are missing us."

Wendy nodded. *Absolutely*. She was absolutely ready to not be alone with Peter.

Peter pulled open the train car door and held it open so Wendy could walk safely in front of him. By the time she had a foot in the train car, Tinkerbelle had sat back down and Nibs and Curly were back in a signed conversation.

Fyodor had apparently found a light and was passing a cigarette back and forth with Tinkerbelle. They looked up as if surprised to see Peter, and Tinkerbelle handed the cigarette back to Fyodor. He took one last hard drag before dropping it to put it out, but Peter snatched it before it hit the ground and shook it warningly in Fyodor's face.

"They'll make your skin look like shit," he said, putting the cigarette out against the window. "You want to look like you're fifty in your thirties, keep smoking like this. If you're really serious about modeling, Fyodor, you need a solid skincare regimen, not this crap."

Fyodor clicked his tongue in the back of his throat and pulled a comb out of his pocket to straighten his pompadour. It was subtle, but Wendy could tell that everyone was relieved she was back. She could hear the mild giddiness in Minsu's voice as he continued talking to Charles. She couldn't tell if this was another fake conversation, because everyone seemed so engaged. It was different when you were a part of a situation and you see the shift from silence to mid-discussion—this felt like walking into a warmth that existed for ages before she got there. The only person who wasn't involved was Ominotago, who had her phone out and was again focused very hard on texting.

"We're close," she said without looking up. "We have to walk for a few blocks, but we have only one stop left."

"Does it have a cover this year?" Charles asked.

Ominotago shrugged. "It might, but anyone who comes in with me is good to go, so it's kind of a nonissue."

Peter had returned to his place behind Nibs and Curly. "I spoke to James before he left," he said. "He won't be bothering us again. It's better this way."

Curly and Nibs nodded stoically, as if they expected this clear falsehood.

Fyodor clicked his tongue in the back of his throat at Wendy to get her attention. "Your uh—from the . . . Can I?" He reached out a hand toward Wendy's hair, waiting for her to give permission.

Unsure what he was asking but willing to give whatever it was a chance, Wendy nodded.

Fyodor leaned over and delicately adjusted the pins holding the sprigs of baby's breath in her hair, which apparently had been thrown into disarray by the screaming wind outside the train car. He didn't press too close or stroke her curls without her permission; he just fixed it and nodded crisply when he finished. Then he turned back to his conversation with Minsu and Charles without needing or expecting appreciation of any kind.

Wendy felt Ominotago's eyes on her, so she stared down at her and Tinkerbelle, who now looked amused as well as relieved.

Ominotago jerked her chin at Fyodor and raised an eyebrow as if to say, *See?*

Wendy did, in fact, see. She pursed her lips at Ominotago, grinning when Ominotago's dark eyes seemed to twinkle in answering amusement.

"THIS IS HOWARD. TRANSFER TO PURPLE-LINE TRAINS AT HOWARD," the train car speakers blared.

"Everybody off," Peter demanded as the train doors opened. "We're already late."

★ ★ ★

The walk from the train station was less tense than the walk *to* the train station, now that Wendy was capable of participating in the "lighthearted discussion that is really just a mask for horrifying tension" thing everyone seemed to be doing. Peter also seemed satisfied that their conversation in between the train cars was enough to smooth over whatever he assumed Wendy had been thinking. He was less hyperfocused on surveillance, and settling in to have a good time.

But Wendy wasn't calm enough to think they weren't still being watched.

She joined Fyodor and Minsu in an argument about college admissions. She laughed good naturedly when Peter teased Ominotago and Tinkerbelle about being joined at the hip, and didn't react to the disgusted tension of Fyodor's jaw or the clenching of Charles's fists that accompanied their own fake smiles. Wendy felt more in tune with these people than with her friends back home as they worked together, synchronized as a well-oiled machine, to keep the mood up. Wendy hadn't known solidarity like this before—and though she still didn't know what was going on, she finally understood just how important it was to continue to keep in step.

They walked for nearly three miles, until the residential and commercial areas faded from bright lights and landscaping to unkempt gravel and boarded-up windows. Wendy could hear the party long before she could see it—its bass reverberating through the night air. The closer they got, the more people their age joined them in heading toward the huge warehouse at the end of the block.

A group of girls in glittery minidresses ran up behind them. One of them boldly slung her arm around Peter's waist and surged up to give him a kiss on the cheek.

"Nice to see you back, Peter," she said sultrily.

Peter pushed her off with a friendly smack to her hip. "Go find some trouble somewhere else. Have a nice night, ladies."

They dashed ahead to wait in line by the door.

Wendy felt sick. How many people did Peter know who

had no idea who he really was? How many "special girls" had met him in the middle of the night?

As if reading Wendy's thoughts, Peter turned to her and said, "I never encourage them, but if they need anything, I'm around. I carry headache meds and umbrellas and these little sticks you can use to make sure no one roofies your drink."

"That's . . . that's nice," Wendy said tentatively, glancing at Ominotago behind Peter's back.

Ominotago shrugged but shook her head like she already knew this and it did not change her opinion of him at all.

Wendy trusted that look more than Peter's explanation and kept silent as they joined the line.

Minsu licked a finger and smoothed down his eyebrows. Charles watched and nodded when he finished. Fyodor pinched his cheeks until they were softly pink and combed his hair back one last time. Wendy thought it was cute watching them primp like this, and judging from the look on Tinkerbelle's face, she felt the same.

When they got to the front doors, the bouncers were tall and broad and did actually look a bit like Ominotago and Waatese. Wendy remembered Minsu mentioning that these were Ominotago, Curly, and Waatese's cousins. They seemed college age, not actual adults, which was a surprise. Instead of forking over a few dollars, Tinkerbelle and Ominotago greeted the bouncers excitedly. The boys scooped them up into tight hugs and slapped Curly on the shoulder. They shook hands with Charles, Minsu, Fyodor, Nibs, and even Peter, though one of them couldn't resist a tight-lipped frown at having to do so.

"This is Wendy," Ominotago said, throwing an arm around her shoulders. "You haven't met her yet, but she's with us, too."

The bouncers stamped everyone's hands and opened the doors.

CHAPTER 12

The lights were off, but the inside of the warehouse could never have been described as dark. Aside from the music, which was as loud and bass-heavy as Wendy had assumed it would be, there were rainbow strobes placed strategically next to disco balls and hanging mirrors that threw flashes of colorful light all over the space, illuminating it like the inside of a kaleidoscope. The warehouse had one large bar in the very center of the first floor and two on opposite sides of the second floor, which was more of a mezzanine that overlooked the dance floor. The machinery had been pushed to the sides of the warehouse ground and walled off with velour drapery and police tape, so no one was able to get close enough to hurt themselves. There was a giant net stretched across the ceiling with tiny holes cut into it, from which tiny slivers of metallic confetti slowly fell as the music and general rowdiness shook the building. Scattered across the mezzanine were couches someone had clearly shipped over from the dump, and there were so many balloons on the ground that you could barely see your own feet. The DJ was set up on a platform of crates overlooking the crowd, and there were large neon signs for the exits and bathrooms. Wendy remembered what Minsu had said earlier—*know all your exits*—and was glad to see they were easy to find.

To be completely honest, if Peter had just taken her straight to the party instead of ruining everything by running her all over the city, she probably would have felt like it was worth the risk of sneaking out. It was better than the cool-kid parties she'd seen on TV back home, and it was certainly much better than she had imagined. The mirror/strobe combination alone was completely out of this world, not to mention the confetti installation. She did *not* feel like this was worth the drama she'd suffered tonight, but it was entirely too late for that.

Fyodor slung his arm over her shoulders and moved closer to yell in her ear over the music. "Ominotago and Tink have to say hi to family," he shouted. "Stay with me. We will go upstairs."

Wendy had been so distracted by the flashing lights that she hadn't noticed Tinkerbelle waving at her.

Five minutes, Tinkerbelle mouthed as Ominotago pulled her away. *Stay with him.*

Minsu and Charles were also leaving. Charles held up his wallet and nodded over at the bar. Fyodor held up three fingers and nodded. Wendy twisted around to see what had happened to Peter, Curly, and Nibs, but only managed to glimpse the bright shock of Nibs's red hair as the three boys disappeared into the crowd.

Fyodor leaned in again as he guided Wendy to the mezzanine stairs. "Hunting," he said.

Wendy didn't know what that meant, but it still filled her with dread. She allowed Fyodor to use his large body to push through the crowd so she wouldn't have to struggle past drunk screaming people on their way up the stairs. He muscled his way to one of the couches, which were all occupied, and sat on the arm. The guy sitting next to the couch arm scooted over to get out of Fyodor's way, and Fyodor took the opportunity to slide down onto the seat. The other kid, clearly unhappy at being way too snugly seated next to a boy he didn't know, got up. Fyodor scooted over even further, brushing up against the kids on the other half of the couch, and smacked the now empty seat next to him. Wendy wasn't sure what was ruder to do, so she just sat down in the vacated space.

Fyodor leaned in again. "Charles and Minsu will be here soon. Then, we talk."

Wendy wanted answers now. "What did you mean by *hunting*?"

Fyodor made a tight expression and looked around before continuing. "This—" he gestured around at all the people, "—is a place where he finds boys to bring home. He can tell, somehow, who is hungry. Who is lonely. He tracks them like a hunter, impresses them. Reaches out with a hand of treats, da? Like he's bringing in a little kitten?" Fyodor put his hand out, cupped like he was coaxing a cat out from under a bush. He looked around again to make sure Peter wasn't nearby.

"Some come out. Some, not so much. Maybe he'll try again later, maybe not." Fyodor shrugged. "He is a picky man and very smart. Dangerous." He raised an eyebrow at her emphatically. "This, you know."

"Is this where he met Curly?" Wendy asked loudly. The music was screaming, and this very much felt like a conversation that should be had in whispers, but it couldn't be helped.

Fyodor shook his head. "Curly came to him. Sometimes there are worse things out at night, on the streets." After the expression Wendy made when hearing this, Fyodor frowned deeply. "Do not judge Curly," he said fiercely.

"I'm not!" Wendy replied quickly. "I'm just worried and scared for him . . . among other things."

Fyodor accepted this and instead looked very, very tired. He rubbed his eyes and put his head in the palm of his hand, leaning over his knee. "It will be good when this is finished," he said.

Minsu and Charles elbowed their way through the crowd, followed closely by Ominotago and Tinkerbelle. At the sight of Ominotago, the kids on the other half of the couch got up and wandered off, clearly recognizing her.

"Sorry," Ominotago said, handing Wendy an apology drink. "My cousins helped set this up, so I had to at least say hi."

"Oh . . . thank you, but I don't drink," Wendy said, looking into the cup suspiciously.

Ominotago shrugged. "It's just soda with some maraschino cherries in it. I didn't want to assume."

"I do," Fyodor said, and snatched one of the shots Charles was balancing on a platter in the cradle of his arm. He threw it back with the desperation of someone who isn't drinking for fun. "How much longer do we have?" he asked, coughing.

Ominotago pulled out her phone. "Twenty minutes. We almost didn't make it in time."

"In time for what?" Wendy asked.

"The police to get here," Ominotago said so quietly that Wendy had to read her lips.

Wendy didn't get a chance to say anything to that whopper of a statement before Tinkerbelle covered Wendy's mouth with her whole hand.

"We can't talk about it anymore," Tinkerbelle hissed. "Just make sure you're with one of us and head for the exits. Don't worry about them grabbing you. I said I'd protect you, and I meant it."

Wendy smacked Tinkerbelle's hand off her mouth and pushed herself up from the couch. "Fuck this. I'm taking my chances and walking home. Thanks for the drink, Ominotago, it's been swell." Wendy whirled on her heel, ready to get the hell out of this situation.

"WENDY, STOP!"

The only reason she turned around was because it was Minsu who had shouted. He sounded more serious than she'd heard him all night, his voice strangled with desperation.

Wendy faced the group. She could see Peter, Curly, and Nibs making their way up the mezzanine stairs on the other side of the building; it wouldn't take more than five minutes for the trio to reach them.

Minsu held out both his hands to her plaintively. "I know you're scared," he said, voice cracking. "Don't you think we're scared, too? You've only been here for a few hours. Curly has been with him for *years*."

Ominotago folded her arms and scowled, but Wendy could tell that she was more hurt than angry. In fact, all of them looked hurt. Charles's wide-eyed terror was beginning to creep back into his face. Tinkerbelle still held her hand where Wendy had slapped it away, her cheeks hot and red. Fyodor's gaze burned as he glared at the ground and refused to participate.

Minsu lowered his hands. "We only have a few chances, and this took ages to plan. You saw how he gets away anytime anything happens! Please, Wendy."

She couldn't hear Peter's approaching footsteps over the thumping beat, but it still felt like she could.

"You promised," Tinkerbelle said, her voice thick with tears. "You spit-shook on it."

Wendy closed her eyes and clenched her fists.

She didn't know these people. Spit-shaking meant nothing to her before tonight. It was after midnight, and her parents were probably already home from the party and furious. Her phone barely had any battery the last time she checked, and it was probably dead by now, so there was no way for her family or Eleanor to contact her. It was still too early for an Amber Alert, so there was no one looking for her. The police—if they were truly coming—would be here to raid this party, not to help her or be on her side. She was never going to see these people ever again after tonight; their problems really weren't her problems. Their suffering was none of her business. This was too dangerous, and the stakes were too high. If she pushed through the crowd and took off at a sprint, Wendy could remember the way to the train station. Peter continued to stride across the mezzanine as the beat throbbed in her ears. She could go home, she could go home, she could go home.

Wendy opened her eyes.

She grabbed her drink back from Ominotago and chugged the entire thing, chewing through the cherries while the entire group watched in suspense. Wendy saw that Peter was only twenty feet away now, his eyes focused hard on the back of Tinkerbelle's head as he wove through the crowd.

"Fyodor," Wendy shouted loud enough for Peter to hear.

Fyodor finally pried his eyes away from the tile and looked up at Wendy solemnly.

"Will you dance with me?" Wendy demanded, thinking quickly.

Fyodor stood and looked Wendy up and down just as Peter broke through to them.

"Yes," Fyodor said, eyes dark and voice rough. He grabbed her hand and pulled her down the stairs.

Wendy couldn't leave the group without glancing back. She saw Peter talking sternly to Tinkerbelle, but Ominotago was watching Wendy and Fyodor leave with a smile tucked in the corner of her eyes and her chin tilted up with pride.

Fyodor wrapped his arm around Wendy's back and nearly carried her down the last three stairs.

They stumbled through the crowd to the middle of the room—in view of all exits, Wendy realized, and far enough from the speakers that the music buzzed in her bones instead of blasting her ear drums.

Fyodor gazed down at Wendy.

Then he pulled his phone out of his pocket and typed for a while, turning it around for her to see, because it was entirely too loud to talk.

You deserve at least one dance.

Wendy looked up to check the mezzanine, to see if Peter was watching them angrily, but Fyodor gently turned her chin back to him.

The music was a punchy rap song, more pop than gritty poetry. The people next to them were jumping up and down with the beat. The strobes enhanced the angles of Fyodor's face, burning an afterglow behind his silhouette as he towered over her.

Fyodor reached out, but paused and jerked his chin at her as if to ask permission. Wendy answered his nod and allowed him to gently take both of her hands and place them on his shoulders. Then he reached a large solid arm behind her back and began to sway her gently to the beat. With a disorienting thrill, Wendy realized they were slow dancing.

Fyodor kept his right hand on the dip of her spine, not taking advantage even when she stumbled; she wasn't used to moving this way. His left hand was tucked behind his back with almost military formality. Wendy couldn't help but watch their feet, focusing on not stepping on his shoes. She realized with flustered hysteria that Minsu had been lying about Fyodor dancing like a scarecrow in a wind tunnel. He had been lying a *lot*. Fyodor was graceful and so skilled that he managed to find the slower beat in the music, turning them both effortlessly as if this was a ballroom and not a warehouse rave at all.

Fyodor stepped closer, until Wendy could feel the heat of his body, and it was nothing like being close to Peter. Fyodor smelled alive: a little like cigarettes, a little like the pomade he had in his blond hair, a little like deodorant, and a little like the metallic tang of panic-sweat that forms on people who have been on edge for entirely too long. No heady flowers, no smoke that reminded her of a house fire, no magic and starlight, just a flesh and blood kid, who moved her out of the way of a flailing dancer—bringing his left hand up fast to block Wendy from getting smacked in the back of the head.

Fyodor flicked his eyes over at the guy who clearly had too much to drink and grinned as if to say, *At least he's having a good time.* He began to drop his arm to tuck it behind his back again, but Wendy caught his hand on the way down and threaded her fingers between his. Fyodor's eyebrows knit in apprehension but smoothed as Wendy moved more confidently now. He squeezed her fingers and shifted into a middle-school-slow-dance style of rocking back and forth. He grinned.

Wendy took the bait, scowling as he dumbed down his waltz style for her. Fyodor grinned wider at Wendy's pettiness, and for some reason seeing the imperfection of his gaping, childish smile and the shadow of a pimple on his forehead filled Wendy's chest with warmth.

Fyodor lifted their conjoined hands and gave her shoulder a nudge. Wendy spun without thinking, and Fyodor caught her with ease, swinging her back into the gentle rhythm. A few of the people nearest them moved away to give them room, with confused and interested glances.

Fyodor chanced a look up at the mezzanine, and Wendy followed his gaze. Peter and Curly were looking down at them, and the expression on Peter's face was what Wendy could only describe as gently furious. Fyodor stepped back from Wendy. The sudden gap left her cold as air rushed in between them.

Fyodor spun them twice and then finished with his back to Peter, blocking Wendy from Peter's prying gaze.

It will be okay, Fyodor mouthed over the music, nodding resolutely.

It will *be okay,* he repeated, then he cupped Wendy's cheek in his large palm and pressed their foreheads together. They weren't dancing anymore, just standing still in the middle of the dance floor.

Wendy arched up closer and closed her eyes.

Her heart tripped over itself as she stood in the circle of Fyodor's arms, with the bridge of his nose just grazing hers. She leaned up even closer for a kiss, but Fyodor pulled back.

He shook his head and pulled out his phone again at Wendy's crestfallen expression.

you have been through too much tonight. It would be taking advantage

Then he took his phone back, swiped around, and handed it over to Wendy completely. He had opened his contacts and selected ADD NEW CONTACT.

Fyodor smirked and wiggled his eyebrow.

Wendy blushed, remembering that Ominotago had called him a flirt earlier in the night. She typed her number into his phone and handed it over.

Fyodor looked over at Peter and clapped his hand on Wendy's shoulder in an overly friendly way, as if she were Charles or Minsu. From the tightening of the expression on Peter's face, it didn't seem to be working.

Peter leaned over to Curly and said something that made

Curly look exasperated. Curly started marching toward the staircase like he'd been given an order.

Before Curly could come down the stairs, all the exits were kicked open, and police poured in. The warehouse filled with sirens so loud, they drowned out the music.

CHAPTER 13

Fyodor acted quickly. He yanked Wendy to the nearest drink table, pushed its cups away, lifted Wendy clean off the ground, and put her on the table just before the stampede began.

"PLEASE LEAVE THE BUILDING IN AN ORDERLY FASHION."

No one was doing that at all. Fyodor was pushed aside violently as Wendy managed to scuttle to the middle of the table, and he was immediately carried away with the crowd. Everyone was running: girls barefoot with heels in hand, partygoers popping the balloons on the floor left and right. It didn't sound quite like gunshots, but it was enough to make the crowd scream and flinch. The DJ yanked their cords midset and the music went off, leaving only the sounds of panic and the authoritative shouting of the Chicago Police Department.

Wendy looked up to the mezzanine, but Peter and the rest of the group were long gone. The police were staying at the perimeter of the warehouse, and, to Wendy's surprise, were actually holding open the doors. They seemed more focused on everyone clearing the building than they were about arresting people or getting in the way of the rushing crowd. *They must be waiting,* Wendy thought dryly, *until everyone gets outside to corral them into police vans.*

Someone roughly bumped the table Wendy was on, and it banged against the back wall, its legs shuddering as if it were about to collapse. She held on and tried to sit as still as possible, and the shaking stopped. The warehouse was clearing fast, and police were pouring in to forcibly push people out. They were dressed almost like a SWAT team, which was a stark difference from the police who'd come to the few house parties Wendy had attended back home. Those cops had mostly looked like trumped-up security guards. This was an entirely different level, even more than what she'd seen at the train station. As the last of the partygoers scampered out the door, Wendy was seized by her arm and dragged off the table by an officer who pushed her toward the door without even saying anything to her. He was rough enough to get the message across wordlessly, so Wendy followed the last of the kids outside. She glanced behind her, just in time to see officers flip over a couch and tear into its cushions as they began to detail-search the building.

It was twice as bright outside as it had been when Wendy and the others had gone inside, and it was extremely crowded. The police had formed barriers around the whole building. They were checking IDs and letting people out in small groups. Some of them were pulling clearly intoxicated partygoers to the side to do breathalyzers and then bundling them into police vans. The rest seemed intent on searching the area, pushing people into lines for ID checks, and tamping down on rowdiness. Despite the massive police presence, the cops were significantly less violent than Wendy would have expected. This wasn't a raid, this was a search party, and the crowd was mostly getting in the way. In fact, now that she was more aware of what was going on, she remembered the explosive police drama earlier slightly differently. The business of it all, the distracted but hawkish look in the officers' eyes, the rush of patting down people and pushing away what looked like easy targets so they could continue their search. Wendy watched as the police let a girl who wasn't completely sloshed, but still visibly drunk, out of the barricade.

Wendy walked across the gravel and joined the back of one of the ID lines. Hopefully they would recognize her as a person who'd been reported missing and escort her home. Which might be a pretty good way to go out, since it wouldn't look like she'd "escaped," and Peter might not hunt her down like Tinkerbelle and the others had hinted he would. The other possibility was that they would just let her out of the barricade like everyone else. Then she could just make an incredibly long walk home or wait at the barrier edge for it to spit out someone she knew.

The lines were moving pretty quickly, but the girls in front of her were complaining loudly about the party being shut down.

Wendy took out her phone and swiped so she could at least use this free time and the last dregs of her battery to contact Eleanor.

She had seventeen text notifications, which wasn't a huge surprise, but she only had 1 percent battery left. She swiped all the way to the bottom of Eleanor's texts, noticing with a spark of humor that they descended from lowercase to caps lock, ending with a final text:

I SWEAR TO GOD I'LL WAKE UP MY PARENTS AND COME FIND YOU MYSELF

Wendy began typing a quick message, but before she could even get I'm okay for now out, her screen froze and then went black. Wendy clicked the home button desperately, but it was over. Her phone was dead. Wendy closed her eyes and whined, taking a moment to feel the full brunt of her own irritation and despair, but got herself back together, unclenched her fists, and kept on going.

"What time is it?" Wendy asked the girls in front of her.

They all turned around and a girl with hair as pink as her dress pulled her phone out. "1:03. Is your phone dead?"

Wendy shrugged. "I think it died about an hour ago, and I've been floating through time ever since. I didn't have time to charge it before I left home."

A girl with wild blond curls like Eleanor's started digging in her purse. "What kind is it? I have a portable charger."

Wendy pulled her phone out. "Oh my God, thank you. It's just a regular micro-USB—"

"Like an Android?" the girl asked. "I have an iPhone, but the base should still work. Does anyone have an Android cord?"

The girls in her group shook their heads, so she turned around and shouted to the rest of the line. "Does anyone have an Android cord?" Everyone within earshot turned around and shouted some version of "No." Which sucked, but definitely wasn't as bad as what happened immediately afterward. The yelling alerted the attention of all the nearby officers, who immediately zoomed in on Wendy. The officer closest to her, a frighteningly muscular white man in combat boots with his face partially obscured by a mask, grabbed Wendy's arm and pulled out a walkie-talkie.

"Got her, moving her now," the officer said as he marched Wendy roughly away from the group. "Anyone else still unaccounted for? Over."

The girls gaped at Wendy as she was dragged away, the nice girl with the portable charger holding it dangling as she watched Wendy go.

The officer took Wendy around the back of the warehouse, where there were significantly fewer people. Standing next to several unmarked cop cars was Detective Hook himself.

He stared hard at her as she got closer, surly eyebrows furrowed dark over his eyes, maroon coat blowing in the wind.

Wendy could see Tinkerbelle, Ominotago, and Curly in one car, Nibs and Fyodor in another, and Charles and Minsu being cuffed and ducked into a last car—which Wendy was getting hauled toward.

But Detective Hook put up a hand to stop the officer

pulling Wendy. The detective looked hard at Wendy's face for a long moment, then waved her on to the car.

Wendy was passed off to a policewoman, who cuffed Wendy with actual metal handcuffs, not zip ties like before. The officer pushed Wendy's head down roughly as she was ushered into the car, and closed the door on her with sharp finality.

Charles and Minsu looked miserable, but also like they were handling this arrest much better than their previous one. Their hands were cuffed behind their backs, and Charles was leaning heavily on Minsu's shoulder again. The officer got into the front of the car, and without saying another word, she started the engine and pulled out of the lot.

Wendy had never been inside the back of a police car before, but the entire situation had incredibly bad energy. She desperately wanted to ask Charles and Minsu if the police had gotten Peter, but even though no one had told her not to speak, she had a general sense that it probably would be a bad idea to start a conversation.

Charles nodded firmly at Wendy. "The good news," he said quietly, "is that we're not far from the precinct. The bad news is that I now know what it's like to be detained."

"They didn't read us our Miranda rights," Wendy said just as quietly. "Can't we sue or something?"

Charles shook his head. "It's not that kind of arrest."

The policewoman driving them glanced at them placidly

over her shoulder, but didn't tell them to be quiet, so Wendy proceeded more confidently.

"Aren't you worried about your school stuff?"

"Shh," Charles said. "If things go the way we hope, that will be the least of our problems."

"My dad is not going to care what kind of arrest this is," Minsu said mournfully. "And I only have about an hour to get home."

"You have got to give up the concept that you're getting home on time," Charles said. "And we should really stop talking."

Wendy sighed and sank lower in the seat. She put her head against the window and let the road rattle her brain around her skull for the rest of the ride to wherever they were being taken. After about ten minutes, they stopped at a large police station.

The officer opened their car door and told Charles, Minsu, and Wendy to join Tinkerbelle, Ominotago, Nibs, Fyodor, and Curly in a line outside the station. Ominotago was at the back, her brown eyes widening as she saw Wendy cuffed with the rest of them. Wendy smiled at her sheepishly and shrugged. Ominotago's face crumpled, and before the officer nearby had time to do anything about it, Ominotago leaned forward and pushed her forehead against Wendy's in sweet apology for the circumstances. Even though the officer turned Ominotago right back around, Wendy could still feel the warmth of her friend's touch, and it grounded her. She was thankful for it as they walked through the hallways of the station.

It was busy inside, but Wendy didn't see any of the kids who had been at the party. Everyone else in here was an adult, from the police all the way to the people she could see on their way to holding cells. She and the others were marched right past the booking area to the back of the station. The officer in front opened a locked door and pushed them all inside, locking it tightly behind them.

To Wendy's surprise, they weren't in a cell at all. It looked like some kind of waiting room. It was sparsely decorated, but there were chairs, a table, a few magazines, and even a water cooler. None of these things would do them any good because they were all still handcuffed, but it was relaxing to know they were in a room where someone cared whether they had something to read.

"What is this place?" Wendy asked. She sat down on a low couch and grimaced at how uncomfortable it was.

Fyodor sat down next to her, smiling mirthlessly and raising an eyebrow. "Waiting room?"

"It's where they put you when they can't decide if you're a suspect or not," Curly said, leaning against the large table in the middle of the room. Nibs mirrored his position; he rolled his shoulders as if he were doubly irritated by the fact that he couldn't use his hands.

"No," Ominotago corrected. "It's where they put you

when they've decided that you're going to be interviewed and they don't know whether you're a suspect yet, but want to have access to recordings of you talking and your DNA from drinking water from the cooler.

"In our situation," she continued, "because we slipped zip tie cuffs earlier and now they can't trust whether we'll follow instructions, they detained us in the 'bad kids but not so bad as to be in cells' area." She lifted one of her legs up and tucked it under her cuffed arms, then did the same with the other so that her arms were cuffed in front of her body instead of behind.

"Don't do that," Fyodor said, scooting low into the couch cushions. "They do not like that."

Ominotago shrugged, looped her cuffed arms over Tinkerbelle's head so they were locked together, then kissed her on the cheek.

Wendy glanced quickly at Fyodor out of the side of her eye. She tried not to turn her head in his direction, but Ominotago—observant as ever—caught her look.

"Since we can't talk about the case in here, let's talk about something lighter. I saw Fyodor putting the moves on you," Ominotago said, smirking. "Glad that's going well."

"Moves?" Fyodor scrunched up his nose in distaste. "What moves? I was very respectful."

"He was," Wendy interjected even though she could feel her cheeks getting hot. "And he's a very good dancer."

"It's very cool and not at all ridiculous how you can get

girls even during the middle of a police sting," Minsu snapped bitterly. "What's the point? You don't even sleep with them!"

Fyodor glanced at Wendy mischievously before answering Minsu's remark. "I will let this thing you've said go because you are so frightened right now. But perhaps when you are less frightened, we will deal with this, da?"

"I'm not aphobic, it's just unfair!" Minsu huffed. "ALL OF US are in ballroom dance. How are you the only one good at it?"

"Why are you in ballroom dance?" Wendy asked.

"Agility practice, for football," Ominotago said, shaking out her dark hair. "And stop changing the subject."

"You changed the subject first. Where the fuck is Peter?" Wendy snapped. She knew they were doing that thing again where they forcibly calmed her down with their charming, witty banter, and she was no longer interested in indulging that.

"We can't talk about that. They're watching us," Tinkerbelle replied crossly, like Wendy was an idiot.

Ominotago clicked in the back of her throat with disapproval. "Be gentle with her, Tink, she doesn't know how any of this works." Ominotago addressed Wendy again. "I meant what I said earlier about getting you home, but under the circumstances, that is no longer possible. But they should be coming to get us soon, and they'll explain everything."

Wendy's outburst had let the wind out of the sails for the entire room. The group broke off into their own quieter conversations. Charles and Minsu gave each other some sort of pep talk in the corner by the windowsill. Ominotago and Tinkerbelle whispered to each other, locked tight in each other's arms. Nibs and Curly were speaking in that near-silent way they seemed to only do when incredibly stressed, their red and dark heads of hair pressed close together.

Fyodor sat silently next to Wendy. He had his eyes closed, and Wendy could see the purple veins above and below them.

Now that she wasn't the focus of the entire group, she took the time to admire how his blond hair had begun falling out of his pompadour at the front. The handcuffs, which were tight on her, were probably even tighter on him. His arms, which had looked very nice when guarding the back of her head from getting smacked, looked even nicer bound behind his back. In all seriousness, Wendy wished very hard that Fyodor had been the first guy she'd met after moving here. He wouldn't have broken into her house—he clearly didn't do things like that. Maybe they would have met on the train, instead. Maybe they would have met while Wendy was on her way home from school. Maybe he would have caught her eye and introduced himself, but she would have ignored him until he said something so funny, she wouldn't have been able to help but laugh. Fyodor would have understood why a strange girl would have been anxious talking to him or going out with him alone. A boy who asks before fixing the flowers in your hair wouldn't think having another girl accompany them was enough to make Wendy feel safe.

Fyodor would have waited for Eleanor to come with them—someone Wendy knew—or introduced himself to her parents, or something like that. He would have taken her to the party and nowhere else. He wouldn't have abandoned her with scores of different groups of people, only swinging back to check on her as an afterthought. Fyodor, who'd saved her from getting hurt during a stampede instead of saving himself, wouldn't do anything like that. He hadn't even seemed like he wanted to be thanked for any of those things. He just did them because he felt like he should, and that was it.

Wendy followed the line of Fyodor's arms from his cuffs back to his face, and his eyes were open now.

He gazed back at her steadily, uncritical of being appraised. Just watching her watch him.

The door of the waiting room opened, and two officers came in. Everyone stopped talking and watched warily as one of the officers hoisted Wendy off the couch. The other officer searched her pockets until he found her wallet. He fished out her ID and compared its picture to her face. When he was satisfied, he put the wallet back in her pocket and walked her out of the room. Wendy kept quiet as they moved her down another hallway with dimmer lights to a much quieter wing of the station.

The officer stopped in front of a door near the back of the station. Wendy flinched in surprise as the officer behind her unlocked her cuffs. They opened the door, lightly nudged her inside, and closed it loudly behind her.

CHAPTER 14

There was only one table in this room, and Detective Hook was sitting in front of it. His maroon jacket was draped over the chair behind him as if he'd come straight to this interrogation from the party. He had a stack of folders to the right of him, but had one single, large image in his hand, balanced between his index finger and the curved end of his prosthetic.

Wendy approached the only other chair in the room and anxiously sat down.

Detective Hook looked at her hard for another moment, then placed the photo flat on the table and pushed it toward her.

"Do you know who this is?" he asked.

His voice was low and rich, a far cry away from his hysterical shouting at the Mermaid's Lagoon. It was disconcerting.

Wendy pulled the picture toward her. With a spike of terror, she realized it was a picture of herself. A mug shot. Or. Actually . . . not her . . . Wendy hadn't been anywhere near a police station in her entire life. She looked up at Detective Hook in confused terror. He sighed and put another photo in front of her, this time a candid, with the subject smiling big and freely with her afro hair permed and flat ironed, and Wendy suddenly knew her.

"This . . . is my mom?" Wendy asked.

Detective Hook leaned back in his seat. "You look like her, you know," he said, crossing his arms. "The hair is

213

different. Yours is curlier, but that might just be a change in fashion. Your ID says your name is Wendy?"

Wendy nodded. She didn't know where this was going, but her blood felt like ice.

Detective Hook sat back up and picked out another folder from the pile.

"You need to sign these nondisclosure agreements before we continue." He placed a few pieces of paper in front of her and handed her a pen. "Ominotago, Fyodor, and the rest have already signed theirs. Your mother has, too, actually. It's about twenty years old, but I could pull it for you, if necessary."

Wendy read the paper carefully and despite her better instincts signed the bottom. It had been a solid seven hours of confusion, but at least if she went to jail, she would go to jail with answers.

Hook put the cooperation agreement in the envelope, and Wendy was pleased to see the paper underneath hers had Ominotago's name on it, so at least he wasn't lying about that.

He put the folder of documents to the left and took another folder off the pile, pulling out another mug shot and placed it in front of her.

"This," Detective Hook said with incredible gravity, "is Peter Pan."

The mug shot was old.

Peter stared back at Wendy from the image, looking not entirely different from when they had met. There were small changes: His eyes were a bit brighter, he had a bit more fat around his face, and his auburn hair was chopped in a rakish mullet—just long enough to still look cool, decades in the future.

Wendy could hear her heart pounding in her ears.

Detective Hook jabbed the center of Peter's face with a thick index finger. "When we took this mug shot, I was still a beat cop. I've been a detective for seventeen years."

Wendy's eyes scanned the image as she sat there numbly. The unbroken nose, the rosier cheeks, no stubble at all.

"I don't . . ." Wendy started, at a loss for words as she tried to do the math.

"Peter Pan is thirty-six years old."

Wendy pushed herself away from the table. She leaned over and tried not to vomit. She put her head on her knees and swallowed hard over and over until her throat burned with the bile she'd forced back down her throat. With that one sentence, the context of everything had changed. She had been alone in her bedroom in the middle of the night with a thirty-six-year-old man. She allowed a thirty-six-year-old man to lure her out of her family home. She had watched a thirty-six-year-old man threaten a child.

She had let down her defenses around him because other kids weren't inherently scary most of the time. Peter must have been using that to his advantage. She remembered with violent clarity the moment they met. When Peter was facing the window in her bedroom, silhouetted by a streetlamp, and she thought for exactly one second that he was a man. But when he turned his face to her, she corrected herself. She looked at his small, cute face and bright wide eyes and thought, *This is a kid like me, this is a boy in my house, this is a boy who might need help. This is a* boy.

Wendy remembered the hot press of his body as he'd climbed down the side of her house and how she'd liked it, and she felt like clawing her own skin off to get rid of the memory of the feeling. Things he had said ran through her mind at rapid speed. *This is Bella's dance, the 'Never Bird.' She's been doing it at this place for fifteen years, I've heard . . . You want to look like you're fifty in your thirties, keep smoking like this . . . I've had this jacket for a very long time . . .* Fyodor calling him a man, Ominotago calling him a man. *Everyone* calling him a man but *her*.

Wendy thought about her mom.

Her mom, clenching the bar tightly on the train, describing this man—describing Peter—in fits and starts, haunted by a ghost that turned out to still be alive. Moving away to escape the memory, waiting until she felt safe, then inadvertently placing her family back into the path of the same predator that had haunted her nights. Her mom. Who would have to learn that Wendy had spent a night the same way she had, with the same predator, when she came to pick Wendy up from the police station.

The necklace Peter made her hours ago suddenly scraped against her skin like rope. Wendy pulled it off and threw it hard across the room.

Detective Hook watched the acorn and string bounce off the concrete wall and land on the floor, and wisely chose to say nothing. He waited patiently until Wendy was able to pull herself together and sit up again. Then he got up and poured Wendy a glass of water from the water cooler and placed it in front of her, along with a box of tissues. Wendy pushed the tissues away but grabbed the water, gulping it down gratefully.

"Who else knows?" Wendy choked out. "Do the others—"

"They know. They learned about a month ago. Genevieve punched me in the face when I told her, so you're handling this better than she did."

"Genevieve?" Wendy asked numbly.

Detective Hook rolled his eyes. "She likes to be called Tinkerbelle, I think."

Wendy could unpack that later. "They let me be close to him when . . . they let him touch me . . . they let . . ."

Detective Hook thumbed through Peter's folder and took out a few more pictures, but this time he held them in a stack instead of handing them over. "They know, but it's not their fault that *you* didn't know. They're all contractually restricted from sharing that information with anyone outside of people working on the case. Also, they spent the majority of their time with him not knowing, either, much longer than you. Peter is very charismatic and convincing; it's not hard for him to trick a group of teenagers. But the thing is that it only works *if* they're *teenagers*. He can't trick people who are much older than you are right now. Whether it's because we're old enough to recognize another adult when we see one, or because the things that make him charismatic stop working after a while, we don't know. But we know that he knows it, too, and that he doesn't allow this situation to happen if he can manage it by keeping the age of people around him low enough for it to keep working. How long have you been with the others? It couldn't have been long . . . a week, maybe?"

"Seven hours," Wendy said, her chest as hollow as a gourd.

Detective Hook grimaced apologetically. "Peter works predictably. He makes friends with vulnerable children, figures out what they need most in the world, and then gives it to them. Food, a home, a brother, a father, a friend. He sticks by them for a couple of years, roughly until they turn eighteen, then he gives them a choice: to leave the city permanently or . . . to leave the city permanently."

Detective Hook set down the photographs he was holding and fanned them out so Wendy could see them all at once. They were candids of street kids, all roughly seventeen or eighteen, ranging from blurry shots of grunge-kids in band T-shirts, all the way up to crisper digital pictures that couldn't have been from more than five years ago. Wendy didn't recognize any of the boys she'd already met, and the names at the bottom of the images weren't any that had been mentioned tonight, either.

"These are his victims. We originally thought disappearances correlated with convenience as a motive, but thanks to Trevor, or well . . . 'Curly'—" Detective Hook took a moment to do air quotes disrespectfully, "—we now know that it actually corresponds with their ages. He rarely takes in two older kids around the same age. Brian—'Nibs'—would have been next to go. His eighteenth birthday is in four months."

"Peter . . . ," Wendy said helplessly.

"Murders his foster children when they get old enough to figure out what he is, or properly challenge his authority," Detective Hook finished. "The first one happened in 2002, which is why we have the mug shot of your mother, Mary Moira, now Mary Darling, one of the original witnesses. We don't think he had a track record from before that incident, but it definitely escalated after that point."

Wendy stared at the images silently.

"Trevor found out a lot earlier than most of Peter's victims do. He witnessed something and passed the information on to Brian. They sat on it for a while before coming down to the precinct, but I'm sure those boys were terrified. I'd already been picking at a different cold case for fifteen years when they dropped this into my lap. A lot of kids go missing without any connection to a serial killer, so it's hard to make a case for these victims individually. You guys get upset, run away, things like that. And even if you all get murdered, who's to say it was the same guy? But I knew I had something with this one."

Wendy looked at Detective Hook as he bragged about

catching on to Peter instead of being concerned about the lost and missing children, and learned to hate him.

"I'd seen Peter with my own two eyes, once when he was seventeen and again when he was probably in his mid-twenties, looking like barely a week had passed. He had the nerve to smile at me and wave, just like he did tonight, that son of a bitch." He paused as if to wait for Wendy to say something, but she just stared at him blankly.

He straightened his collar and leaned close to her. "Look, kid. I know this has been a rough seven hours for you, but it's been a rough *fifteen years* for me. Do you know what it's like to know someone's out there killing boys? To have everyone around you keep ignoring your warnings until he straight up smashes off your hand? I know this whole thing is 'a lot for you,' and I respect that, believe me I do, but, sweetie: You're not actually the victim here.

"We've been trying to bust open this case and bring him home to roost for months now." He shoved the pictures of the dead boys into their folder, then opened up another. "Curly and his friends are the first lead into this group that we've ever had. Peter was completely untouchable for fifteen years, then out of nowhere he starts acting out, getting sloppy. Maybe he could see the difference between his families that he creates and a real solid group of good kids, and it made him lose it a bit. I don't really know; I'll send you a copy when we write the book on this one. But something shifted, and all of a sudden it was easier.

"Those kids down there are putting themselves on the line every day with that murderous son of a bitch, because they get it. They know what needs to be done to make this stop, and they're the only ones who can do it."

He pushed the folder over to Wendy. It was a stack of printouts of digital records. She scanned them quickly. Tinkerbelle was only sixteen years old. Ominotago was seventeen, and her parents had signed for her permission to help the investigation. Fyodor's file had notes in it about expediting his citizenship status in exchange for participation. Minsu's had a request that he be protected from media investigation in both a positive and negative circumstance; his focus was mostly on discretion. Both of their cooperation agreements were unsigned by their parents—but they were also both eighteen. Curly and Nibs, sixteen and seventeen respectively, had both recently filed for emancipated minor status—probably to avoid the foster system after Peter's eventual capture. Charles had paid in advance to have his record scrubbed in the likely event that he would be arrested in conjunction with this, and had requested witness protection if they were unable to catch Peter.

She hadn't known him for long, but it was so like Charles to take those precautions that Wendy felt a spark of amusement. After she'd finished reading, Wendy gathered the printouts, stacked them, and slipped them back inside the folder. "If the others are directly involved in Peter's capture, why did they get arrested earlier this evening?" she asked calmly.

Detective Hook rubbed his mustache, clearly trying to decide whether he wanted to share this information with Wendy. "Peter moves his home about twice a year. It's difficult to keep track of his base, and Trevor hadn't been able to come back to the precinct since before their move, so we had to use our own intel for locating Peter's home. We had APBs out for unaccompanied male youths in the area, and at least two of the boys fit the basic description. They were cuffed and detained while the officers checked their IDs against police records. If Peter hadn't disrupted that process, their identities would have been confirmed, and they would have been released. I had direct contact with Ominotago, and was monitoring their location via her, but officers can't use burner numbers to contact the station. And the phone I provided her is a burner. They wouldn't be able to use it as a reference to confirm her identity and wouldn't be able to use her association with me as protection. They would have to look up police records and Ominotago doesn't have a record. She's clean."

"You scared Minsu half to death!" Wendy spat.

"And the Chicago Police Department will offer an apology for that," Detective Hook said, leaning back in his chair. "*After* we capture the perpetrator."

"Did you call my parents yet?" Wendy asked.

Detective Hook looked Wendy up and down in a very "cop" way, then folded his burly arms on the desk. "I received a hysterical call from a girl named Eleanor Rodgers earlier this evening concerning you and—once I figured out who you were and just how special you are—I made the executive decision not to call your parents. Wendy Darling, I have a proposition for you."

He opened another folder, plucked a single piece of paper out, and held it up in his prosthetic. "We think that Peter is in a vulnerable state. He's beginning to behave erratically after years of discipline, and that disorganization has opened up a few weaknesses. For fifteen years he never approached women, and he's since had contact with two: Genevieve and Ominotago. He doesn't usually take in very young children, but we've heard that he has a seven-year-old boy. We think he used to be able to blend, psychologically, with his victims and relate directly to their shared experience. However, we think that he may be outgrowing his MO and starting to search for a more stabilizing environment that he can control."

"What does that mean?" Wendy asked dubiously.

Detective Hook grimaced before laying the sheet of paper down in front of her. "We think he's looking for a partner. Or something like that. Peter has been able to play brother to his victims successfully for almost twenty years, from the age of seventeen to the age of thirty-six. But the man is facing down forty; he's probably not going to be able to pretend to be a teenager for much longer. We think he's begun looking for a mother for them. Instead of a found family, he wants to create . . . a real family." Detective Hook shrugged. "So to speak."

Wendy squeezed her thighs hard in both hands as she tried, successfully, to keep from heaving.

Detective Hook waited for her to recover before continuing. "We do not think he's interested in actual romantic relationships with any of these women. It's more like Peter is looking for an accomplice to support his illusory family unit. Obviously Ominotago and Tinkerbelle were both unsuited for that role once they figured out his motives, and quickly broke Peter of the illusion that they would be interested in anything other than a normal relationship with a normal person—thank God." Detective Hook muttered that last part half to himself.

"What do you want from me?" Wendy asked.

"I want you to give him what he wants," Detective Hook said, quietly tapping the agreement he'd placed in front of her. "You're a descendant of a witness to his first victim. A killer's *only* anniversary. You'd be more than he'd be able to resist, if he knew who you really were. We need a full confession, and we think that you'll be able to get it out of him. We ran four different stings tonight, and he's managed to slip out of every one of them. Running is Peter's greatest strength, but he's a narcissist and he'll incriminate himself if given the slightest chance to brag about his accomplishments. He hasn't had enough time to regroup and process the events of the night, and he's on edge and low on resources; if we take one more shot tonight, he might be weak enough to buckle. Now, will you help us close the pages on this?"

Wendy pushed herself away from the table and stood up. This was her decision, but first, she had something to do. Tinkerbelle and Ominotago had been given this choice and took it. The rest of the boys had just made it their business to do what was right for justice's sake. Wendy wasn't any less brave than they were, and she had much less to lose. She cared about people, even if Detective Hook didn't seem to. She had burned through her reserves of terror for the night and now felt only disgust and anger. Wendy knew she could use that pain for something good.

"I need twenty minutes to talk to the group," she said.

Detective Hook looked furious for a second, but managed to suppress it. "You have ten." He barked at the door. "WILSON!"

The officer who had brought Wendy to this room immediately unlocked the door.

"Bring her back in ten minutes," Hook said, waving his hand in dismissal.

Wendy walked toward the doorway on shaking legs.

"Stop."

She paused.

"If he gets away tonight . . . it's on you," Detective Hook said, breathing hard with anger.

Wendy didn't turn to face him. "No. It's not," she said firmly. "I'm just a kid, asshole. And you should have called my parents."

CHAPTER 15

Everyone looked up when the officer opened the door. Ominotago and Tinkerbelle had drifted to Fyodor's side. Fyodor was white as a ghost from stress. Charles had managed to get his cuffed hands in front of him like Ominotago and had an arm around Minsu's shoulders. Nibs and Curly were sitting on the floor between Fyodor and Minsu, Curly's chin on Nibs's shoulder. Curly looked like he'd been caught whispering in his brother's ear.

Wendy stared at Tinkerbelle for a long moment, ages after the door had closed behind her. "You told me to stay home."

Tinkerbelle's eyes filled with tears, and she hid her face in the curve of Ominotago's neck. Wendy crossed the room in three long strides and swept Tinkerbelle into a tight hug.

"I'm sorry!" Tinkerbelle cried, muffled into Wendy's hair.

"No," Wendy said resolutely. "Thank you for trying."

"Did you sign the NDA?" Ominotago asked gently.

"Yes. We have ten minutes before I have to tell Detective Hook whether I'm going to join you all or not."

"Okay, you need answers," Ominotago said seriously. "And you need them fast." She squeezed Wendy's shoulder with her cuffed hand. Then she scooted over to create room on the couch for Wendy to sit between Tinkerbelle and Fyodor. Charles and Minsu joined the group, sitting on the floor in front of the others and completing the circle.

Ominotago nudged Tinkerbelle. "You go first."

Tinkerbelle took a moment to get her breath under control and began. "Peter wasn't looking for you specifically; it was a coincidence. The whole thing with his jacket threw the timing of the entire night off. So I was angry when we met because you were already ruining things before you knew it. We were supposed to get to the train station twenty minutes earlier, and the cops would have been able to grab Peter on the train platform, where there are limited places to run. They probably panicked once we didn't arrive when they expected, so they started trying to make barricades, but it was too late. Peter watches where we go, so Curly, Slightly, Nibs, and me can't ever meet with the police in person. He also pays our cell phone bills so he has access to our call and text records, so we can't talk to them that way, either. We were relying on Ominotago as direct contact for timing, and we missed our connection point. I'd been hoping that you'd get scared off by my story, but you stayed, anyway. You could have gotten away, back—"

"I know, Tinkerbelle, it's okay." Wendy squeezed Tinkerbelle's hand.

"The next opportunity was at the Mermaid's Lagoon, but by that time, Peter probably knew something was up. The cops chase him every several months or so, but they only tend to do one attack at a time, not many in a single night, so he probably thought he was in the clear—"

Curly interrupted Tinkerbelle. "Peter has been paying the Crocodile off to create interference for as long as I've known him." He nudged Nibs, and Nibs agreed. "The Crocodile takes in a decent chunk of money to keep the police off our backs and texts Peter about where the police will be so Peter can avoid them," he said. "However, if the Crocodile turns Peter in, he'll get a lump sum reward, so he's not 100 percent trustworthy. He's just holding out to see how much he can get off Peter in the long run before bringing him in."

Curly frowned, then the corners of his mouth started wavering as he forced himself not to cry. "They met that night with me and Slightly and James at the train party, when Hook almost caught us. The Crocodile agreed that he would protect us all, so long as Peter paid him on time. Not that it did James any good. The Crocodile never said he'd protect us from Peter," Curly finished bitterly, wiping his eyes on the shoulder of Nibs's jacket.

Wendy felt a frisson of terror as she reassessed the events of the night. "So Peter really . . . James . . . I'd hoped that . . ."

"You didn't see James again, did you? Did anyone? Peter probably pushed James off the train," Fyodor said. He closed his eyes, swaying in a way that made Wendy genuinely concerned about his health. "Is he alive?" He continued, "Perhaps. But also, perhaps not."

"Oh my God. Oh my God. Oh God. Oh my God," Wendy mumbled, horrified.

"We don't have time for you to process this," Ominotago said firmly. "You probably only have six more minutes before the cops come back. Let's keep this going. My family knows about Peter and knew the cops were coming to raid the party. The decor was less elaborate, and we had fewer places for someone to hide so that finding Peter in the building might be easier. But he slipped out of there somehow. What else?"

"He never touched me when we were dating," Tinkerbelle said hollowly. "It was like he didn't know how."

"Same," Ominotago said quickly. She snapped her fingers at the group. "What else?"

"When did you guys figure out all of this?" Wendy asked.

Ominotago pointed at herself and Tinkerbelle. "Three months ago for the both of us. Charles had suspicions slightly earlier, but he got confirmation from the police with me and Tink. We told Fyodor and Minsu soon afterward. Curly?"

Curly looked like he was in agony. "Almost a year," he said curtly, voice thick. "Alexander . . . another brother before James . . . went missing, and I saw Peter washing his hands in the sink. He said Alex had run away, but later I found Alex's cell phone on the floor in the bathroom behind the toilet, like it had been dropped. Alex wouldn't have left without it. I told Nibs a month later, and it took him three more months to believe me."

Nibs clenched his jaw so hard that it looked like it hurt.

"I know it's not your fault," Curly continued sharply.

"It's none of our faults," Tinkerbelle said.

"I know." Nibs hung his head. "I'm still sorry. I'll always be sorry."

"What did Detective Hook want you to do?" Omino-tago asked. "He wouldn't have told you anything important unless he wanted something from you." Her eyes were glued to the small window on the waiting room door, watching to see if the officers had returned.

Wendy paused. She wasn't sure if she was comfortable sharing this information with everyone. It was a bit personal, and she knew it would change everyone's perception of her immediately upon knowing her direct connection to this situation. Everyone was waiting patiently for her to go on, but Wendy could feel their restlessness.

"Are you not allowed to say?" Minsu asked. "We would understand if—"

"It's not that," Wendy interrupted. "Peter . . . ," she started, then stopped.

Ominotago was beginning to look frustrated, and Tinkerbelle was clearly not far behind.

Wendy clenched her hands into fists on her thighs and took a deep breath. "You have to promise you won't yell or make a big deal about this," she said anxiously.

"No one will make a big deal," Fyodor replied softly.

"For Peter, I'm special. He . . . knew my mom," Wendy said. "She was a witness to one of his first killings." She paused, expecting the others to react in some dramatic way, but they just sat there seriously, waiting for her to continue. "When Peter was still an actual teenager, he and his friends lured my mom and some of her friends out to a cemetery.

Then later on, he separated one of his friends from the group and killed him. Detective Hook thinks it was Peter's first time, and he doesn't know if Peter really remembers my mom at all. But he thinks that if I tell him who I am, he might be so startled or excited that I could maybe get a confession out of him or something . . . I don't know."

The room was dead silent. Fyodor shook his head slowly back and forth. Ominotago and Tinkerbelle were staring directly at each other, clearly having a rapid silent conversation.

"Fuck," Minsu said, looking properly horrified. "Did you, like . . . anger a witch?"

"What?" Wendy said.

"You have extremely terrible luck," Minsu said. "This is supernaturally terrible. For you. I mean, for us also, I guess, since we are A) still here, B) in handcuffs, and C) also know and have to deal with serial killer Peter Pan. But, like, you literally could have missed out on being a part of this situation by a couple of days. If you'd moved here last week, or even next week, it would have been too early for this chain of events, or too late."

"I know," Wendy said.

"What did you say when you found out?" Charles asked. He looked just as scandalized as Minsu. His eyebrows were so knotted in confusion and horror that if it weren't for the situation, she'd have thought he was exaggerating his expression.

"He just showed me a picture of Peter from when he was actually sixteen, and it was the scariest thing on earth," Wendy replied. "And then he showed me a picture of my mom at fourteen and was all: 'Do you know who this is?' like some creep getting off on the drama of a big reveal. I was so shocked; I don't think I said anything. Plus, I thought the picture of my mom was a picture of me for a second, before I—"

"That's fucked up," Minsu interrupted.

"Yes! Thank you! It *is* fucked up!" Wendy exclaimed hysterically. "Then he started talking about how Peter wants a mom for the boys or whatever."

"He does," Ominotago said suddenly, her eyes sliding away from Tinkerbelle's to Wendy. "He hasn't always . . . but he does now. Peter is like a kid in many ways. He needs to be praised and validated constantly. He's impulsive and self-centered. His concept of 'rules' and when to stick to them is . . . a bit like a third grader's. He's sensitive like one, too. It's not an act for him—he's not pretending to be like this. It genuinely just *is* him all the way through."

Ominotago waited for a moment before continuing. "And . . . he's cruel, not mean. There is a difference. He's cruel in the way kids are cruel before they can really understand that their actions affect others. Peter does things not to hurt other people, but more because they serve his own needs. He picks boys like Curly and Nibs because they're easy. He kills them because not doing so would make his own life difficult. He started looking for a mother figure because in some way, he realized he needed one to continue having what he wants."

"And what he wants is to keep killing people," Wendy said.

But Ominotago shook her head sharply. "No. What he wants is a family. A timeless, perfect home, where no one can tell him what to do. Where there is no bedtime, and you don't have to eat your vegetables if you don't want to. Where there is no homework and no rules, except for the rules he makes. Where there is no school and no work, and you survive by being clever and having fun. Killing people is just the means. Preserving this situation is the ends.

"But if he had *you*," Ominotago continued, tilting her head in consideration, "if he had someone who understood that and understood him, who he thought would stay by his side and help him continue this endless illusion, someone innocent-looking, but as smart and cruel as he is . . . then maybe, just maybe he could have a few more years of being a boy wonder at the center of the family that he always wished he had."

To Wendy's surprise, Fyodor shifted in his seat and raised an eyebrow at Ominotago. She quieted and allowed him to pick up the narrative.

"Tinkerbelle did not work, she wasn't a mother, she is a daughter in all ways that matter to him," Fyodor said. "Too vulnerable, da? Ominotago is smarter than him and could never be cruel in the way he wants. With her, he would have to *push* in a way that a man does, not a boy. Unsuitable to Peter's tastes, these actions."

"But Peter doesn't know you," Tinkerbelle interjected softy. "He hasn't decided if you fit. Detective Hook is a bastard, but he's good at his job. We know his profile on Peter; he's been working on it for years. He might just be right."

"What do you mean?" Wendy asked warily.

Ominotago bit her lip and thought hard, her brown eyes shifting left to right. "If you . . . ," she began hesitantly, "were able to get Peter to talk about James . . . If you were able to get him to brag about James or even tell you what happened, maybe that would be enough to take him in. He needs validation. He's been holding his viciousness in for a long time, and you're—"

The door to the room swung open and Detective Hook swaggered inside, flanked by two officers. "It's not a bad idea," he said, rubbing at his mustache. "Of course, it's a shame to hear about your friend James. Really a shame. You have my condolences."

"We already knew you were listening to us," Ominotago snapped.

Detective Hook grinned down at Ominotago smarmily, clearly enjoying upsetting her. He waved a hand at the officer to his right, who immediately began uncuffing Charles. He made his way through the group until everyone was freed.

"Did you enjoy your time in confinement?" Detective

Hook asked, rubbing his hands together. "Next time we'll stick to the schedule, won't we?"

"I hope there will not be a next time," Fyodor said. "What do you want from us?"

Detective Hook smiled brightly, but it didn't reach his eyes. "From you? Nothing. In fact, you, Charles, Minsu, and Ominotago are free to go. You've served your purpose tonight. Genevieve, Trevor, and Brian, come with me." He turned sharply on a heel and walked out into the hallway.

Wendy followed them all out of the room, pausing by the door as Tinkerbelle stopped in front of Ominotago. Tinkerbelle gave her a quick kiss on the cheek and hugged her tightly.

To Wendy's surprise, Ominotago hugged her. "You've got this, Wendy," she said quietly. "It was an honor to meet you." Ominotago kissed Wendy on the cheek and squeezed her shoulder hard, then followed the officer.

Charles stuck out a hand for Wendy to shake, but she pulled him into a hug anyway.

Minsu wrapped himself on the outside of Charles and Wendy's hug. "You're the real deal, Wendy. Even if you are named after a sandwich restaurant," he said tenderly into the side of Charles's neck.

Charles smacked him on the back of the head.

"Fine. Sorry." Minsu laughed. "It was NICE to MEET you, TOO. You can add me on social media or whatever; I have them all." He followed Ominotago down the hall.

Charles rolled his eyes fondly and went after him. "Good luck," he called over his shoulder as he walked away. "You can add me, too."

Fyodor had been hanging behind on purpose. Curly, Nibs, and Tinkerbelle all watched gleefully as he sauntered up to Wendy, arms tucked behind his back.

"It was really nice to meet you," Wendy offered. She could feel her cheeks getting hot again.

Fyodor nodded. He gestured to her face. "Another to match, da?" he asked softly. The tips of his ears were bright pink.

Wendy was confused. "What?"

"HE WANTS TO KISS YOUR CHEEK," Minsu shouted horribly from fifty feet down the hallway.

"Oh my God," Wendy said as embarrassment burned up her entire body. "Oh my God, oh my God."

"Just do it," Curly said in anguish, also red with second-hand embarrassment. "Detective Hook is gonna come back."

Wendy turned to Tinkerbelle in mild panic, but she was just grinning unhelpfully and watching them like it was some kind of show.

Fyodor raised an eyebrow, as if to ask for permission, then cupped the side of her jaw.

"I SAID FOLLOW ME. DO YOU IDIOTS WANT TO BE PUT BACK IN CUFFS?" Detective Hook shouted from the interrogation room down the hall.

Fyodor wasn't the type of person to bend to threats. He

gentled his grip to a caress and leaned down slowly, making sure not to crowd Wendy, waiting cautiously for any signs that she didn't want this.

"Yes," Wendy said finally, though it felt bad to have to force the word out of her throat while Curly, Nibs, and Tinkerbelle, were all watching.

As soon as he had permission, Fyodor nuzzled the side of Wendy's forehead with his own, and pressed not one, but three quick kisses to the cheek that Ominotago had left bare. He pulled back just an inch and gazed at Wendy, eyelids low and cheeks rosy. "You call me, da?" he said breathlessly.

"Yes," Tinkerbelle said, grabbing Wendy's hand and dragging her limp body toward the interrogation room. "She will absolutely call you, Fyodor."

Detective Hook was just as irate as he'd sounded from the hallway. He was standing behind his desk, pacing back and forth, but stopped to look up as Tinkerbelle and Wendy entered the room.

"We're wasting time," he snapped. "The longer Peter has to regroup after these attacks, the better he is at avoiding them. You should know that, Genevieve. You're not like Wendy—you have no excuse."

Tinkerbelle raised her chin at Detective Hook and folded her arms. "I *am* like Wendy, that's the entire point. Me and Ominotago are just like Wendy because if we weren't, she wouldn't be here. He wouldn't have picked her."

"That's not the point!" Detective Hook shoved his index

finger in Tinkerbelle's face, but she didn't flinch; she wasn't afraid of him at all.

"You know what I'm talking about," Hook said. "You've been doing this longer than she has. If Ominotago would have worked for this, I would have gone with her—she's clearly the smartest of you lot—but she visibly hates Peter too much for it to work. You're all just generations of the same trap for him, and both of you are going to be expired to him soon."

"God, you're such a dick," Tinkerbelle spat. "I notice you're not wearing your wedding ring anymore. Big surprise on that front."

"Tinkerbelle, no," Wendy gasped, thinking of all the ways Detective Hook could make them regret that.

"Tinkerbelle, YES," she replied aggressively, putting her fists on her hips.

Detective Hook rubbed his temple and, to Wendy's surprise, seemed to calm down. He pulled his desk chair out and settled into it. Then he tipped his head back and combed his hand through his hair, even though the gel made it stick up crazily when he'd finished. "I have daughters, you know. About your age," he said. "And I know they only lash out for the gut like you just did when they're scared. And you have every reason to be.

"But I'm tired. It's late, and this is important. I know my verbal filter goes when things are on the line, but I promise you, we'll have men at your back. Wherever Peter takes you, we'll be tracking and following at a block's radius. If your safety is at risk, we'll hear it on the wires and move in, even if it means we lose him again."

He sighed and looked up at the ceiling like he was looking at God. "Lord knows you won't be the last girls on earth Peter can find who're like you three." His gaze shifted back to Wendy. "But time is lives, and who knows when he'll find you."

Wendy could tell he was shifting responsibility to guilt her into accepting this assignment, and she wouldn't have it. "That's not our fault, and it's not our problem. Protecting children from killers is your job, not ours."

Detective Hook let that land, then took a folder off the stack and opened it. He slid the cooperation agreement inside across the desk. "Are you going to do this, or are you going to keep wasting my time?"

"The others got to have things in exchange for accepting," Wendy said as she pulled the paper close to look it over. "I have requests, too."

"Fine. What do you want?"

"Preferential treatment for the boys left in Peter's home. They need to be adopted or fostered. I don't know how any of that works, but you need to make it easy for them."

Detective Hook breathed out hard, like Wendy was asking him to move mountains, but then he snatched the paper back from her and turned to his computer to add a last-minute addendum to the contract. "Don't know how it works, indeed," he muttered. "You don't know how anything works, if that's what you're asking for. Could have asked for money; I know I would."

"I don't want money," Wendy said, loud and angry. "I want them to be safe. Can you promise me that you'll make an effort and not just throw them away, hide them, or toss them somewhere just to get them off your hands? They're people, and this is affecting them! It's not a joke for them, or a glory moment. These are their *lives*."

Wendy could feel Tinkerbelle looking at her.

"Yeah, yeah," Detective Hook said. "Whatever you want, just make sure you do a good job. Grab that copy from the printer to your left and make sure your signature is clear."

Tinkerbelle grabbed Wendy's arm before she could move to the printer. "Me too," she said hoarsely.

Detective Hook looked up from his computer with irritation. "What?" He put his reading glasses on like he needed them to hear her better.

"Put me on the list for that, too," Tinkerbelle said. Quieter, but more insistent.

"But I already printed it out," Detective Hook griped, taking his reading glasses back off.

"PUT HER ON THE LIST," Wendy shouted.

Detective Hook startled, jerking back in his chair at the force of Wendy's rage. He turned back to the computer, wordlessly typed Tinkerbelle's legal name into the document, and hit print.

Wendy marched across the room, snatched the paper out

of the printer, and brought it to Detective Hook's desk. She took a pen out of his "World's Okayest Dad" novelty mug and signed the contract.

"Head to the next office and get fitted with your surveillance equipment," Detective Hook said, chastened.

Wendy turned on her heel and headed for the door, with Tinkerbelle close behind.

"If it's any consolation . . . ," Detective Hook said to Wendy's back. Wendy stopped to listen, not moving even when Tinkerbelle bumped into her back. "You're better than he is. Remember that. He's smart but he's alone, and he always will be."

Wendy didn't reply. She just pulled the door open and left.

CHAPTER 16

Curly and Nibs were waiting for them in the front lobby, Curly bouncing his leg anxiously. He jumped up immediately when they rounded the corner. "He texted me. He wants to meet us in Edgewater."

"Do you have any more money for the bus?" Tinkerbelle asked.

Nibs shrugged. "They gave us a couple of fare cards."

"Oooh, I wonder if it will work after tonight," Tinkerbelle said, eyes brightening.

"They wouldn't give us a fare card we could use indefinitely," Curly said. "I'm pretty sure it will stop working as soon as the sun comes up. Or it only has enough for, like, two rides on it."

"It's better than nothing," Tinkerbelle said. She threw an arm over Wendy's shoulders and they all went outside to catch the number twenty-two Clark Bus.

The ride this time was quiet and tense, but it was a different kind of tension than before. Wendy's heart was steady, but her veins felt like they were full of lightning. She wasn't shaking and scared—she was ready.

"Peter is going to send us home as soon as we get there," Curly said suddenly after they had been riding for a while. He unbraided his hair and combed his fingers through it a few times. "He likes to isolate people, so just let him. We won't really leave; we'll follow you at a distance. Peter knows when he's being tailed, so we'll have to keep pretty far away."

"You don't have to if you don't want to," Wendy said. "The police will be following and listening in, and if anything happens—"

Curly shook his head sharply. "We never leave Tinkerbelle alone in the night."

Oh yeah. Wendy had forgotten about that. The train ride to Peter's house seemed like it had happened so long ago, but it was barely 2:15 a.m.

Tinkerbelle leaned the side of her head on the bus seat and closed her eyes. Nibs reached over and ran his hand through her short blond hair.

"It's almost over, Wendy," Tinkerbelle said sleepily. "Whether you succeed or not. How do you feel?"

"Nervous. Determined . . . exhausted." Wendy laughed. "I stay up this late pretty often, but I'm usually in bed and on the Internet or playing video games. I think I've walked more tonight than I have in the past month."

Tinkerbelle smiled softly and closed her eyes. "I know we might not, but I hope we see you again. Even if it's just in passing or on the train."

Beside her, Curly began rebraiding his hair, pulling tightly so his braids were stiff and shiny.

Wendy wondered how they got ready for bed normally, if they spent some time together as a family and watched TV, or read books out loud so the younger boys could listen.

If Peter had never entered their lives but they'd all found themselves living under the same roof, Wendy believed they could have survived without him. They would have been much happier, too.

When their bus stopped at the corner of Clark and Albion, Nibs shook Tinkerbelle to wake her up. Curly pulled the string to stop the bus, hopped out the back door, and held it open for them. When the bus pulled off, Peter was there, standing across the street.

He was stock-still, watching them with his hands tucked in his pockets. They waited for the traffic light to change, then crossed the street to meet him on the other side.

Peter looked them up and down. "It's been an interesting night, hasn't it?" he asked, without any inflection whatso-ever in his voice.

Curly and Nibs didn't say anything. They waited as if in military rest for Peter to say or do something instead.

Peter's golden eyes were fixed on Tinkerbelle as he stared her down in suspicion. "Go home," he said.

Curly and Nibs turned and began walking down the side-walk without a second glance at the girls they were leaving behind. Tinkerbelle watched them leave, then met Peter's gaze.

"I'm taking Wendy back," Peter said quietly. "Then, when we get home, you and I are going to have a talk."

Tinkerbelle flinched like he'd hit her, hands visibly shaking.

Wendy's heart was pounding in her chest. Only the scratch of the wire's tape against her skin and the knowledge of what was at stake gave her the bravery to speak. She stepped closer to Tinkerbelle, edging herself into Peter's line of sight to hopefully break his focus and resettle it on herself. "Tonight had nothing to do with her," Wendy said firmly.

Peter's gaze flickered in Wendy's direction for a second, but then resettled onto Tinkerbelle. A predator rarely gets distracted.

Wendy steeled herself and tried again. "Stop scaring her. You don't do anything to girls. You never have and never will."

Peter's neck snapped so fast in Wendy's direction there was an audible crack. For one incredibly horrifying second, an expression shifted over his face that was so full of the promise of violence, Wendy almost stepped back.

But she didn't. She filled herself with the last shreds she could reach of Ominotago's boldness and said, "Do you know who I am? I know who you are. I've always known." *By the grace of God keep my voice still, keep my knees steady, keep my face blank,* Wendy chanted silently.

Peter's golden eyes shifted back and forth as he clawed through his memory, Tinkerbelle almost entirely forgotten.

Wendy tilted her head to the side and looked at Peter like he was being amusing. There was such a thin line between throwing him off guard enough to trick him and saying something that would make him react as quickly and danger-ously as she'd seem him already tonight.

"Wendy, no," Tinkerbelle whispered.

"Wendy, yes!" Wendy exclaimed, grinning at Peter. "Only my last name is probably throwing you off. God, if she knew how easily she'd slipped your mind, she wouldn't have stayed away from this city for almost twenty years."

Peter's arm shot out so fast it was a blur, grabbing Wendy's forearm with crushing pressure. He swung her around and slammed her so hard against the brick wall of the building behind them that stars danced across her eyes. Tinkerbelle screamed, but there was no one on the street to hear her. It was too late at night, but also too early in the morning.

In spite of the pain, Wendy giggled and bared her teeth in her closest approximation of the feral smile Peter had given Detective Hook earlier. "I've been told I look like her," she said.

"Mary Moira," Peter replied roughly, ghosts swimming across his vision. He looked more haggard and more his age than Wendy had ever seen him—auburn curls finger-combed and frizzed, lack of sleep, setting spray for his makeup let-ting the circles beneath his eyes show through.

Wendy ignored the throbbing in her upper arm and the scrape at the back of her head. "She was running from you, but I've been *looking* for you," she said, tilting her chin up to gaze at him beneath lowered eyelids.

Peter clenched his teeth angrily, but the rest of his face

crumpled into the expectant despair of a man who knew he couldn't keep getting away forever. "What do you want? Did you come here to kill me?" he rasped, shaking her shoulders roughly.

Wendy clenched her left hand into a fist as she struggled not to react to the skin on the back of her arm tearing as it scraped against the brick. "I came to watch you," she said.

Peter instantly let go of her arm in confusion. He backed away from her and began pacing, like a tiger as he circled her.

"Sorry for the girl next door act, but I had to see for myself if you were really him. Or if you had . . ." Wendy looked him up and down wolfishly, then continued, ". . . depreciated or retired. You're very rare, Peter. No one who meets you can ever forget."

Peter hissed air through his teeth angrily, and Wendy tried not to flinch. She started again: "I've grown up hearing stories about you for as long as I've been alive. No one can catch the great Peter Pan," she lied triumphantly. "No one would ever want to."

"They *can* catch me, and you're a liability," Peter said firmly. He grabbed Wendy by the top of her dress and Tinkerbelle by her sleeve and marched them into an alley where there would be even less likelihood of witnesses.

"I'm not a liability," Wendy said quickly as they stumbled into the darkness. "I'm an asset."

Tinkerbelle had begun to cry, and it took everything in Wendy's power not to reach out to comfort her.

Peter looked at Tinkerbelle and sneered in disgust. "Stop it, you're being too loud," he shouted at her.

Tinkerbelle covered her face with her hands and worked to quiet herself.

Wendy felt a spark of anger, and it was enough to fuel her. The fact that he was shouting when he wanted quiet was just more proof that as dangerous as Peter was, he was fallible, and he was messy.

"How long do you think you can keep this up?" Wendy asked, challenging him. "Can you even still do it, or are you retired already? It would be such a letdown for me."

Peter paused, clearly surprised that she would ask that. "I'm not retired," he said with no small amount of offense.

Wendy put her hand on her hip. "Really? Because it would be very disappointing to have come all this way and gotten to meet you only to learn that you were done."

"And why does that even matter to you?" Peter asked darkly. "Do you want an autograph or something?"

It was Wendy's turn to pretend to be offended. "No. I want to help."

Peter gasped. Then he threw his head back and laughed at her, his delight crawling up the alley walls and spiraling out into the night sky. He held his stomach and laughed until tears leaked out of the corners of his eyes.

Tinkerbelle nudged Wendy in the side and nodded at a beer bottle on the ground while Peter was distracted.

Wendy made a decision. "Fine. I thought you might be

looking for a protégé, but I guess not. I'll get started on my own then," she said loudly, nodding back at Tinkerbelle in understanding. She crouched down, snatched the bottle off the ground, and smashed its end against the wall. Then Wendy turned and stabbed it close to Tinkerbelle. Tinkerbelle shrieked as the sharp glass edges skittered off the brick near her head.

Wendy reared her arm back to stab at Tinkerbelle again, but Peter lunged forward and slapped the side of Wendy's arm so hard that she smashed the bottle to pieces against the wall, rendering it useless.

"No," Peter growled, stepping close to her, all traces of levity gone from his beautiful face. "Tinkerbelle is mine."

"Then take me seriously," Wendy said, keeping her face blank. "I've taken *you* seriously."

Tinkerbelle was gasping in feigned terror, crouched on the ground. Her hands were shaking like they usually did when she was afraid, but Wendy could tell she was doing it a little bit too fast. She was acting.

Wendy's chest squeezed hard and her throat felt hot. They just might succeed. They just might be able to do this.

Peter reached down and wrenched Tinkerbelle up, then shook her hard with one hand. "It is too dangerous for you, and it's late. You need to go home," he said.

Wendy remembered what Fyodor had said. *Peter would have to push in a way that a man does, not a boy.* Peter didn't kill women and he didn't beat women, only boys.

Wendy didn't want to test the theory, but it seemed to be holding fast. "I want her here," she said, thinking quickly. "If you're both taking me home, I want my parents to see Tinkerbelle with me at the door, not you. Be practical."

Peter let go of Tinkerbelle and brushed his hands down the side of her arms as if in apology. "You can't be impulsive," he said to Wendy, even though he was looking at Tinkerbelle. "I admire your enthusiasm, but fucking hell. You can't just go out swinging or you'll never last long enough to get good at this. You have to plan and be graceful about it."

He paused to pluck a few pieces of glass out of Tinkerbelle's hair, then brushed the finer pieces away with the side of his sleeve. Then he cupped Tinkerbelle's face in his hands and thumbed the tears off her cheeks.

Tinkerbelle sniffled and leaned up into his gentle grip, away from Wendy like Tinkerbelle was scared of her.

"Say you're sorry," Peter demanded of Wendy. "You can't scold me for scaring her if you're just going to turn around and scare her, too."

"I'm sorry, Tinkerbelle," Wendy said, rolling her eyes.

"You have to be nice to people, too," Peter said, already in teacher mode. "The world won't give you things easily if you have a bad attitude."

"Look, I don't even know if you're retired yet or not," Wendy said with just as much attitude as before.

Peter looked at her sharply. "I'm not retired."

"Prove it."

Peter scowled. "Why would I do that? We literally just fucking met."

"Fyodor has an opinion about what happened to James tonight," Wendy said boldly. "I think you might be able to guess what."

Tinkerbelle made a noise of pain and despair, selling the illusion of her ignorance.

"If you did get rid of James," Wendy continued, "he should be nearby. If you don't take me to him, I'll still walk away knowing it happened and approximately where to find him. Which would make me, in your own words, a liability. Then, well, you could get rid of me, too . . . but then you'll have sullied your streak and done something I'm beginning to understand you don't ever want to do. Alternatively . . ."

She ran a finger up the side of Tinkerbelle's arm, and grinned when Tinkerbelle flinched. "You could bring me with you and give me a lesson in etiquette. We could come to some kind of arrangement."

"Why are you doing this?" Peter asked.

Wendy smiled. "It's what I've always wanted to be when I grew up. Surely you had dreams of what you wanted to be when you grew up."

Peter frowned softly. "No. I didn't. The only dream I had was . . . I just wanted—"

Wendy interrupted him. "I know."

Peter glanced out of the alley into the street. A single car drove down the road, passing them and flooding the alley with bright light for a split second. Peter put his hands on his hips and matched Wendy's gaze for a long and excruciating moment. He rolled one shoulder, the shoulder that wore the jacket sleeve that she had been sewn earlier in the night. Wendy heard an echo of his words: *I've had this jacket for a very long time. It used to belong to a friend of mine—the very first friend I ever had.*

Peter took a deep breath and let it out in a long, shaky sigh. "You can have anything in life if you will sacrifice everything else for it," he said into the quiet of the night. He raked his hand through his auburn hair, then stretched his arms up and behind his head to crack his back. Then Peter smirked. He reached inside his jacket and took out a switchblade comb and began putting himself to rights.

"The first time was an accident," he said, and Wendy didn't believe him for a second. "But it gets easier after that."

Wendy swallowed and kept herself from looking at Tinkerbelle. After a night of gazing at the other girl for reassurance, it was harder than she thought. "Do you do it for fun?" she asked, leaning casually against the brick. "I'd do it for fun."

"No." Peter's response was quick and agonized. The wind blew hard into the alley, and the light of another passing car illuminated his silhouette as he blocked the only way out of the alley. "I forget them afterward." He clenched his hands into fists. "When you grow up, you become not yourself in so many ways. I couldn't bear it if I passed one of them on the street completely grown and completely unlike himself. No interest in anything but work, incapable of having adventures, tired, like all the light has been sucked out of him. This is easier in many ways."

That was an unexpected response. Wendy didn't quite know what to say to that. She'd have to switch tactics. "You told us James left without saying goodbye," she said. "If he'd already left, then what was the problem?"

Peter laughed mirthlessly and rubbed his eyes with both hands. Wendy took this second of relief from being pinned under Peter's surveillance to quickly shoot a reassuring expression at Tinkerbelle.

Tinkerbelle's shoulders dropped a fraction.

"James left a year early," Peter said, letting his arms fall to his sides so hard in exasperation that they hit the sides of his thighs. "He robbed us of a full 391 days of being with him, 390 mornings of being together to make breakfast, 391 nights of listening to him read out loud. Everyone who leaves gets a chance to say goodbye—even the ones who don't leave voluntarily. But James fled in the middle of the night and he . . . he broke Curly's heart."

Tinkerbelle sprang to action and took control of the direction that this was going. She rubbed the sides of Peter's arms as his eyes got red again.

"What is it with you?" he said to Wendy, choked up. "You've made me cry three times tonight."

"I'm sorry. I think you just needed to; it's been a long

time for you, hasn't it?" Wendy asked softly. "I'm sorry for trivializing what you do. I didn't understand why you did it, I didn't know . . ."

Tinkerbelle allowed Peter to rest his head on her shoulder. She curled an arm around his back and held him tight as he sniffled into the side of her neck. She rocked him back and forth and made soft hushing noises. Peter let her move him gently until she had rocked him almost ninety degrees in a semicircle, until Peter's wet, accusatory eyes were no longer facing Wendy.

Tinkerbelle hushed gently at him for a second more, then looked directly at Wendy over Peter's head and nodded. Wendy nodded back and gave Tinkerbelle a quick thumbs up. Tinkerbelle nuzzled into the side of Peter's head in faux reassurance and rolled her eyes.

"It's different for Wendy," Tinkerbelle explained, gentle like she was talking to a child. "You have to put yourself in her shoes, Peter. She's waited so long to see you—you're practically a celebrity to her. There was no way she could have had the right context for our lives and there's no way she would have known how much this means to you. It's not fair to stay angry at her if she didn't do any of it on purpose. Right?"

Peter nodded into the curve of Tinkerbelle's neck, but didn't lift his head.

"I'm sure a smart, kind girl like Wendy would be willing to try, though?" Tinkerbelle asked. "You remember how happy Slightly was that she liked his soup and Curly was when she loved his bread?"

"I remember," Peter said, his words muffled by Tinkerbelle's skin.

"The boys like her so much. If anyone would understand, it's Wendy, but you have to give her a chance to try."

Peter sobbed into Tinkerbelle's shoulder and said something hysterically that Wendy couldn't make out.

Tinkerbelle hushed him again sweetly and held him tighter. "I know, Peter, I know. But sometimes people don't mean to hurt people. Wendy already apologized to me, and I accepted her apology. It was a mistake. You make mistakes sometimes, too. How would you feel if someone didn't accept your apology?"

Wendy watched with no small amount of horror and amazement as Tinkerbelle masterfully manipulated Peter in his regressive state.

"We could have a home together with her," Tinkerbelle said tenderly, stroking the side of Peter's cheek. "She came to you all on her own, just like Curly, and she wants to stay with you—she said so herself. You are so lucky, Peter. Don't waste this opportunity; it's like she was practically made for you."

Tinkerbelle locked eyes with Wendy again and gave a small, helpless shrug. Wendy waved her hand in forgiveness. It was a creepy thing to say, but none of this conversation could possibly be taken seriously between them. Wendy vaguely wondered where the police were and if Curly and Nibs were perched nearby and able to see them.

Peter seemed to be calming down. He nodded one last time into Tinkerbelle's neck and pulled his face up, then he turned and reached out a hand for Wendy to take.

"I will take you to see James, but you have to promise you won't leave like he did. If you make Slightly, Curly, Nibs, and the rest like you and then you leave us, it wouldn't be fair," Peter said, his voice rough.

Wendy noticed that he didn't say that he would kill her for it, but that was hardly a relief.

"I know," Wendy said carefully. "I won't."

Peter stepped out of the alley and began to lead Tinkerbelle and Wendy toward the train station. "You don't have to live with us if you don't want," Peter said gingerly. "Your parents clearly love you. But I know the littler ones would like to see you again, and you can't go in and out of their lives recklessly. It hurts them."

The cognitive dissonance between watching Peter desperately weeping and needing to be comforted like a child and having him dropping childhood developmental psychology tips like he was an authority on what children need was dizzying. Something inside this man was incredibly broken. He was just thousands of shards of what he may have been in his past, taped haphazardly together, all his sharp edges rubbing and grinding against each other.

It would be sad if it wasn't simultaneously activating her fight-or-flight instinct.

The night was still dark, but Wendy could tell that it was getting late enough for the sky to start shifting. The wind had picked up, like it was getting ready to rain, and the dress Wendy borrowed from Tinkerbelle was no longer enough to keep her warm. She tried to suppress a shiver, but Peter noticed immediately.

He let go of her hand, took his gray jacket off, and draped it over her shoulders. "Be careful with it. Don't let anything fall out of the pockets," Peter said quietly.

Tinkerbelle looked shocked behind him, but quickly fixed her face when he grabbed both of their hands and started walking again.

It would have been too conspicuous to dig around inside the jacket, but Wendy could feel things inside it that she hadn't been aware of back when she was angrily sewing his sleeve back on, objects sewn into the linings of the cuffs and the bottom of the jacket that scraped against her as she moved. It was heavier than it looked, concentrated mostly on the left front, where it would be quick to slip a hand inside. A magic jacket, indeed. Wendy was warm, but at what cost?

Peter turned them down a residential street, and they traded the comfort of the main road for darkness. They crept along the side of the elevated train tracks, shadowed by trees and the high wall that separated the train from the grass.

"I don't bury anyone. It doesn't feel right to hide them,

to keep them from the sunshine," Peter admitted. "It helps with forensics, as well. You can never make a scene clean enough, but if you leave it messy, things get muddled, so there'll be questions."

"How ma—" Wendy started, but Tinkerbelle shook her head hard, so Wendy shifted direction. "How close are we going to get to him?"

Peter hummed and considered it. "Close enough to see, and that's it. I don't disturb the bodies; it feels disrespectful."

It! Feels! Disrespectful?! Wendy wanted to scream. This line, specifically, would be going right into the mental box where she was planning to keep her trauma regarding this forever.

They were getting farther from the main road, and Wendy was beginning to worry about whether the police would be able to swarm down on him like she'd been hoping. She hadn't heard any helicopters, and there weren't a lot of places to park. If they were coming for him, they'd have to drive into the grass. At the very least, what Peter had said was pretty close to a confession, so if they couldn't arrest him tonight, maybe they could take him in for questioning tomorrow.

Peter stopped walking. He held out an arm to block Wendy from getting too close.

Roughly fifty feet away, there was a dark smudge in the grass. They were far enough away that Wendy couldn't see any details, but close enough that she could tell that it was too large to be roadkill. Wendy glanced up at the elevated tracks, where Peter had pushed James from the train. It was about twenty or thirty feet up. Tall enough for an immediate fatality. Or worse, James may have fallen, been grievously injured, and lain there in pain in the dark until he eventually succumbed to his injuries while Wendy and the rest of the group were dancing at the party.

Wendy's heart lurched with disgust and horror and she felt almost like she was going to throw up before disassociation properly kicked in and she began floating above herself. She watched herself gazing at James's body and vaguely felt herself hoping he was just unconscious.

Tinkerbelle covered her face. Peter pulled Tinkerbelle to his chest, allowing her to turn away from what he had done. Wendy watched from above and couldn't imagine how unbearable it would feel to be in the cradle of Peter's arms right now.

"Is that him?" Wendy asked. It felt like she was speaking underwater.

Peter turned as slow as time and fixed her with his golden gaze. "He didn't even scream as he fell." He sighed. "It was like he knew he deserved it."

Wendy folded her arms in Peter's jacket and stared at the dark smudge. Nothing was happening police-wise, so she knew she hadn't finished the job. "I want to stay with you," Wendy started. "But I need you to help me. I want to be a part of your family, but in order to give Slightly, Curly, Nibs, Prentis, Tootles, and the twins the mother they deserve, I need to understand why this is such a big part of who you are."

Peter paused, then tilted his head back until he was look-ing at the stars. "I never had anything like this when I was younger. I always had to build my families from scratch. There will always be people like me who have nothing and no one, who have to burn themselves alive to stay warm. It's always easy for me to find other people like that because we know one another on sight. When we finally have the oppor-tunity to belong to each other and build a community, it's something rare and special. We are the ones who make the rules; we are the ones who build our own home. We take care of one another, and our word is our bond, and nothing but that matters.

"But it's hard to keep that going forever. You don't stop needing your brothers when you turn eighteen, you need them even more. But the world isn't built in a way that allows people to really hold on to one another how we should. Everyone gets to a certain point where they grow up, and suddenly they don't think they need anyone. They want to leave and find new people to share their time with, and they rarely come back to visit. The world becomes so big for them, and they look down on the places they stayed and the people they made memories with. It's such a monumental betrayal to the people they've left behind."

Peter closed his eyes.

"I haven't talked to anyone about this before," he admitted.

"It's okay," Wendy lied. *Good God.*

Peter stood still for a moment, looking at James's body

from a distance. He seemed to deflate a bit. "I've heard that people come home to visit their mothers. You know, during the holidays and all of that. No matter how old they get, they always come back home to see her. You see on TV when they say things like, 'This tastes just like how Mom makes it!' or, 'Mom used to do this with us,' and you can tell they really want to go home and see her. You don't hear that about dads, you don't hear that about brothers. Mothers are special somehow. I just think . . . maybe if we had one, my brothers wouldn't leave and never come back. They might want to come and visit, even if it was just for her," Peter finished, his eyes fluttering closed.

The breath felt like it had been punched clean out of Wendy's lungs. She watched this monster of a boy, backlit by a blanket of stars, and felt herself falling to pieces. "If—if you knew they would come back," Wendy stammered, "would you still keep . . . like . . . James . . . ?"

Peter's eyes snapped open and he frowned. "It's too late for James. I killed James because—"

The instant that phrase was out of his mouth, Wendy heard two loud bangs, and Peter fell jerkily to his knees and screamed. Tinkerbelle wrenched her hand out of his grip and pulled Wendy backward.

It took Wendy a second to figure out what had happened. Peter was kneeling and panting hard. The back of his calves began to darken with blood. Wendy looked up and saw a sniper, who had been nestled on the elevated train tracks, climb to his feet. Almost immediately sirens began going off in the distance. Peter gasped and tried to pull himself to his feet, but he collapsed back down to the ground.

"Tink . . . Tinkerbelle, please," he groaned, but Tinkerbelle shook her head and backed away from his flailing arms.

Wendy held on to her hand tight as they watched Peter try to rise to his feet.

The police cars drove over the grass and were getting close quickly.

Peter Pan hissed and compressed his wounds with hands slick with blood. "I hate you," he spat at Tinkerbelle and Wendy.

"You're disgusting!" Tinkerbelle shouted.

"I am many things," Peter panted, smiling in the face of their betrayal. "I'm youth, I'm joy, I'm a little bird who has broken out of the egg."

With terrible speed, he snatched a blade from somewhere Wendy didn't see, and threw it fast.

Wendy clenched her teeth and shut her eyes, but Peter's deadly aim had been marred by panic and pain, and the knife cut the sleeve of Tinkerbelle's dress instead of any precious bit of her.

The police poured out of their cars and surrounded them, immediately cuffing Peter and holding him down on his knees.

Nibs and Curly emerged from the dark side of the tracks; they marched straight past James's body without glancing at it and picked up speed. Nibs outpaced Curly, heading directly for Tinkerbelle, who began crying, arms open to receive him. Curly kept running behind them. The police parted, making way for him as he got closer, holding Peter upright and facing his challenger. Curly pulled out the bar he'd used to pry Ominotago out of the police car.

"No, Curly, wait," Peter said, eyes white with terror.

"Shut up and die," Curly yelled. He leaped into the air, swinging the bar like a bat, and smashed Peter across the face with incredible violence. Peter's jaw made a crack that was absolutely bone-shattering, and his scream of agony would haunt Wendy for the next decade of her life.

The police watched in silence as Curly dropped the bar and flung himself into Tinkerbelle and Nibs. No one yelled at him or made any move to restrain him at all, they just watched.

The officer holding Peter's arms behind his back jerked him upright but didn't pull him to his feet.

Wendy took off Peter's jacket and threw it on the ground.

"Is that evidence, or is that yours?" a nearby officer asked.

"Evidence," Wendy said, stepping away from it and wrapping her arms around herself.

Tinkerbelle, Curly, and Nibs held each other tightly. They had turned completely around and had their backs to Peter, while he gasped through his ruined face.

Another car drove up to the scene recklessly fast, stopping with a loud screech. Detective Hook stepped out and strode quickly across the grass. He eyed Wendy, the boys, and Tinkerbelle warily, but didn't stop to speak to them. He headed straight for Peter.

As if Peter could sense Detective Hook nearby, he stopped whimpering pathetically and sat very still and silent, his head bowed and still bleeding.

Detective Hook stood over Peter Pan and stared down at him. Then he stooped to one knee, put a meaty hand in Peter's hair, and wrenched his face up.

"Who did this?" he called out loudly.

No one spoke. It was quiet except for the wind and Curly's and Tinkerbelle's grateful weeping.

Wendy began to shiver. She looked around at the officers, but their expressions were stern as they focused on the detective.

Detective Hook wrenched Peter's head to the left and then to the right as he surveyed the damage Curly had inflicted. His eyes wandered a few feet up to the bar that Curly had tossed down and followed it up to the huddled three.

"It looks like you fell," Detective Hook said, loud enough for the other officers to hear. Then he leaned close to Peter so only the other officers couldn't hear him. "Unfortunate," he growled. "I've always known you to be graceful."

Peter spat at Detective Hook, spraying him with blood spatter. Detective Hook didn't wipe his cheek; instead he grinned broad and white. Peter gasped involuntarily in pain for a long moment, then he lifted his face of his own volition and met Detective Hook's grin with one of his own.

"Yes, James Hook, it is all my doing," Peter wheezed cockily.

"Proud and insolent to the end," Detective Hook replied. His expression didn't change as he reached down and grabbed Peter's jaw with his prosthetic. He yanked Peter's head, exposing the purpling side of his face to the light of the moon so he could appraise the effects of Curly's blow.

Peter gasped in agony as the metal ground into his flesh, flinching away from the hand he'd made necessary and the grip that he'd earned.

Curly jolted at the sound, and Nibs and Tinkerbelle held him tighter.

Detective Hook dropped Peter's face and climbed to his feet. He met the eyes of the officer holding Peter's arms behind his back. "Take him in."

CHAPTER 17

The drive to the station was quiet. Detective Hook drove them himself. He let all four of them sit in the back even though there was only room for three, and Wendy was thankful for it. She was still floating above herself, but she didn't think she could take having to sit next to Detective Hook while he had Peter's blood and spit on his face, dripping down to stain his white shirt, and drying sticky and dark on his prosthetic.

Nibs, Curly, and Tinkerbelle were so wrapped up in the trauma of their escape, they hadn't paid Wendy an inch of attention since Curly broke Peter's jaw. They huddled close together like little rabbits, shaking. Wendy was cold and still dealing with the drama of the night, but she could understand the difference between her terror and the old fear that had lurked in every movement for these kids since she had met them.

Wendy leaned against the car window and tried to relax. Now that the adrenaline of trying to trick a grown man into confessing and the entire night in general was wearing off, she could feel waves of exhaustion on the horizon. The sky was the light purple that was more morning than night, and her stomach was beginning to cramp with hunger from staying up too late.

When they pulled into the precinct parking lot, Wendy

opened her eyes, and with a jolt of horror and relief, saw her dad's car parked in front.

"I think my parents are here," she said quietly.

Detective Hook looked over his shoulder at her and grunted. He didn't elaborate; he just parked and unlocked the car. Instead of taking them in the front door, Hook led them through a side door and straight to the room where he had shown Wendy the folders of evidence and Peter's mug shot. Curly and Nibs were separated from them and taken somewhere else. Wendy stared blankly as an officer removed the wire she was wearing, then went to go sit beside Tinkerbelle, waiting for her to finish having hers removed, as well. Wendy was chilled and sluggish and didn't feel capable of reacting to anything else tonight.

Tinkerbelle looked much the same. Her blond hair was spiked in all directions from being mussed by Curly and Nibs's embrace. The circles beneath her eyes were so deep they almost looked like bruises.

When the officer finished removing the tape from the wire and Tinkerbelle had her dress back on and zipped, she trudged over to the seat next to Wendy and flung herself heavily into it. "What a night, huh?" She closed her eyes and dropped her head onto the wall behind her.

"Yeah," Wendy said, physically incapable of thinking of something better to say.

Tinkerbelle took a deep breath and let it out all at once

in a sharp huff. They sat in silence next to each other. A few minutes later, there were the sounds of many feet running.

"You got him!" someone shouted.

The entire precinct broke out into muffled cheers and applause.

Wendy closed her eyes against the noise, but opened them again when she felt a soft nudge. Instead of turning, Wendy just let her eyes swivel over to Tinkerbelle.

The corner of Tinkerbelle's mouth ticked up as they listened to the officers cheer Detective Hook for his big catch, while the detective himself yelled for them to calm down already.

"Do you think they're gonna get him a cake?" Tinkerbelle asked quietly, her smirk slowly blossoming into a true smile.

Wendy couldn't help but smile back. "Best day of his life." She snorted.

Tinkerbelle closed her eyes again and shook her head, still grinning. "God, it better be someone's."

"Punch me if it's too early to ask," Wendy said, exhaustion making her bold, "but what are you going to do now?"

Tinkerbelle pursed her lips, then turned her head until it was lying against the top of the chair. "Live, I guess. They'll be taking us out of Peter's house and putting us in a hotel for the night, and then maybe we'll get doled out to foster families afterward. Whoooo." Tinkerbelle raised her arm in fake celebration.

"I'm so sorry—" Wendy started, but Tinkerbelle shook her head.

"No. You shouldn't be saying sorry; I should be saying thank you," Tinkerbelle told her honestly. "You really held your own out there. Almost had me scared for real, for a moment."

Suddenly, without knowing why, Wendy's throat got hot and tight, and her eyes began to prickle. "I went to theater camp," she managed to choke out before starting to cry.

Tinkerbelle scooted closer and put an arm over the back of Wendy's chair so Wendy could lean on her.

"I . . . don't know why I'm . . . nothing is even happening to me anymore!" Wendy wiped at her face roughly, half angry at herself and more than a little embarrassed.

Tinkerbelle patted Wendy's shoulder and sighed again, her thousandth sigh of the night.

"It's like that sometimes," she admitted. "It's easier to cry afterward when you finally know that you're safe."

Tinkerbelle held her like that for a long time, completely unlike the way she'd held Peter while he was crying.

Wendy kept wiping her face until it was dry, and the bees quit buzzing in her chest.

Tinkerbelle waited until Wendy gathered control of her breathing before she began tenderly removing the dried flowers from Wendy's hair. She plucked them out one by one, untangling them from Wendy's curls and laying them in her lap. Then she wiggled the pins that had held Wendy's hair back from her face until they came free. Tinkerbelle dipped her fingers into Wendy's hair and shook it lightly until it fell around Wendy's face, messy and free.

"There," Tinkerbelle said. "Now you're yourself again."

Fresh tears sprung to Wendy's eyes, and she covered her face with both hands, but Tinkerbelle tugged her wrists until she dropped them to her lap once again.

"You're a very brave friend, Wendy," she whispered.

The door to the interrogation room opened again, and Detective Hook was standing there, cheeks red and jolly, eyes sparkling. "Come on, Wendy, your parents are waiting for you in the lobby. Your mom remembers me, can you believe it? Fifty pounds and twenty years, and I've still got it!" He gleefully smacked a hand over his gut.

Wendy shot him a dirty look and stood up, letting all the dried flowers and pins fall on the floor.

Detective Hook glanced at the mess, then at both Wendy and Tinkerbelle—who stared back in placid amusement.

"Normally I'd yell at you about that, but there's literally nothing that can ruin my good mood," he said chipperly. "We've even sprung for a two-star hotel for the orphans."

Tinkerbelle scowled at being referred to like that.

"Merry Christmas!" Detective Hook exclaimed before turning on a heel and heading back down the hallway.

Wendy's heart raced at the thought of facing her parents after what had happened, but Tinkerbelle stood up and stretched, yawning loudly. "Okay. Let's go get yelled at," she said, and trudged out the door.

Wendy followed Tinkerbelle through the precinct and out to the front lobby. To her surprise, Fyodor, Charles, Minsu, and Ominotago were all back and reunited with their families.

Charles's mom was large and muscular, like she played football, herself, but his dad was tall and thin. They both looked incredibly glamorous for having been awoken at three a.m. to come collect their child from a police station, and both were crying and holding him. Fyodor's parents were both much shorter than him, and while his mom was round and sweet-looking, his father had a face more chiseled than Fyodor himself, and the sort of hair that would make an angel weep. Fyodor's mom was shouting at Fyodor in quick, angry Russian—clearly trying to yell some sense back into him, while Fyodor argued back with tears in his eyes, pointing at Ominotago and Curly emphatically. By the time Wendy had stepped fully into the lobby, Fyodor's mother had begun to cry, too, and Fyodor pulled her quickly into his arms.

Curly was standing dejectedly by Ominotago and getting a soft talking-to by a man who had to be Ominotago's father. Waatese, who looked more than half asleep, had been dragged back into the night and was slumped on the shoulder of a woman who looked a lot like him. It was clearly Ominotago's mother; she looked Wendy over with suspicion, but her expression melted into something much softer as she laid eyes on Tinkerbelle and realized who Wendy must be.

Minsu's parents were sitting in near silence as an officer explained the situation, which Minsu translated into Korean. They were dressed extremely fancy, in spite of the late hour. Wendy remembered how Minsu had said his father wouldn't care why he was arrested and would be angry anyway. But Minsu's father was looking between his son and the officer in confused wonder at what his son had helped achieve. Minsu's mother's hands were clasped tightly between her husband's. Minsu looked nervous, but Wendy was sure that everything would probably be all right.

Wendy didn't see her own parents, so she went to go sit in one of the empty plastic chairs by the front door.

Nibs, who was also by himself, came and sat next to her. He nudged her shoulder with his and nodded at Curly and at Ominotago's father, who was standing by him.

"That's Curly's family, too, right?" Wendy asked.

Nibs nodded firmly. "They're giving him another chance, and they said they'll let me stay with them, too. I can tell they're wary, but he's not going to mess his chance up. Not again, not after this."

"What did he do the first time?"

Nibs shook his head. "If you want to know, you have to ask him. He's not proud of it, and it's not my story to tell."

Wendy began to apologize for prying, but was startled by a yell from the doorway.

"WENDY!" Mrs. Darling shrieked.

Wendy looked up, startled.

Mr. and Mrs. Darling were coming out of the back of the precinct, from the opposite direction Wendy and Tinkerbelle had come from. Wendy had only a moment to wonder why they were that deep into the building when Mrs. Darling sprinted across the room and slammed into her. She crushed Wendy in her arms in hysteria, dragging Wendy to the ground as she scream-cried. Mr. Darling jogged up behind her and knelt down on the floor so he could get his arms around the both of them.

Mrs. Darling clawed at the back of Wendy's dress, nearly incoherent. Wendy closed her eyes and buried her face in her mom's sweater, inhaling her familiar mom scent, and the noise of the precinct and the screaming and crying faded away.

She knew she was in trouble, and it was the big kind, but that hardly seemed to matter. Wendy held on to her mom and thought about how Mrs. Darling really didn't need CrossFit because she was crushing the air clean out of Wendy's lungs. She hoped that when her mom let go, she would still feel this ache, and know that she was home and she was loved. Wendy had never wanted to go home more in her life. She was so, so tired.

"You're grounded for thousands of years," Mrs. Darling sobbed.

"I know."

"You're never leaving the house again!"

Wendy's eyes smarted and she nodded, just holding her mom and dad closer. "Yeah, okay . . ."

It was getting louder outside of the hug she was in, but Wendy didn't want to pull back to see what was going on. She stayed nearby, until the noise was much closer and starting to slap at her back.

"Wendy! Wendy!"

"Young lady, if you don't back off—" Mrs. Darling started, but Wendy knew the voice she'd heard. She wrenched her head around to find Eleanor and two tired, angry people who had to be Eleanor's parents. Eleanor was still in her pajamas, but her parents were fully dressed and looking down at the Darling family like they were sure Wendy was a bad influence.

"This is bad timing, but I'm Eleanor, and I called the police," Eleanor said proudly. "As I'm sure you've been told, I'm a fan of safety and good decisions. Nice to finally meet you all at four o'clock in the morning in the middle of a police station."

"You're very rude," Mr. Darling said.

"Noted. Now, I've had a very long and anxious night; can I get this hug I've been wanting for a couple of years?"

Mrs. Darling recovered the quickest. She let go of Wendy and shook hands with Eleanor's parents. "Mrs. and Mr. Darling, nice to meet you. Sorry about this; we were really hoping to meet you both under much better circumstances."

While their parents began introducing themselves, Wendy let Eleanor's spindly arms rock her from side to side. She was taller than Wendy had thought she'd be—no one can ever really imagine that correctly with online friends—but otherwise she looked the same. Eleanor stepped back to take all of Wendy in properly. She gently patted Wendy's shoulders, then her cheeks, then the side of her hair. Up close without a screen between them, Wendy could see Eleanor's freckles and a bit of red in her blond hair.

Eleanor looked sleepy, but her eyes were bright and happy. "What's up, buttercup?" she asked with a soft grin. "Not very romantic to have our first meetup like this. Although I must give you points for drama and originality."

Wendy laughed and felt much better. So much better. "How long are you grounded for?" Wendy asked.

Eleanor glanced over at her parents, who were now smiling and talking to Wendy's parents enthusiastically. "A month for enabling," she replied, turning back. "How about you?"

"Thousands and thousands of years, apparently."

Eleanor groaned. "So, right back to normal, then?" She pulled Wendy back into another hug, this time laying her curly head in the hollow of Wendy's neck.

Wendy rubbed at Eleanor's back remorsefully. Over Eleanor's shoulder, she could see Tinkerbelle watching them curiously.

"Not even close, Eleanor," Wendy said. "Not even close."

"On these magic shores children at play are forever beaching their coracles. We too have been there; we can still hear the sound of the surf, though we shall land no more."

Peter Pan, by J.M. Barrie

EPILOGUE

The sun was so bright that Wendy could see it through her eyelids. She turned over and wrapped her blanket over her head and groaned. Why did the blinds have to be all the way up? It was a Sunday for God's sake. A day of rest.

"You should really be awake by now," Tinkerbelle said. "Eleanor is going to be here in half an hour."

Wendy tugged her blanket off her head and stared directly at the ceiling. There was no way she would have agreed to share her room with Tinkerbelle if she had known what a yoga freak the other girl was. Meanwhile, Prentis stayed asleep until twelve p.m. every day of the weekend. *And he's neater,* Wendy thought ruefully.

Tinkerbelle finished stretching and hopped up to sit on her bed, bouncing happily on the firm expensive mattress—the first she'd ever had. "You should really get dressed."

Wendy turned over completely so her face was buried in her pillow. "Eleanor doesn't care if I'm in pajamas, and I'm not allowed to leave, anyway, so why should I put on real clothes?"

"She might be bringing Fyodor—I don't know," Tinkerbelle said coquettishly. "You wouldn't want to *not* get dressed and wish that you *had*."

Wendy flipped over again and sighed loudly and angrily at the ceiling. "You wouldn't say that unless you knew for certain he WAS coming," she snapped. "Why don't you go downstairs and bother the twins? They're always spoiling for a fight."

Tinkerbelle shrugged. "Teasing boys isn't the same. You should know, they're your brothers now, too."

Wendy scowled and let her legs fall out of bed. Instead of getting up, she just slithered limply off the mattress to the floor like wet spaghetti and lay there, arms and legs akimbo.

Tinkerbelle bounced down from her mattress and settled somewhere near Wendy's head. She squished Wendy's cheeks between both hands, and Wendy let her. Petulantly.

"You're so spoiled." Tinkerbelle giggled.

"You are now, too," Wendy said through her tightly held cheeks. "Only, you actually get to enjoy it. They're not going to let me outside until I'm buying my own home."

Tinkerbelle hummed. "Sucks to suck. It's only been four months, you've experienced worse things in life." She squished Wendy's face tightly one more time, then stood up and began peeling off her exercise gear to change into her new everyday clothes. After her adoption, Tinkerbelle had given up her giant wardrobe of many-size pieces and sheepishly let Wendy's parents buy her new clothes that actually fit. With more money to actually choose things she liked, Tinkerbelle had developed a cute, mod style with little minidresses, colored tights, and bold fake eyelashes. Her hair had even grown out a bit, but she'd already warned Mrs. Darling that she would be getting it cut short again soon and not to get used to it.

"I'm going to visit Slightly," Tinkerbelle announced.

"They're putting Curly's bottle sculpture up in the Chicago Cultural Center, and he wants us to help. Slightly said his great-cousin would make us lunch if we stopped by first. Are you sure you don't want to sneak out and come?"

Wendy missed having Slightly around, but the allure of seeing Fyodor again was too much to resist, so she shook her head. Slightly had only stayed at the Darling's house until they were able to reunite him with family. To everyone's combined relief, Slightly's only living relative, his great-cousin, who was only twenty-seven, herself, offered to take in Tootles as well. Mr. Darling made good money, but five kids was a squeeze, and seven had been entirely too much for their little house.

Tinkerbelle shoved her feet into her platform go-go boots and zipped up the sides. Then she ran a brush over her spiky blond pixie cut and spritzed her neck with perfume. "Fine," she announced. "I'm going to tell Slightly you don't miss him anymore, and he's going to show up here with Tootles, and Tootles is going to be so excited to see us again that he'll run around screaming and touch all our stuff." She flounced out the door.

"TINK, NO—" Wendy scrambled to her feet.

Tinkerbelle squeaked and stumbled forward, clumsy in her platform boots. She slid across the hallway and clomped loudly down the stairs with Wendy hot on her heels. Wendy snagged the back of Tinkerbelle's turtleneck dress and tugged her backward, trying to beat the other girl into the kitchen, but Tinkerbelle was more determined. She wriggled between Wendy and the wall so she could jump down the next four stairs. Tinkerbelle and her heels crashed onto the landing in the middle of the staircase with a noise so loud that Wendy knew her dad would be checking the wood for dents later. Tinkerbelle stuck the landing at first, but her ankles wobbled and she pinwheeled her arms to steady herself, but it didn't look like it was working. With a spike of concern, Wendy lunged forward, grabbed Tinkerbelle around the waist to save her, and almost immediately lost her balance as well. They both slid down three more stairs dangerously quickly before Tinkerbelle was able to halt their descent by clinging to the railing.

"What the . . . fuck?" Prentis asked.

Everyone in the kitchen was frozen and staring. Prentis and the twins, who had real names now but rarely used them, were eating breakfast. Second had paused with his fork halfway to his mouth and was giving Wendy a harsh look that immediately reminded her that she was still wearing the Inuyasha pajamas that Eleanor had given her last Christmas as a joke.

Mrs. Darling was by the stove frying eggs, but she'd turned around completely, her arms folded tightly over her chest, spatula still in hand. Mr. Darling, who had clearly heard Tinkerbelle's shoes collide with their brand-new wood floors, was in front of the open front door, gazing up at them in dismay.

Finally, standing in the open doorway with their bikes partially inside the house, were Eleanor and Fyodor.

Tinkerbelle, unphased by all the attention, shrugged herself out of Wendy's grip. "Language, Prentis," she said prissily, and she flung herself into a dining room chair.

"There had better not be scuffs on those stairs—" Mr. Darling began, but Eleanor shrieked over him excitedly.

"YOU'RE WEARING THEM!"

Wendy looked down at her pajamas in horror and then back up at Fyodor, whose pretty cheeks were lightly pinking like they always did when he saw her.

"They look nice," Fyodor said politely.

Wendy didn't dignify that with a response. She slapped her arms over the cartoon faces on her chest and ran back up the stairs without another word.

"You can't run from our love!" Eleanor shouted.

"And you should have gotten dressed!" Tinkerbelle added ruthlessly.

Wendy slammed her bedroom door behind herself and screamed.

She hated this fucking family.

ACKNOWLEDGMENTS

First, I would like to thank my lovely editors as well as the Imprint team for taking a chance on this as a proposal. Making books with you is always such a joy. Thank you to my lovely partner, Kyle, for the unwavering support. To my amazing beta readers: You really helped me make the best of the last rays of daylight before the dark: Eli, Aija Rose, E. Adkins, Anna Didenkow, Noah Smoyer, Colby Dockery, Makenzie Marts, Maddie, and Jack Simonds. To all the authenticity readers who helped me reach my goals, you're the true MVPs for writers who insist on representational diversity in their work. Project Gutenberg, thank you for my copies of all Peter Pan and Peter Pan–adjacent media. God bless all the masters and PhD students whose dissertations I read to research this book; all forty-three of you are absolutely bonkers obsessed with Neverland, and that passion was so valuable to the design of this manuscript.

Last but not least, thank you to J.M. Barrie for such a strange and tender story, smartly written and beautifully expanded. It's a masterpiece.